FALL OF A KINGDOM

SINS Series Book 8

EMMA SLATE

Tabula Rasa Publishing

Prologue

From the journal of Barrett Campbell:

No MATTER how much you change, you will still have to pay the price for what you have done.

Chapter 1
BARRETT

"Good evening, Madame," the *maître d'* greeted in French.

"Good evening." I smiled, enjoying the way his eyes attempted to remain on my face but instinctively drifted lower.

The white satin gown hugged my curves, dipping in the front and back. It was a tease of a dress, clearly designed to entice.

My auburn hair was twirled up and pinned back, highlighting my cheekbones and long neck. Something primal happened to men when they saw a beautiful woman composed and put together. They wanted to rattle their cages and break free for the hunt and find out what sort of sensuality was concealed beneath the armor of hair spray and makeup.

"Do we have the pleasure of you dining with us tonight?" he asked.

"I don't have a reservation, I'm afraid." Though the height of the Monaco tourist season was long over, tables at *Le Roi* were booked solid for months. "I'll head to the bar."

"Enjoy," he said. "And please, let me know if there's anything you need."

I smiled.

There was nothing intimate about *Le Roi*. It had been designed to impress, to overwhelm. It verged on being almost too much, gaudy even. Golden drapes garnished the glass doors that led out to the terrace, where one could dine while overlooking the Mediterranean.

I strode through the restaurant, recognizing celebrities and rock stars who dined on fresh oysters and expensive champagne. There were others I recognized too. The truly powerful movers and shakers who made the world turn, whom you've never heard of.

My right hip twinged, but I ignored it. Tonight, I'd worn heels instead of flats. They instilled the greatest sense of confidence. Heels showed that I was feminine, desirable, and waiting to be impressed.

I felt it in the air. The promise. The power. The *want*. Hunger stirred deep in my belly.

Diamonds the size of small marbles adorned my ears. They were the only jewelry I wore.

I approached the bar, noting the man with broad shoulders. He filled out his gray suit jacket, and dark hair almost brushed the collar of his crisp white shirt.

I sidled up next to him but didn't look at him.

"Buy you a drink?" came his rumbly, thick voice.

I turned my head to look at him, meeting his cobalt blue eyes. My gaze slid to the glass of amber liquid in front of him. I reached across the bar and grasped it. Without taking my eyes off him, I brought it to my nose and took a delicate sniff.

"Balvenie DoubleWood, 17 year."

His eyes lit with humor. "A woman who knows her scotch. I'm impressed."

I sipped from his glass and arched a brow.

He signaled to the bartender for another.

"So," he began.

"So," I repeated.

"Are you married?"

"No."

He looked at my naked ring finger. "Why not? A woman who looks like you and knows her scotch…you must be one of a kind."

My smile widened. "Glad you think so. It would take a very special man to get me to settle down."

"You mean like the kind of man who owns his own scotch distillery?" he asked.

I shrugged.

"So, the scotch lover is not impressed?"

"Not really."

The bartender set another glass of liquor in front of the man and then discreetly moved away.

"I could sail you around the world on my catamaran. She's a massive vessel, fit for a king and queen. I could take you to places on this earth regular people don't even know exist."

"Tempting." My gaze slid down him like the alcohol slid down my throat. Warm. Heady. "But I'm looking for something—*something*…"

"I could give you a life you've never dared to dream," he continued, his blue eyes flickering like twin flames. "I could give you the most beautiful children in all the world… I could give you my heart."

I took a step closer to him, and with my free hand, I placed it against his chest. "You sound pretty cavalier about your heart. Do you trust me to keep it safe for you?"

His smile was slow, heated. "Not even a little bit."

I grinned. "Smart man. I like smart men."

His hand snaked out to rest on the curve of my hip, and he pulled me closer. "Have dinner with me."

"Now?"

"Aye, now. Apparently, I'm going to need a few more hours to seduce you."

I leaned forward and whispered in his ear. "I'm a simple woman. Feed me, then fuck me."

His crack of laughter boomed across the restaurant, and he signaled once again to the bartender.

"Sir?" the young man asked.

Flynn looked at me and grinned. "My wife is hungry. Bring one of everything on the menu."

"Well?" Flynn asked several hours later.

I sipped on an amaro. "Well, what?"

"Well, how was it?"

"I've had better," I stated.

"You're referring to the food, aye?" he asked with a glint of amusement.

"Yes. The food. I'm a fan of the company and the conversation."

Our bodies were turned toward each other. We had an innate intimacy born from several years of marriage and raising children together. But we still reached for excitement and new opportunities. Hence our teasing banter when we'd pretended to be strangers meeting for the first time in a bar.

"I agree with you about the food." Flynn dabbed his lips with a black cloth napkin and set it aside. "The Monaco Rex will be a smashing success."

"Agreed."

Flynn had whisked me and the children away from the dreary winter in Scotland and sailed us to Monaco. He was interested in acquiring a property that would become the newest addition to The Rex Hotel empire. We'd brought the boys along, but they were currently on the yacht with the nannies and the rest of the crew. *Le Roi* was no place for children. And I always enjoyed having my husband to myself. Dinner out at a fancy restaurant reminded me of our early days together, when we discovered we couldn't breathe without the other.

I still felt that way. After all these years.

"What are you thinking about, hen?" he asked, reaching for my hand and stroking his thumb across my knuckles.

"How much I love you."

His eyes darkened. "Prove it."

"My place or yours?" I teased.

Chuckling, he reached into his breast pocket and extracted his wallet. He quickly laid down several bills.

He settled his hand in the small of my back and guided me toward the exit. I shot the *maître d'* a wink which made an appreciative smile bloom across his face.

"My wife, the flagrant flirt," Flynn remarked dryly.

"Oh, and you don't flirt?" I demanded. "How easily could you replace me with any of the young women who drool in your vicinity?"

The attendant outside of *Le Roi* gestured to the waiting black Rolls-Royce and then opened the back door so we could slide onto the massive rear seat.

I scooted in first and then Flynn followed. He settled in next to me and placed his large palm on my thigh.

"The marina, s'il vous plaît."

"Right away, Mr. Campbell," the driver replied.

Flynn pressed a button on a small control console and a black privacy screen rose to conceal us from the driver. Flynn pressed another button, and a light indicated the microphone and speakers had been turned off in the back, to give us complete privacy.

"Irreplaceable," Flynn said.

"Hmm?" I asked, turning my attention away from the street traffic to look at him. "What did you say?"

"I said *irreplaceable*. As in, you're irreplaceable."

"So, you won't be trading me in for a younger model any time soon?"

"No. Grow old with me, Barrett."

"Gnarled and shriveled," I promised. "But until then…" I grasped his hand and gently slid it up my dress.

"Wicked woman," he whispered when he realized I wasn't wearing any underwear. "Perfection."

His fingers inched along my skin. I spread my legs as much as the dress would allow, letting him have his way with me in the back of the Rolls.

My cheeks heated with desire as I kept my eyes trained on his.

"I better not go any further," he said, his voice husky with want. "You're wearing white. Besides, I have something planned for you."

He gently removed his hand from beneath my skirt. I nearly lamented it, but knew he'd keep his word and make it up to me later.

A small light flashed overhead, and a bell chimed softly, indicating we had arrived at our destination. Flynn unlocked the car but waited for the driver to open the rear door. We walked hand in hand along the wooden planks to our yacht. I paused for a moment to stare at it.

"Still think it's too big?" he asked with a wide, boyish grin.

"Men and their toys." I snorted. "And no. You were right. It's perfect."

"Just like I was right about the jet and the house."

"No one likes a braggart, Flynn."

His resonant laugh echoed across the marina. I slid off my heels and let out a low moan of relief. The yacht was lit up well and we easily traversed the steps and boarded astern the starboard hull of the massive catamaran.

"I know they hurt you, hen, but damn…they make your legs look a mile long."

"That's why I wore them," I said, absently rubbing my hip. "The pain is worth it. Especially when you look at me the way you do."

He brought my hand to his lips. "Check in on the lads?"

"Yes."

They were three peas in a pod. They slept in one of the yacht's forward cabins, the twins on a set of bunk beds and Hawk in a single bed on the other side of the room. Flynn and I had the yacht custom designed with the children in mind and had placed them in an area where they could spend time together when they wanted away from us.

Flynn and I crept quietly so as not to disturb them, but they slept soundly, and our presence went unnoticed. They had burned off hours of energy playing on the beach, and nothing took it out of them like the sunshine and sea spray. Even after their baths, they still smelled of sun and sunscreen. Their mouths were slack with the deep sleep reserved only for children.

I still couldn't believe they were ours.

Flynn's eyes caught mine and with the aid of the moonlight streaming through the porthole, I could see the love for his children permeate his expression.

He gently tugged me from the cabin, and we headed back toward the aft stateroom and closed and locked the door. It was expansive and lavish, more so than a normal sailing vessel. But that was how we lived. We had a crew and a Captain that saw to our every need and ensured we stayed on course.

"What do you have planned for me?" I asked as I turned my back to him and gestured to my zipper.

He gently tugged it down and then grazed his lips along the sensitive skin of my neck, causing me to shiver.

"Get into a bathing suit. The black one that barely covers anything."

Laughing, I spun and wrapped my arms around his neck. "How do you know I even brought the little black one?"

He grinned. "I made sure it was packed before we even set sail."

I kissed his lips. "Your wish is my command."

Flynn's arms tightened around me. "You're so compliant tonight, hen. I'm not sure how I feel about it."

"You like it."

"I do. But I don't trust it." He winked.

I slithered into the black suit that drove Flynn wild, and then turned to look at myself in the mirror. He stood next to me, wearing a pair of navy-blue trunks. I marveled at the scars on both our bodies.

"Can you believe it?" he asked quietly, his eyes meeting mine in the glass.

"Believe what?"

His fingers danced across the bullet wound marring my abdomen. "We're both alive."

"We are," I agreed, taking his hand and bringing it to my mouth.

He looked down at me, studying me. "There's something on your mind."

I hesitated and then nodded.

"Something big?"

I nodded.

"Something you've been thinking about for a long time?" he prodded.

"Define long," I asked evasively.

He rubbed the back of his neck. "Hot tub. You can tell me underneath the stars."

I left my phone on the nightstand and let Flynn lead me out of the cabin. The water was calm tonight and it would be perfect for relaxing in the hot tub.

The stars were out and winking from above. The air was chilly, as was the slight breeze. I shivered as Flynn pressed a button and the hot tub's cover opened. I stepped into the steaming water, letting it envelop me. Flynn followed and sidled up next to me. We leaned our heads back to stare at the sky.

"Hen?" he prodded.

"I want another baby."

He didn't say anything, and I looked at him. His expression was indecipherable. "How long have you been thinking about this?" he asked finally.

"I'm not sure. A while, I guess. I think it's been in the back of my mind for longer than I realized." I paused. "Sterling sent me a photo of the nursery and I just…"

"You just what, hen?"

"I want another. I don't feel complete."

He reached his arm around me and tickled the top of my shoulder with his finger. "I've had a vasectomy."

"Yes."

"You've had substantial injuries and can't—"

"We could adopt. I'd be fine with adopting."

"I thought our family was complete." He frowned.

"It was," I agreed. "But lately, it feels...incomplete."

"Let me think about this."

"All right."

"I'm not saying no, but I'm not saying yes, either. Give me time."

I reached behind my neck and removed the tie, the top of my swimsuit falling into the water.

The lights of the yacht were bright enough that I could see the banked fires of lust in his eyes.

There was no point in talking about it anymore. I told him what I wanted, and he was taking time to process it. That was all I could ask for.

I floated my body toward his and plopped down onto his lap.

"I love you," I whispered just before my lips brushed his.

And then my mind short circuited as my lust for Flynn took over.

Chapter 2
BARRETT

I stepped out onto the deck the next morning to bright sunshine and crisp air. I tugged up the collar of my sweater as I made my way to a table that was covered in white linens and five place settings.

Hawk bounced on the settee as he shoved a piece of toast smothered with butter and jam into his mouth. That was all my seven-year-old needed: carbs and sugar.

Flynn sat between our six-year-old twins, but that didn't stop Iain from misbehaving. He was currently throwing raspberries at his brother.

"Stop!" Noah shouted.

"Iain," Flynn boomed. "I told you to behave. If you can't, you will leave the table."

Iain popped the raspberry he'd been about to hurl at Noah into his mouth and then he slunk down in his seat, his expression glum at being chastised.

Flynn reached for his espresso cup.

"Morning, hen," he greeted, his voice rumbly and delicious.

It reminded me of the previous evening, when he growled low in my ear as he pleasured me.

"Morning." I stole my hand across the broad expanse of his shoulders and then took the empty seat next to Hawk.

"You boys sleep all right?" I asked as I placed the white napkin in my lap.

Noah nodded. Iain swiped his dark hair off his forehead and reached for a piece of bacon on Hawk's plate.

Hawk glared at his younger brother.

Iain gave him a cheeky grin.

"Mam, may I be excused?" Hawk asked.

My eldest son, and the one who looked most like Flynn, had jam splattered across his cheeks. His blue eyes were bright with energy, and he was unable to sit still.

"You may," I allowed.

"Me too?" Iain asked.

"Aye," Flynn said.

Hawk and Iain pushed back from the table and then ran toward the salon, the sound of their boat shoes hitting the deck as they sprinted into the living room area of the vessel. Noah continued to eat his parritch, not caring that he'd been left behind.

A member of the crew dressed in a black sweater and khakis appeared with a cappuccino on a tray. He set the coffee cup in front of me and stood back. "May I get you something to eat, Mrs. Campbell?"

"Crab Benedict would be wonderful," I said. "Thank you."

"My pleasure," he said. "Sir?"

"I'm fine, thank you." Flynn lifted his espresso cup to his mouth.

The attendant left, striding back inside. I took a sip of my cappuccino and nearly purred.

"Mam, I'm finished," Noah said. "Can I be excused?"

I smiled at his manners. They came far easier to him than Hawk and Iain. "Sure. Are you going to go join your brothers?"

He shook his head. "I want to visit the captain. Can I?"

"You *may*," Flynn said. "But be mindful that you don't get in his way, aye?"

"Aye," Noah agreed. He shot me a toothy grin and then slid back his chair.

He was gone in a blur, and I stared after him wistfully.

"You look tired, hen," Flynn said quietly.

"What an unchivalrous thing to say," I teased.

His grin was lopsided. "I know why you're tired."

I snorted. "Yes. Someone decided to wake me up in the middle of the night…"

"I don't see you complaining."

"I'll never complain," I assured him. "But I might have to take a nap later today."

Flynn finished off the rest of his espresso and then leaned back in his chair. "Hadrian called."

"Did he?"

"He invited us to stop off at his island on our way home."

"Hmmm. He *invited*? With our brood? He wants to talk business, doesn't he?"

"Of course. You know how he is. The man prefers not to communicate via technology if he can help it."

The eccentric, reclusive Scottish billionaire lived on his own private Shetland Island with his wife and preferred to remain in his own domain. Hadrian counted Ramsey Buchanan as his best friend and part of his inner circle, therefore Duncan and Flynn were included by extension.

"I wouldn't mind seeing Sterling," I said, mentioning

Hadrian's wife. "And the boys are on break from school until the new year, so that's not a concern."

"Not that it matters," Flynn remarked dryly. "We pull them out of school frequently enough."

"Yes, and we also donate enough to their school that the headmaster doesn't say a word when we do," I pointed out. "Do you think the boys are missing something by not being in school as much as their peers?"

"They don't seem to be missing anything. I'd rather have them with us when we travel, and besides, they're young enough that the only true thing they miss from primary school is social interaction. They're already ahead in reading and maths. If it causes problems for them in their later years, we'll pay for their therapy."

I let out a laugh. "I would apologize for being able to live by different rules because of who we are, but I'm not really that concerned about it, to be honest."

He fell silent for a moment and then he said, "The boys are at a perfect age. They can entertain themselves and they don't need us every hour of every day."

"You don't want another baby," I stated. "That's what you're saying."

"I love our family, Barrett. You know I do. But I feel like it's complete."

"I thought you said you'd take the time to think about it."

"I have thought about it."

"Have you?" I raised my brows. "How can you have thought about it and come to this conclusion all in the span of eight hours when I've been thinking about this for weeks?"

"Weeks?"

"Months, actually. I've been thinking about this for months."

"What is it you want me to say, Barrett?" He all but growled.

"I want you to consider what I asked. *Really* consider it. Don't just placate me and tell me you considered it when all you did was wait a few hours and then say no."

"How long should I have taken? How many hours need to pass before I can say no?" he pressed.

I threw up my hands. "You're basically saying you won't even change your mind." I shoved back from the table just as the crewmember brought my breakfast.

He jumped out of the way as I blew past him like an ocean storm. I needed to escape. I wanted to be in my own space, to have some privacy.

Even though our yacht was massive, I was still trapped. There was no way off.

"Barrett," Flynn called. "Stop."

I came to a halt and grasped the railing near me.

"What is this really about, hen?"

"A baby."

"No. I don't think it is." He sidled up next to me. "This is something else. The baby is just a mask for something deeper. Are you unhappy, love?"

"Unhappy?" I repeated. "I'm the farthest thing from unhappy."

"Then what is all this about? You've been…restless."

Flynn and I traveled the world. We had three amazing boys, wonderful friends, a rich life full of laughter and excitement and enough money to do anything we wanted.

"I know how it sounds," I began. "Nothing is missing from our lives, but you know that feeling when you're about to leave the house, and you pat yourself down to ensure you have everything you need, but you feel like you're forgetting something? I feel like I'm forgetting some-thing, Flynn."

"And you think another baby is the thing you're forgetting?"

I could tell he didn't understand. Not that I blamed him. I wasn't sure I understood it, either. But it was a feeling, a sense that I was an incomplete puzzle, and that without another child I would never find that last center piece.

"I don't know," I admitted. "I just—I don't know, Flynn. I can't explain it any better than I have."

"What if I say yes, Barrett? What if I agree and we make it happen and then you realize it's not about a baby at all? What if it's something different?"

"Tarnished metal," I said quietly.

"What?"

"I feel like tarnished metal. I feel worn out and dull. I want something new and beautiful. Something that lights me up. Something that gives me a purpose."

His brow furrowed. "You don't think you have a purpose? What about the SINS?"

"What about it?" I asked, raising my brows. "We are more than just the SINS, Flynn."

"Just like we are more than just parents."

"Touché."

"You were lost for so long," he said, pitching his voice low. "With the lads, I mean. You made no secret of that fact. They changed our lives, for the better of course, but there was a time that you weren't—that you…"

"I wasn't myself," I finished for him. "I know."

"That could happen again. With a new baby."

"Maybe." I turned my head to look in the direction where the boys had run to. I couldn't see them, of course. No doubt causing havoc and chaos.

"I'm concerned," he said. "You're not what I'd call *maternal*. Not in the traditional sense, and yet you'd do anything for your children. But they can't fill the void inside you. I don't think another baby will change anything for you. It'll just change us. Our entire dynamic and life will change all over again."

He took me into his arms. "Really think about why you're asking for this. And if you come to me and you can look me in the eye and say clearly and for sure why you want this, then I'll seriously consider it."

Chapter 3
FLYNN

I sat down on the plush leather couch in my private study and had to stifle a moan of relief. Tonight, I would sleep in my own bed. After weeks on the yacht seeing to business with Hadrian, I was glad to be home. The yacht was comfortable. I'd made sure of it. But there was nothing like the sanctuary of your own house.

"You look exhausted," Duncan said from the other couch. "We should've waited to have a family dinner until you were settled in."

"It's fine," I assured him.

The lads were currently with my aunt and uncle in Ireland, so the house was unusually quiet. Having Duncan, Ash, and their children over to our house for an evening meal had been a buffer between me and Barrett. We hadn't been on the same footing since she'd brought up the subject of another baby nearly a week ago, and we hadn't talked about it since.

"How was Monaco?" Duncan asked.

"Productive. We start construction on the new hotel in the spring."

"And Hadrian?"

"Lovesick." I grinned. "He barely lets Sterling out of his sight."

Duncan chuckled. "Possessive."

"That's putting it mildly." I grinned. "He's buying some mines in South America and asked if we wanted to diversify."

"And you said?"

"I said yes."

The world was changing quickly. I often wondered what it would look like by the time the boys were of age and took their place alongside me.

"Something else is weighing on you," Duncan said.

I sighed. "Is it that obvious?"

"I read you better than anyone. Except for your wife, of course."

"My wife," I murmured. "The source of my tension."

"Are you fighting?"

"No."

Duncan frowned. "Then what is it?"

"I'm getting Barrett's equivalent of the cold shoulder."

"Why? What did you do?"

"Me?" I raised my brows. "What makes you think *I* did something?"

"I'm assuming."

"Barrett wants another bairn," I stated.

Duncan lowered his glass of SINNERS scotch from his lips and peered at me, his eyes silver in the low firelight. "Well, that's an interesting turn of events, considering you had a procedure that's effectively neutered you."

"Thanks for reminding me," I remarked dryly. I reached for the cigar box resting on the Biedermeier end table and held it out to Duncan. He shook his head in polite denial. I took out a bold and spicy Cuban cigar, a gift from Mateo Sanchez. The bastard wanted to fuck my wife, but at least he possessed the gentility to offer fine cigars and top shelf liquor to his business associates.

I quickly cut off the end of the cigar and lit it.

"Barrett is welcome to one of ours," Duncan said with a wry grin. "Tell her to take the baby. He won't sleep the night through and I'm dying."

"I'm not sure she really wants another baby," I said. "I think she thinks she wants another one because she doesn't really know what she wants."

"Say that again? In plain English this time."

I sighed. "Why now? Why another baby now? It doesn't make sense to me, Duncan. She says she's willing to adopt…"

"Maybe this is more than a whim," Duncan said. "Maybe she really does want another bairn."

"Maybe. I want her to be happy. You know I do. You know I'd do anything if it made her happy."

I set my cigar in the antique crystal ashtray next to me. I rose from the chair and walked to the fireplace and rested my forearm against the mantle, clenching my fist as I stared into the flames.

"I'm sensing a *but*. How do you feel about another baby? About adoption?"

I looked at the man I considered a brother, even though we didn't share the same bloodline. "I love our life the way it is. I don't want it to change."

"Then say no. You have three lads already. And they're a handful."

I sighed in frustration. "She says…she says our family doesn't feel complete. That something—someone—is missing. I can't be the reason she doesn't feel complete, Duncan. But I'm not convinced this is best for us."

He stared at me for a long moment.

I sighed. "I think I feel pangs of guilt,"

"About what?" he demanded.

"Bringing her into our way of life. Her whole world changed when she decided to be with me."

"*Your* whole world changed, too," he reasoned.

"It's not the same. I grew up in the SINS. She didn't."

He lifted his glass of scotch to his lips and sipped. "I guess you have to ask yourself the real question then: will she resent you if you don't give her another baby?"

"I don't know."

"Are you afraid you won't be able to love a child that's not of your blood? Not of Barrett's blood?"

I fell silent.

"Ah," he said with a slow nod. "I see. You really should've discussed this with Sasha. He could give you better insight on the matter."

I scratched a thumb across my stubbled jaw. "I thought about calling him. But he and I—most moments, most situations, I can forget that he once loved my wife and wanted her for his own. I know he's in love with Quinn. I know it. But talking to Sasha about bringing another child into my family feels…"

"Cruel."

"Aye. Cruel."

"Loving Barrett has changed you. Made you softer."

"Hey," I warned. "I'm not soft."

"I didn't call you soft. But some of your—how shall I say it—your rougher edges, have been filed down a bit."

"This is why we have to ensure we raise tough men. Because when we're old, we'll be soft and used to comfort, and we won't remember what we spent our lives fighting for."

"Do you think Da was soft in the end?" Duncan asked.

"No. Malcolm wasn't soft."

I returned to my seat. I needed more time to think about what Barrett was asking for.

"Whatever you decide, it will be right," Duncan said.

"Shut up, ye bastard," I said with a laugh. "What if it were Ash? And she wanted another?"

"If Ash wanted to adopt because we couldn't have another, I would do it," he said without pause. "There are children that need a home, and we've got one. Family is everything, brother, and you know as well as I do that sometimes family isn't made by blood. Family is clan... family is life. Look," he continued, "even if wanting another baby is just a mask for something deeper, in the end, you'd be doing something meaningful. How bad could it be?"

We fell into a pensive silence. We drank the rest of our scotch, and I finished my cigar without speaking. His words resonated in my bones, and I replayed them over and over in my head to the sound of a crackling fire.

Family.

Aye.

There was *nothing* more important than family.

Chapter 4

BARRETT

"I NEVER THOUGHT Wee Duncan would fall asleep," Ash said as she kicked off her shoes and plopped down onto the couch of the castle turret. She pulled a blanket around her even though a wood fire had been lit and lent warmth and a cheery atmosphere to the otherwise cold stone.

"He did seem a bit fussier than usual," I said.

"He's teething."

"Ah, been there," I said in understanding.

"Thank you."

"For what?"

"For inviting us to stay the night. It would be much quieter for you if we went home, though."

I smiled. "I'm their godmother. I love having them here. I love the insanity."

"You do not," she said with a wry chuckle.

"I do," I promised. "And if the boys were here, it would be a three-ring circus and I'd be the ringmaster."

"You miss them," she concluded.

"I do." I sighed. "The quiet is...too quiet."

"They'll be back soon." She looked around my private refuge. "I love the remodel."

"Thank you." I had dreamt for years of filling the room with ancient texts and leather-bound books so I could spend my time deciphering history, wishing to glean insight for the future, but as the wife of Flynn Campbell, as the mother of his children, I had other duties. So I'd turned the turret into a lounge, a place to sit quietly and dream.

"Do you think it would be easier if we all lived in the same castle? The Buchanans could have a wing and the Campbells could have the other?" I asked in amusement.

"There's a thought." She grinned. "We do spend more time together than apart. That's weird, isn't it?"

"Probably. But I love it," I admitted.

"Good, me too."

Ash wasn't just my best friend; she was the sister I never had. We'd been through so much: deaths, births, and emotional turmoil. We'd seen each other at our worst. There were things she knew about me, things I never would've shared with her if she hadn't married Duncan… if she hadn't come into this life.

We had both fallen in love with men who lived in the morally gray, and now we were bound by loyalty and history. Bonds that were too strong to be broken.

I would stand in front of her and take a bullet if I had to, just as I would for any of my own children. Or my husband. Or Sasha and Quinn, Ramsey, Duncan, and Ash's wee ones.

Kin.

The fire crackled as flames licked the burning wood.

"Wine?" I asked her.

"Please."

I got up and went to the liquor cart and opened a

bottle of red wine, courtesy of Angelo Moretti. He was a bastard, but the man knew how to make wine.

"What do you think our men are talking about?" Ash asked.

The cork slid out of the bottle with a soft pop and poured two glasses. "Probably about the fact that I want another baby."

Her blue eyes widened. "You *what*?"

"Want another baby," I repeated, handing her a glass and then lifting mine to my lips. It was rich and complex, and I could almost taste the ancient soil of Naples.

"Barrett?"

"Hmm?"

"You can't just stop there," Ash stated. "Are you serious? You want another baby?"

"I do."

"But Flynn's vasectomy and your pelvis injury—"

"I'm talking about adoption."

"I see."

She didn't push me to continue speaking, choosing instead to silently wait as I gathered my words.

"I didn't get to decide," I said softly. "My children were…unexpected." I looked at her.

She nodded.

"Unexpected, but *so* welcome." I smiled. "From the moment they open their eyes in the morning until they fall asleep at night, I cherish every moment with them."

I took my wine and went to the window, pulling back the heavy black velvet drapes to stare out across the acreage. Thunder rumbled like an angry toddler.

"I thought I was finished… No, I thought *we* were finished having children. But something happened a few months ago. I don't even know what it was, but I started to want another one."

"Did you get bored?"

"Bored?" I snorted. "As Flynn Campbell's wife? Please."

She chuckled, but then sobered. "Then what is this? Where did it come from?"

"No idea. It's just…there. Like this feeling that there's a missing piece of my life and I have to have it."

"The sheep doesn't fill that void for you?"

I grinned and turned to look at her over my shoulder. "No. Betty doesn't fill that void."

"And what about Flynn?"

"He's happy the way things are. He doesn't want our life to change." I bit my lip and then took a sip of wine. "He also has concerns."

"Concerns about what?"

"About why I want another baby in the first place."

She frowned. "This doesn't sound like you."

"And what am I supposed to sound like?"

"I don't know. You're Barrett."

"What the hell does that mean? Is this about my maternal side?"

"No." Ash shook her head. "It's just—your boys are potty trained, they're in school, they have nannies, and are starting to find their own interests and activities. You kind of have your life back, a bit, you know? You could do something else with all your free time. Get back into history. Hell, you could teach Scottish history. It's what you were going for when—"

"When my brother changed the course of my entire life and I fell into Flynn's nefarious clutches?"

"Well, yeah. You finally have the chance to focus on yourself again. New avenues. Old avenues. Whatever… I mean, I'm kind of with Flynn on this one. I don't understand."

"I don't *need* you to understand," I said in exasperation. "I need you to support me."

"Okay, I support you." She paused. "Will you push Flynn to do this?"

"No. I won't push Flynn."

"He'll come around. Flynn has never been able to deny you anything."

"Maybe." I frowned. "I can't—no, I *won't* back him into a corner. If he doesn't want another baby, I won't resent him for it."

"Just as easy as that, huh? You won't resent him for not giving you what you need?"

I faced her and took a sip of wine. "He doesn't resent me for my relationship with Sasha."

"But there's nothing between you and Sasha now except deep friendship," she pointed out.

"Still, if the shoe were on the other foot and there was a woman in Flynn's life, a woman he was as close to as I am to Sasha, I don't think I'd be as understanding."

"Marriage isn't about keeping score."

"No?"

She shook her head. "No. Otherwise, Duncan could've held a lot of things against me, but he hasn't."

"How do you know?" I inquired. "How do you know he hasn't held anything against you?"

"Blind faith."

"Blind delusion, you mean?" I laughed, but it sounded sardonic.

"Are you happy?" she asked bluntly.

"Happy," I repeated. "Right now? Yes."

"Are you sure?"

"But there's this feeling of *more*. Like, purpose or something. I'm dying for a purpose."

"Children, though a blessing, are not your sole reason

for living. You can't look to them to fill that space inside of you. They'll grow up and move away. They'll form their own lives, and then where will you be?"

I frowned into my glass and then tossed back the rest of my wine.

She studied me for a long moment and then asked, "Another bottle?"

I grinned, forcing the moment to be light when I felt anything but. "Do you even have to ask?"

Chapter 5
FLYNN

I strode into the kitchen the next morning and asked, "Has anyone seen my wife?"

Ash gazed at me in confusion as she reached for her mug of tea. "I thought she was still asleep. We were up late and had a lot of wine."

"Aye, I know."

Barrett had climbed into bed and turned toward me, sliding her body over mine. Her skin glowed in the moonlight as we came together in a fit of passion.

I'd fallen asleep with her in my arms and woken up to find her gone.

"She's probably out at the stables," Duncan suggested. "It was a bad storm last night. No doubt she wanted to comfort the beasties."

"Good thinking."

I strode outside, not bothering with a coat, and trekked to the stables. Old Hugh was brushing a gray Highland pony, but he looked up when I approached.

"Good morning, Mr. Campbell," he greeted in a thick Scottish burr.

"Morning, Hugh. Have you seen my wife? Did she come out to spend time with the horses?"

Hugh shook his head. "No, sir. I haven't seen Mrs. Campbell."

I held in my sigh of frustration but couldn't ignore my gut reaction that Barrett was no longer on the grounds.

Patting the gray pony, I spent the next few minutes talking to Hugh, which was no easy feat considering the man was tacit on a good day.

And today was not a good day.

"Was she there?" Duncan asked when I came back inside.

"No." I exhaled and rubbed the back of my neck.

"Maybe she just went for a drive?" Ash speculated. "Isn't that a possibility?"

I looked at Duncan and his expression tightened in understanding.

"I don't think she went for a drive, Ash," I muttered.

"Wait, do you think she just *left*? With us here? Without a note or a phone call?" Ash shook her head. "I don't buy it."

"She did seem a bit distracted during dinner last night," Duncan pointed out.

"Do you think…" Ash began, and then ceased speaking.

"What?" I commanded.

"Is this about her wanting another baby?" Ash blurted out.

"I don't know. Maybe." My brow furrowed. "This baby thing… It feels like it came out of nowhere."

"We've all been through a lot the last several years," Duncan remarked quietly. "Is it possible the stress of it has finally gotten to her and she just needed some time to herself?"

"It's possible, but why didn't she call or text?" I pondered everything that had led us to this point in time. "It's not just the baby thing. She's been…restless. I thought with enough romantic getaways, enough hotel openings, enough time with the bairns, it would go away." I met Ash's gaze and found truth in her eyes. A truth that could not be concealed or brushed away like dust on a fireplace mantle.

"You noticed it too," I stated. "Her changing?"

Ash nodded.

"Where did she go?" Duncan mused. "To *him*?"

I adamantly shook my head. "I don't think so."

"She runs to him every time something's wrong," Duncan pointed out. "We all know this."

"He would've called me. If she was there, he would've called me," I insisted.

"Sasha's loyalty is to her," Duncan said. "Barrett comes first in his mind, always."

"Not anymore. Quinn is his woman now," Ash said.

If I'd been alone, I would've poured a glass of scotch, damn the time. But I wasn't alone. Even though I considered Ash and Duncan family, I still didn't want them to witness my lack of control over this situation. Thank God the lads were with my aunt and uncle. It would've been hell trying to explain this to them.

Maybe she'd waited to leave until they were visiting family. I didn't believe she'd leave her children for any length of time.

"Have you called him?" Ash asked.

"And let him know my wife is missing?" My tone was bitter. "And give him a chance to gloat?"

"Sasha wouldn't gloat," Ash insisted. "Not after…not now. He's changed. As Duncan pointed out, we've all changed."

One thing I knew as a constant was Barrett and Sasha. It was eating me alive not knowing where she was, but I'd be damned if I would call and ask if she was with him.

We were all silent for a moment and then realization dawned. "I'm such an eejit. God, how could I have been so stupid?"

"What?" Duncan asked with a furrowed brow.

"It's the anniversary," I announced. "The anniversary of his death."

Emotion roiled through me as I realized that today was the anniversary of the day Barrett killed Igor Dolinsky.

Chapter 6
BARRETT

"Mrs. Campbell!"

I brushed the snow from my peacoat and smiled. "Good afternoon, Hildie," I said in her native tongue. "How many times do I have to tell you to call me Barrett?"

"It wouldn't be appropriate. Come in, come in," the housekeeper replied in Russian. "You were supposed to be here hours ago!"

"Ah, yeah. The plane had trouble landing due to visibility, and on the drive here, the snowstorm hit."

Hildie looked behind me, her already wrinkled forehead creasing even more as she frowned. "You drove yourself from the airport?"

"*Da.*"

Hildie's mouth closed and then she shut the door. I was immediately enveloped by warmth and familiarity.

"I've had borscht on for a few hours and a loaf of bread has just finished baking."

I cradled her papery cheek in my hand. "You're a doll."

"No luggage, I see."

"Why pack when I know I have everything I need here?" I asked with a droll smile.

"How long will you stay?" she asked, ushering me into the foyer.

"A few days."

"And your husband? The children? Will they be joining you? Will I finally get to meet them?"

"So many questions, Hildie." I chuckled. "Just a quick solo trip. Flynn is at home in Dornoch. The children are spending time with their great aunt and uncle in Ireland, and then we'll have a quiet Christmas together."

I headed for the staircase. Hildie meant well, but I was attempting to be evasive about my reason for being alone and I could tell she knew.

"How was Monaco?"

"Wonderful. We break ground on the new hotel in the spring."

She shook her head. "Where do you find the energy to travel the way you do? I'd prefer to spend my time next to a roaring fire with a good book."

It had been a long time since I'd sat and enjoyed something so simple. I wasn't even sure I knew how to live in the stillness, preferring instead to stay busy. It didn't stop me from thinking, though. Nothing ever did.

"I'm going to take a bath and then I'll eat in the dining room."

"There are fresh sheets on the bed, and I've had your cashmere pressed."

"What would I do without you, Hildie?" I asked.

"You never have to find out, Mrs. Campbell."

Grinning, I took the stairs, my hand gliding along the wooden bannister. It was like no time had passed since I'd last been to this place. Sasha had bought Dolinsky's home years ago, but he never came here. I had full run of the house and the grounds. I was the one who kept in contact with Hildie.

It was strange. I knew it was. My relationship with Sasha. Our connection to this home. The fact that Flynn didn't know.

The door to my room was open and the four-poster bed had already been turned down. I walked to the ornate armoire and pulled out a gray sweater and black trousers. In the chest of drawers, I found undergarments and a pair of warm woolen socks.

I placed them all on the bed and then stripped on my way to the bathroom. The drapes were pulled back to reveal the heavy, fat snowflakes that had begun falling halfway through my drive. After slowing to a crawl on the icy road, I was glad to have arrived safe and sound. It had been far too long since I'd driven myself. It wasn't as easy, now. Not with the limp.

My hip and knee were sore. I drew a bath and sprinkled my favorite bath salts and effervescent pods into the water. I tied up my hair, wishing I had the hairpin that Flynn had given me. But I'd left it in Dornoch.

My soak in the tub was leisurely and I thought of the people I loved back home. They swirled in my head like the steam from my bath. They were never far from my mind, even when I attempted to push them away. Guilt swarmed my insides, feasting on the blackened part of me that had long ago been my heart.

No doubt Flynn was going insane, wondering where I'd gone. To leave him like that, without a word… What must he be thinking? But I couldn't—didn't—have anything left in me to give him at that moment. Maybe it was selfish. Fuck, I *knew* it was selfish, but I just couldn't bring myself to contact him.

It wasn't about the baby. It wasn't about him denying

me. I could've pushed harder, demanded it from him. But that wasn't my way with Flynn. He rarely denied me a thing. We had a beautiful life together.

For days, weeks, I'd felt like I was moving through a fog. And then I'd woken up in the middle of the night after being with him and it was so clear what I had to do.

I had to come here.

"You're a cruel, beautiful woman," Igor Dolinsky's ghost said to me.

"I'm aware," I replied.

His brown eyes delved into mine as he leaned against the sink, standing there like a monument to what he once was. Honesty pierced the moment. "Not a day goes by that I don't miss you." His English was accented with Russian. He was cultured, dapper. Old world. A monster that had turned me violent, ruthless, and lethal.

Even now, years later, my feelings for Igor were complicated. When he was alive, he'd brought my baser instincts to the surface. I'd learned to manipulate emotions, exploiting the weakness of lust. And in the end, I'd killed him. His death by my hand didn't weigh me down. It was everything that had come before it. I'd told myself time and time again that I'd been pretending he was Flynn when I kissed him. But it hadn't been the truth. I'd found pleasure in Igor's arms, and for that, I'd never forgive myself.

Igor smile was pained. "M*oya krasotka.*"

"Don't call me that," I snapped.

"Why? Does it remind you of what could've been? If you'd chosen me?" He took a step toward me and crouched down next to the tub so that we were eye level. Igor reached out and trailed his finger across my collar bone.

I slapped his hand away, but his words made me tremble. They rearranged my heart, split apart my soul, and opened it, revealing an avalanche of grief, desire, and guilt.

"When you shot me in the heart," he paused, as if weighing his words, "did you kill only me? Or did part of you die that day as well?"

"Stop it, Igor."

"You prove me right, again. I'm part of you. You know this. Everything I ask out loud, you've asked yourself a dozen times already."

"I killed you because I loved Flynn…I *love* Flynn."

"You love me, too."

"What I feel for you isn't love."

"Then what is it?" he demanded.

"Hell if I know."

"We could've been happy together. If you'd chosen me."

I mulishly clamped my mouth shut, but it didn't stop the truth from leaking into my expression.

"You came here, to this house, the house I once brought you to. Why? Because you can't let me go. You say you want to, but I know that you don't. You come here once a year on the anniversary of the day you took everything from me." He cocked his head to the side. "You haven't told your husband. You've kept this a secret from him. It's a betrayal. This house that you share with Sasha but not your husband."

"This would hurt Flynn. I wouldn't even know how to explain it to him. And I'm allowed to have secrets. He doesn't have to know *everything* about me. I guarantee there are things I don't know about him, even after all this time."

"Secrets," Igor murmured. "*Da.* But this isn't the only secret you're keeping from him, is it?"

The water had long since turned cold, but my body

was hot. Feverish. On fire. From the words and truths spewing from a ghost I'd been unable to exorcise.

"Do you ever think about it?" Igor asked.

"Think about what?" I asked as I stood up from the bath and reached for a towel and wrapped it around me.

"What a life together would have looked like?"

"No, I don't think about it," I said, stepping from the tub. "My life is exactly as it should be. When I think of you, I only think of the woman I was before. She was innocent and naïve. She was a pawn. She was stupid. I refuse to live with regrets. And I have no remorse over pulling the trigger."

"I'm the reason you became a queen," he pointed out. "I'm the reason your husband keeps your council. Because of me, you stripped away a level of your humanity. You earned your respect of some of the most powerful men in the world. You have a place at their negotiation table. Make no mistake, because of me, your value has increased."

Igor followed me out of the bathroom and into the bedroom. "What could we have done together? The world will never know."

"So maudlin," I muttered.

"We would've had a girl first," he said.

"Stop," I commanded as I reached for my clothes.

"I always liked the name Rose."

I quickly pulled on my trousers, sweater, and then my socks, and then I fled the room. Igor trailed behind me.

"I would've hired someone to paint you," he said. "Wearing nothing but mink and diamonds, round with my child."

I traversed the staircase, my hand on the bannister.

"After about a year, I would've gotten you pregnant again. This time with my heir."

I was on the verge of asking what his name would've been, but I bit my tongue, wanting—*needing*—to stop myself.

"Ivan," Igor said, answering my unasked question.

I went into the dining room. The gleaming wooden table sat twelve, but there was only a place setting at the head of it. "Hildie!" I called.

The older woman pushed through the swinging door. "Mrs. Campbell?"

"I'd love a bowl of that borscht." I forced a grin, trying to ignore the ghost at my shoulder.

"Right away," she said. "There's a bottle of Merlot—"

"Yes, perfect." I sat down and reached for the black napkin that had been folded into a swan and set it across my lap.

Igor took the chair next to me, his gaze unwavering. Thankfully, he remained blessedly silent.

Hildie returned with a bowl of red borscht and a thick slice of dark brown bread. She set the food down in front of me and said, "I'll get that bottle of wine."

I smiled up at her. "Thank you for taking such good care of me."

She touched my shoulder in a silent gesture of gratitude and retreated to the kitchen. She came back a moment later, the bottle already uncorked. Hildie poured the wine and when she went to take the bottle back to the kitchen, I said, "Leave it, please."

Hildie set the bottle down. "Anything else I can get you?"

"No, thank you. You can go home." Hildie lived on the grounds with her husband in a carriage house that had been converted.

"Are you sure?"

"I'm sure."

"What about the food? I can put it away before I go…"

"Don't bother. I'll do it."

She paused. "All right," she said finally. "You'll call? If you need anything?"

"I will," I said. "Thank you, Hildie. For … everything."

Hildie looked like she wanted to say something more, but at the last moment, closed her mouth. She nodded and then quietly disappeared, leaving me alone with my ghost.

I gently set my spoon in the bowl and ladled a small bit of borsht into my mouth.

"Ivan would need a second in command," Igor said, as if no time had passed. "We'd give him a brother—Alexei."

I bowed my head and ate.

"And after a few years, when Rose was five, and the boys four and three, we'd have another one."

My spoon clattered against china, and I glared at him. "Is that how you see me? As your brood mare?"

His brown eyes bored into mine, peering into my rotten soul.

"That day, in the warehouse, if you'd shot Campbell instead of me…do you know what I would've done after?" He didn't wait for me to reply. "I would've whisked you away to St. Petersburg where we would've dined on fine caviar and champagne. I would've had a Fabergé egg commissioned for you and I would've taken you to world-class symphonies and wiped the tears from your cheeks as you cried at the beauty of the music."

"Why me, Igor?" I asked softly.

"Why *not* you, Barrett?"

No longer hungry, I rose from my chair. I grasped the bottle of wine by the neck and walked into the custom designed, state-of-the-art kitchen. The only thing truly modern in this opulent, imperial home.

I went out the back to the covered patio. It was bone-chillingly cold, and the snow hadn't stopped falling.

The hot tub was covered and already warm. I stood on the wooden steps, lifted the top, and then pressed a button to start the water bubbling.

"What are you doing?" Igor asked.

I set the bottle of wine on the ledge and then pulled my sweater over my head, tossing it aside. My trousers were next. I climbed into the hot tub, dressed only in moonlight. I sank into the hot, bubbling water, wishing I could see the stars, but the snow and clouds concealed everything.

It reminded me of the night on the yacht with Flynn. It seemed like so long ago. Touching and holding one another, the beauty of the stars above us, the promise of a future of unknown possibilities.

Now I'd gone and destroyed it all because of my inability to let go of the ghost of my past.

"It's good we didn't wind up together," I told Igor. "I would've become exactly what I am now, only much sooner."

"What's that, Barrett?"

I grasped the bottle of wine and brought it to my lips. I took a long, slow drink. "Soulless."

Chapter 7
FLYNN

A few days passed without a word from Barrett. It was the dead of night, and the library door was open just a crack. Still, the sound of their voices swept across the hallway. Soft, like a hushed whisper of intimacy.

"I've never seen him this way," Duncan said.

"Never?" Ash asked. "Not once in all your years of friendship and brotherhood?"

My mouth quirked up into a sinister smile. I reached for the glass of scotch, wondering what number I was on. It didn't matter. Day was night, night was day. None of it had any meaning.

"Never. Even when Dolinsky kidnapped her, Flynn didn't unravel," Duncan replied.

"I can hear you!" I called out from behind my desk.

Their conversation ceased and then the library door opened, and they entered.

"It's like a tomb in here," Ash muttered, reaching for the light switch.

"Don't," I snapped.

There was enough firelight in the library to illuminate the room.

Ash's hand fell away from the switch.

"You can both go," I sneered. "I don't need you watching over me like I'm a child."

Duncan pulled Ash to his side and whispered something too low for me to hear. Nodding, she cast one last glance at me before departing.

"I don't need your pity!" I yelled after her.

"Flynn, enough." Duncan's brow furrowed. "Da would be ashamed of you right now."

His words, meant to injure, ricocheted off me like I was wearing armor.

Duncan was right.

Malcom would be ashamed of me. But he was dead and couldn't witness my downward spiral.

She'd left her hairpin, a gift I had bought for her for our six-month anniversary. It was a dagger, built from a solid piece of metal, the handle adorned with intricate scrollwork. It was a weapon of beauty and high-quality craftsmanship.

I'd picked it up off her bedside table and brought it with me into the library. It currently rested on the edge of my desk. I grabbed it with one hand and then pressed my other palm flat, spread my fingers wide, and then proceeded to stab the spaces between my flesh, marring the desktop beneath my hand.

"You're ruining a twenty-thousand-dollar desk," Duncan said flatly.

"It's mine to ruin."

He fell silent again and watched as I continued my game. I wondered if I'd feel anything if I accidentally stabbed myself with the hairpin. Maybe the blood would distract me from the all- consuming anguish.

The door to the library opened and Ash strode in with a plate of food.

"What the hell are you doing?" she demanded over the sound of the hairpin sticking in wood.

"Living dangerously."

She stomped toward the desk and set the plate down. "Eat. And then shower and shave. You look like hell, and you smell like a distillery." Ash glared at her husband. "Fix this. He's Flynn Campbell for shit's sake."

Ash marched from the room.

"She's right," Duncan said, shoving his hands in his trouser pockets. "The Flynn I know wouldn't be sitting around in two-day old clothes, stubble on his face, reeking of scotch and seething humiliation. If you don't get your shite together and go after her, then you don't deserve her."

"I don't even know where she is." I growled. "I know she left of her own accord." I'd confirmed it with Tony, my head of security of the estate.

Duncan walked to the front of the desk and slid my cell phone toward me. "I'm still convinced he'll know where she is. What do you want, Flynn? Your pride? Or your wife back?"

He didn't wait for me to reply. Duncan walked to the door, and then stopped and turned to me and smiled. "You can eat that if you want, but be warned, Ash's cooking leaves a lot to be desired."

"I heard that!" she yelled from the hallway.

"I meant you to, love!" Duncan called back.

He left.

And I found my first smile in days.

Barrett was hurting. I needed to find her so I could make it better. She was the rudder of our family's ship, and without her, we'd all drown in this storm.

I picked up my cell phone, pressed a few buttons to unlock it, and then opened my contacts list. I touched the screen and put the phone to my ear.

He came on the line after one ring. "Campbell."

"Petrovich." I inhaled a deep breath. "I need your help."

There was a pause on the other end of the line. No doubt I had shocked him into silence.

After a long moment, he finally said, "You never ask for my help. You hate asking for my help."

"I'm asking under extreme duress. Please don't make me feel worse about it."

"Is it Hawk?" he demanded. "Iain? Noah? I'll get on a plane—"

"It's Barrett," I gritted out.

"Barrett?" he repeated slowly, as if he couldn't quite believe it. "What's wrong with Barrett?"

"She's gone. Left a few days ago. Hasn't checked in." I paused. "It was the anniversary of Dolinsky's death."

"*Da.* I know the day. I never forget the day, though I try to."

"How do you get through the day?" I inquired.

"Drink, fight, fuck."

I thought of the years past, trying to remember how Barrett handled the anniversary of Dolinsky's death. But it all ran together, and when the bairns were younger and needed her close, she was never far from them. Were there times that she snuck away, just for a few hours, reconciling the past? Or trying to bury it?

Why had she never spoken to me about it? Why had I never thought to ask? Why had I never noticed? When did I stop *seeing* my wife?

"Do you have any idea where she could be?" I asked, shame coating my tongue.

He fell silent.

"You know, don't you?" I demanded, already knowing the answer.

He knew, and it felt like a betrayal. Like Barrett didn't trust me the way she trusted *him*.

"She didn't call me," Sasha explained. "I swear it, Flynn. But I think I have an idea of where she is."

I pinched the bridge of my nose.

Sasha paused and then said slowly, "I think she's at his house in Vermont. Where he...kept her."

"Why would she be there?"

"Because I bought it years ago. I never go there, but she does."

"That sounds an awful lot like you bought my wife a house."

"I suppose you could see it that way."

"Why don't you ever go there?"

"I have no need to."

"Then why do you own it?"

"Flynn," he began.

We rarely called one another by our first names. Only in moments of extreme importance.

"It's not what you think," he insisted. "I did not buy her a house."

"Is this one of those Sasha and Barrett things that I'll never understand? That I'm not privy to?"

"Give her a chance to explain."

"She should've told me about it. About the house."

"Why?"

"Why what?"

"Why should she have told you about it? So you could read more into it than what's really there? She knows how much it hurts you to be reminded of him and what he took from you. Took from you both. She didn't want to burden you with it."

Dolinsky was always a sore subject. He was an abscess. Still, after all this time.

"Does Quinn know? About the house?"

"No. She doesn't know."

Secrets. Barrett kept them from me. Sasha kept them from Quinn.

I rose slowly from my desk. "What's the address?"

"I'll text it to you."

I swallowed my pride and then said simply, "Thank you." I hoped he could hear the sincerity in my tone.

"I would've called you," he said. "If I'd known she was gone."

"Aye?"

"*Da*. Be well, Flynn."

He hung up. A moment later, my phone pinged with the address.

I stalked from the library, the scotch I'd consumed pumping out of my veins and replaced with adrenaline. I made a quick call to my pilot, waking him up out of a sound sleep to tell him to ready the plane.

After I hung up with him, I threw the phone on the bed and then went to shower. I scrubbed the last few days from my skin, my mind churning over every possible reason she'd fled to Dolinsky's house, and why she hadn't told me.

I was tired of the secrets. Tired of the lies. It all needed to be brought into the light.

Now.

I'd wallowed long enough, letting my pride get in the way of what I needed to do. My wife was hurting. And she was doing it alone. But that wasn't the way marriages worked. I didn't care what she told me. I didn't care if her words gutted me. I'd listen and then hold her, and we'd find a way through this.

Duncan was sitting on the bed when I came out of the bathroom, a towel wrapped around my waist.

"You didn't shave."

"Don't care much about shaving," I said, padding my way to the closet. "I showered. Isn't that enough?"

"What did Petrovich have to say."

I opened the top dresser drawer and grabbed a pair of boxer briefs in navy, Barrett's favorite pair.

"He says she's at Dolinsky's home."

"Dolinsky's home… The one in Vermont, you mean?"

"That would be the one." I quickly donned the trousers and then a blue V-neck sweater.

"But how? Why?"

"Apparently, Petrovich bought the house years ago. He owns it, but never goes there. But Barrett does."

"Holy shite."

"I know."

"He bought her a *house*?"

"He claims it's not like that."

"Then what the hell is it? If another man bought Ash a house, I'd—" He quickly switched to Gaelic and let out a surge of curses.

"My sentiments exactly." I walked back into the bedroom, holding a pair of socks.

I had to be strong enough for both of us now.

Strong enough to exorcise Igor Dolinsky, once and for all.

Chapter 8
BARRETT

"You look tired," Hildie said as she placed the half grapefruit in front of me, along with a heavily toasted and buttered English muffin on a plate.

"You couldn't lie to me?" I asked with a smile. "Or pretend you don't notice every little detail?"

"Lying doesn't do you any good, and I think you've had too many people in your life lie to you."

I leaned back in my chair. "That sounds like an accusation."

"No, it was an assessment. When you get to be my age, you learn that holding your tongue is useless."

"So, you can just say whatever is on your mind?" I asked in amusement.

"When I think it will help someone I care about, then yes."

"Thanks, Hildie." I sighed. "But you're wrong. There are people in my life who tell me the truth. I just haven't listened to them."

"You weren't ready to listen to them, but you'll listen to me."

"What makes you think I'll listen to you?"

"Instinct. Eat your breakfast and then take a walk across the grounds," Hildie said. "Maybe some fresh air will do you good and then you can take a nap."

I reached for my espresso. "This should do the trick."

"I'll leave you to it, then. Enjoy your breakfast." She turned and left.

I sipped on my espresso for a moment and then I picked up my cloth napkin and set it on my lap.

I ate my food without much excitement or appetite. When I finished, I stood up and walked out of the dining room to the front closet.

There were snow pants, boots, and a heavy coat in my size. I quickly got into the outdoor clothes, grabbed a pair of gloves and a hat, and was out the door.

The snowstorm had blown itself out sometime in the middle of the night. Now the sun was shining, and the sky was clear. Cold air filtered into my lungs, causing my chest to burn. I shivered as I trekked through a foot of snow.

"Why are you doing this?" Igor asked, suddenly by my side. He was dressed in a black parka and a red hunting hat.

A Russian Holden Caulfield, I thought with derision.

"Doing what? Slogging through the snow?" I asked.

"No. I meant, why are you torturing yourself?"

"I'm not torturing myself. I'm being tortured by *you.*"

He shoved his hands in his pockets. "I'm nothing, Barrett. I'm nothing but a memory. I'm ashes in the wind. Why don't you want to be happy?"

"Do I deserve to be happy?" I murmured. "After all I've done?"

"You killed me in the name of your family. In the name of love. Or so you keep saying."

"It's still killing," I pointed out.

"And you'd kill again to protect Flynn. To protect your sons."

"Yes."

There was no hesitation at all in my answer.

"So, it's not the killing that has you twisted up inside, is it? It's not even your unresolved feelings for me. It's something deeper. You know what you've tried to conceal, it's finally sprouted from the grave you tried to bury it in. So, pull the vine out of your soul or it's going to strangle you as it grows."

"Go away," I groused in misery.

"I can't. Not until you're truly ready to let me go. And I don't think you want to let me go. You like having something between you and your husband."

I whirled to face him. "What the hell is that supposed to mean?"

"You're afraid he won't love you anymore. Not after you tell him the truth. Not after you tell him what you've kept from him all this time."

"Go. Away."

His cheeks weren't red with from the chill, and there was no breath from him visible in the cold. He was just the ghost of a man I once knew. It reminded me that he wasn't real.

But my suffering was real. That was the only truth I knew—and I couldn't keep living like this.

I needed to talk to Flynn. I needed to come clean. And if he still loved me after the truth…then maybe we would be stronger. Maybe we'd survive.

I'd been running long enough. It was time to face my husband. I'd say goodbye to Hildie and drive back to the airport and catch a flight home.

The weight I'd been carrying around lifted from my

heart because I realized I was going to tell Flynn everything.

I turned back toward the mansion, exhausted from the emotion roiling through me, but I was committed to the course now. The agony of limbo was worse than potentially burning everything to the ground and starting over.

Tears threatened to cascade down my cheeks when I thought about losing it all. My throat constricted. I couldn't picture a life without Flynn.

A lone figure stood on the opposite end of the snow-bathed lawn. When I was closer, I knew immediately it was him.

I paused, but only for a moment, and then I was running in heavy snow boots to Flynn as if my life depended on it. I tripped and fell to the ground, but I scrambled back up. He came for me too, showing me, even now, that he would always meet me halfway.

I ran and didn't stop, not even when I was close enough to see the cobalt blue of his eyes. I jumped into his arms and wrapped myself around him, burying my nose against the side of his neck, breathing deeply, wanting to inhale every piece of him.

His arms went around me immediately. "Hen," he whispered.

The tears I'd attempted to hide fell, and they came from somewhere deep inside, springing from my heart. I trembled against him. "You came for me."

Flynn's arms loosened, and I slid down his body. When I stood on my own two feet, Flynn's hands came up to cradle my cheeks and forced my gaze up to his.

"You daft woman," he rumbled softly. "I'll always come for you."

Chapter 9
FLYNN

She shuddered in my embrace.

"Hen?"

"Just…give me a minute." Barrett clung tighter to me, as if she were afraid that I would disappear if she let me go.

We stood there in the cold, the pristine snow all around us as she curled her body into mine.

Barrett needed me. It had been so long since I felt like she'd needed me. I loved that she was strong and independent, but damn it all to hell, all I wanted to do was protect and care for her.

Why wouldn't she let me?

"Are you ready to go inside?" I asked, leaning my cheek against her head.

"I guess we should." She sighed and then pulled back to peer up at me. "I still can't believe you're here. How did you—"

"In a bit, hen," I interrupted. "All that can wait."

I took her gloved hand in mine and headed for the

house. The front door opened just as we tromped up the steps.

"Mr. Campbell!" the older woman greeted in surprise.

I frowned and looked down at Barrett.

"Hildie," Barrett introduced. "She and her husband live in the converted carriage house and take care of the place."

"Pleasure to meet you," I said, holding out my free hand to the woman.

"It's nice to finally meet you, sir." She took it immediately and gave it a hearty shake. "I thought you weren't joining Mrs. Campbell."

"Change of plans," Barrett interjected quickly.

"Did you bring the children with you?" Hildie asked with an eager smile, looking over my shoulder as if I'd stashed them somewhere out of sight.

"No, they're still with their great aunt and uncle in Ireland," I explained.

Barrett said, "Hildie has been wanting to spoil the bairns ever since I showed her photos of them."

Hildie stepped back to let us into the house. I looked around the foyer, seeing it for the very first time.

I was in Dolinsky's home—the place he'd brought Barrett all those years ago.

It was beautiful and opulent. The wooden bannister had clearly been carved by an expert craftsman. The crown moldings, along with the architecture itself was unrivaled. I knew this place held dark memories for Barrett, but I wondered if they were all unhappy. This was the place she'd discovered that she could be as ruthless as any man.

"I'll bring tea to the salon," Hildie said, jarring me out of my reverie. "And a plate of ham and cheese croissants."

"Thank you," Barrett said as she began unzipping her coat.

Hildie looked at Barrett and then at me before nodding and turning away to head down the hallway.

We removed our outer wear and boots in silence. My eyes drank her in. We'd been separated for only a few days, but it was enough for me to see a change in her. Her normally luminous skin looked wan. When she started walking toward the salon, she rubbed her hip. I wondered if it actually bothered her, or if it was more of a reflex.

The salon was lit from large, open windows that let in the low winter light. A cheerful fire glowed in the fireplace. Logs crackled and popped, and the scent of oak filled the warm, dry room.

Barrett took a seat on the L-shaped gray couch and curled her wool sock clad feet beneath her. She grabbed a black blanket next to her and covered her lap.

I settled beside her.

"I expected you to yell," she said, staring into the flames instead of meeting my gaze.

"I can yell, if you want."

"I deserve it," she said flatly. She paused a moment and then finally looked directly at me. Her hazel eyes appeared watery, like she was about to cry.

"Aye, you deserve it," I agreed.

We fell silent as Hildie entered the salon, carrying a tea tray laden with two saucers and a pot of steaming water, cold milk, and honey. The ham and cheese croissants were arranged in a neat pattern on white china with rose gold edging.

I hadn't eaten in hours and despite the unresolved tension between me and my wife, I was hungry.

"Thank you, Hildie. It looks delicious," I said.

"You look like you need some good hearty food, and a

nap, too," Hildie remarked as she set the tray down on the wood coffee table. "You look almost as tired as Mrs. Campbell."

I raised my brows and glanced at Barrett. She leaned over and began fixing two cups of tea. "Hildie offers her observations without reserve, and at no additional cost."

She plopped two lumps of sugar into a teacup and stirred it before handing it to me.

"I have some things to take care of back at the carriage house," Hildie said.

Barrett nodded. "Thank you for the tea and croissants."

"Call if you need me. Otherwise, I'll be gone all afternoon."

I watched her touch Barrett's shoulder in a show of silent affection and then leave the salon. Hildie's footsteps faded down the hallway and we were alone again.

"She's right," Barrett said, reaching for a ham and cheese croissant and wrapping it in a white linen napkin before giving it to me. "You do look like you need a nap."

"So do you," I pointed out as I took the croissant from her.

"You didn't shave."

"Didn't think it was important. When I found out where you were, I showered off the scotch and then got on a plane."

She winced. "You called Sasha, didn't you?"

"Aye."

"I'm guessing you know he owns it?"

I nodded. "Why didn't you tell me?"

Barrett lifted the cup of tea to her lips. "I wasn't sure how to explain it. I wasn't sure it would make sense."

"So, you decided to keep it a secret from me. Not just that he owns the house, but that you have complete access to it." The anger that had been pushed aside due to the relief of holding her in my arms came roaring back. "Why do you keep things from me? Haven't I forgiven you enough in the past? Sometimes I want to shake some sense into you, Barrett. I'm your husband, and yet you keep me at arm's length. Have you ever truly let me in?"

She turned her head and glared at me. "That's not fair, Flynn. We didn't meet under normal circumstances, and don't pretend there weren't times you haven't been honest with me."

"No," I said, my tone darkening. "You don't get to make excuses. When you found out who I was, who I *truly* was, you chose to stay. You do not get to punish me for that now."

Barrett bowed her head and nodded timidly. In that moment, she appeared smaller. Like the world had battered her down.

"Do you want a divorce?" I asked suddenly. "Is that what all this about?"

She lifted her gaze swiftly to mine. "No. I don't want a divorce."

"Then why, Barrett? Why do you come here? Why did you run off without an explanation? Why didn't you at least let me know you were safe? And why the hell do you and Sasha have secrets that I'm not privy to?"

Barrett set her cup of tea down on the tray and rose. She wrapped the blanket around her shoulders and then strode to the fireplace to stare into the flames.

I wanted to go to her, but the anger poisoned my veins and unleashed white-hot rage into my body. I couldn't move. I could barely breathe. I was afraid if I went to her, we wouldn't talk. I'd drag her into my arms and kiss the breath out of her. We'd fall to the floor and fuck in front of the fire, and nothing would be resolved. We'd be back where we started without resolution. But the cracks in our relationship had reached the foundation. One earthquake and we'd be nothing but rubble.

She turned her head to look at me. Her hazel eyes were shiny, and a lone tear slipped out of the corner of her eye to roll down her cheek. "I'm consumed with guilt."

"Guilt over what? Dolinsky? Needing to still mourn the anniversary of his death? What? For fuck's sake, what the hell is this all about?"

She exhaled a shaky breath and then squared her shoulders. "We were supposed to have another child, Flynn. But I lost it."

Chapter 10
BARRETT

His eyes widened. "What the hell are you talking about?"

"We lost a baby, Flynn."

"When? For shite's sake, Barrett. I want the entire fucking story and I want it now!"

I nodded. "It happened when we went to rescue Katherine from Andrew."

Flynn stilled. "You fell…"

"Yes," I whispered. "The fall caused me to miscarry."

"Did you know? Before all that happened with Andrew, did you know you were pregnant?"

I shook my head. "It was early, Flynn. Really early. I hadn't missed my period yet. Later the doctor… he told me…due to the trauma of the fall, I miscarried." I swallowed my tears. "And then he told me I wouldn't be able to have any more children because of the way my pelvis broke."

"But I'd had a vasectomy—"

"It failed."

Flynn closed his eyes and remorse rolled across his face. When he finally opened his eyes to look at me, they appeared unusually bright. "You still haven't explained why you come here? Why do you torture yourself? Losing the baby was out of your control."

I played with the dainty wedding band on my finger. It had belonged to Flynn's mother. I didn't feel like I deserved to wear it.

"This is the place where I lost myself, Flynn. Dolinsky brought me here and I left a different woman." I stared back into the flames, unable to endure the hurt that spread across Flynn's expression. "I think I deserved to lose our baby. I think it was punishment. For my sins."

"If we were punished for our sins, then I should be dead many times over." He stood up and came to me and gripped me by the upper arms. "You should've told me about the baby, so I could've been there for you. And you shouldn't feel guilty for losing our baby."

I gripped his sweater, trying to infuse him with understanding. "Don't you get it? I've killed to protect my children. But I couldn't even protect the life growing inside me."

"You have to let it go." He pulled me to his chest and wrapped his arms around me. "You saved Katherine, love. Your only mistake was not confiding in me."

"I didn't know how. I didn't even…"

"What?"

"I didn't even write about it. During the year that I was healing I poured my grief and anger into my journals, but I never admitted I was pregnant. Not even to myself. I just buried it."

"What *did* you put in those journals, hen? You never let me read them."

"You never asked."

"I respect your privacy."

"Maybe you shouldn't."

He tugged on my hair and forced me to look him in the eyes, and then from somewhere deep within him, he rumbled, "Maybe you should stop thinking you have to carry all your burdens alone."

"I don't want to hurt you."

"You hurt me more when you live your life without me. Just *tell* me, hen."

Tears seeped from the corners of my eyes, and he brushed them away with his thumbs.

"Why are you crying?"

"Because you love me in a way that's hard for me. It's so unconditional. At times I can't bear it."

He smiled and it was tender and sincere. Far more tender than I deserved. "Aye."

"I don't know why I cause you pain and then run."

"That has to stop. Promise me now, Barrett. I won't tolerate it anymore. If you have a problem from now on, you come to me. When you dream about the men you've killed, you wake me up and talk about it. I love you more than you know, but that all stops now."

My eyes widened. "How did you——"

"You talk in your sleep."

How long has he known?

What exactly does he know?

Did he know that I didn't always just dream of killing Dolinsky? That my dreams were painted with blood, sex, and destruction? Did he understand that it was the feeling of power that surged in my veins, more potent than any aphrodisiac or even adrenaline itself?

"Swear it to me, Barrett. Now. Swear that you won't run from me again. No matter what goes on in your head. No matter what demons chase you. You come to me. Always."

"I swear it," I whispered helplessly.

He looked at me for a long moment and then he bent his head and touched his lips to mine. His tongue demanded entrance.

I opened to him, wanting—needing—him to prove his love for me in a manner deeper than words.

Flynn had always been good at showing his love with words.

He was better at showing me with his body.

Flynn released me, but only so he could fling the blanket from my shoulders. We fumbled like two teenagers trying to get our clothes off while attempting not to break contact with our lips.

Finally, the both of us grew too demanding.

I ripped my mouth from his and stepped away. My fingers went to the buttons of my pants, and I hastily shucked them off. I yanked the sweater over my head and cast it aside.

Flynn's eyes glittered with desire as he hastily removed his own clothes.

When we both stood completely naked, we stared at each other. The years we'd spent together had been kind to him. Except for a few scars from being shot, he looked the same as when we'd met.

I was softer.

I bore the scars of carrying his children.

My body had been through many wars in the name of protecting my family.

"You're beautiful," he whispered gruffly.

"I'm broken."

He stepped closer and traced my belly with his fingers. "You're a warrior."

His hands plowed into my hair, and he firmly pulled my head toward him and brought my mouth to his again. I closed my eyes and reveled in his touch. I breathed him in, wondering why this man had chosen me.

"Stop thinking," he said against my lips. "That's your problem. You think too damn much."

"Help me not think," I pleaded.

Flynn slid his arms around me, and we sank to the ground on the dark rug next to the firelight. He lay me down on my back and looked at me.

"Touch me, Flynn."

His hands skated up my body to caress my breasts. He flicked my nipples and then pinched them between his fingertips.

I moaned with desire at what was coming.

Then he leaned down and took one of the tightening buds into his mouth. He swept his tongue across my sensitive breast while his hand teased the other.

I tried to reach down and grasp him, but he batted my fingers away.

"I own you, Barrett," he growled. "Tonight, I'm taking my pleasure the way *I* want it."

My eyes rolled into the back of my head as I succumbed to his caresses and dominant words.

His lips left my breasts and skimmed across my belly, kissing every curve, every line on the way down. He didn't stop until he was at the heat between my legs.

I expected to feel his tongue stroke me, but when it didn't, I opened my eyes.

He was staring at me like I was the most precious, most beautiful treasure in the world to him.

"You don't seem to believe me when I talk. Maybe you'll believe this."

His finger danced across the apex of my thighs, twirling and teasing before slipping inside of me. He gently grasped my leg and angled it so that he could push deeper, stroking the spot that was elusive to lesser men.

My back arched in pleasure.

"Who do you belong to, Barrett?"

"You," I whispered.

His thumb taunted the primed bud between my legs. He exerted just enough pressure to drive me wild, but he refused to let me go over the edge.

A wail escaped my lips when he left me. Without breaking eye contact, he slid his fingers into his mouth and licked them clean.

Before I had a chance to demand he satisfy me, he took his other hand and grasped himself. He stroked his erection, gave it a few pumps before guiding it into my eager and welcoming body.

Flynn went slowly at first; torturously slow.

His eyes were on mine as he rested his weight on his elbows and gently rocked into me.

"Flynn…"

"Hen?"

"I need you."

"I know."

He slid out of me and then pushed back in, angling his pelvis so he hit all the right spots. I arched up to meet his thrusts, gasping, moaning, beseeching as he pushed deep and hard.

I clawed at his back. Our skin was slippery with sweat and hot to the touch.

It would never be enough.

No matter how many times he sank into my body, no matter how many times he made me come, it was never enough.

I wanted him now and forever.

He slammed into me, and I clasped Flynn as the pleasure rolled through me. I felt it all the way down my spine. My scalp tingled and my toes curled. I trembled and cried out my release.

"Fuck," Flynn shouted as he plunged into me one final time before stilling.

I pressed my hand to his thundering heart, feeling the strength that coursed through his body.

Flynn was strong when I needed him to be strong. He owned my body the way I needed to be owned.

We paused for a moment and caught our breaths, and then I gently pushed against him, and Flynn eased out of me.

"Barrett," he whispered, taking my lips in a punishingly sweet kiss before flopping down on the rug next to me.

With a wicked grin, I climbed on top of him. He was still hard, and I angled him back inside of me.

"You may own me, Flynn," I said, leaning down so my hair brushed his face. "But that means I get to own you, too."

His smile was slow, full of heat and want. "Own me, Barrett. For the rest of my life."

Chapter 11
FLYNN

BARRETT PULLED AWAY from my side and sat up. I gently grasped her arm and attempted to haul her on top of me.

She sniggered and collapsed against me for a moment.

"I just wanted to get us a blanket," she said, kissing my lips.

"We could move upstairs to a bed," I suggested. "It might be more comfortable."

"You sound old, Flynn."

Barrett's eyes were clear and free of turmoil. I swept a damp curl away from her cheek. "Do I need to prove to you how young I really am?"

Her grin was cheeky and impish. "Yes. I think you should."

I laughed and gently swatted her backside. "Be quick about it."

She got up and went to retrieve the blanket she had discarded and dropped to the floor in our haste to be with one another. She favored her right leg, and I was instantly contrite. "I should've taken you upstairs."

Barrett looked at me over her shoulder as she grabbed the blanket. "Why?"

"Your hip."

"My hip is fine." She came back, then laid down, nestling herself against me, and pulled the blanket over us.

Her fingers trailed over my chest before settling her palm against my heart. I covered her hand with mine.

"Explain something to me," I said after a few minutes of silence. "If my vasectomy failed, how have you prevented pregnancy?"

She paused before admitting, "Birth control."

"I see. You kept that from me, too."

"If I told you why I was on birth control, then the truth would've come out. I just…didn't know how. I wish you didn't know," she said softly. "I wish I had been able to grieve on my own and move on. I didn't want to burden you with this. I thought I had dealt with this. Truly. And then a few months ago…"

"Is that why you wanted another baby? Because you feel like the miscarriage is somehow your fault and you want to rectify it?"

"It *is* my fault," she said. "I was pregnant. And then I wasn't."

"It's not your fault," I stated.

I knew she didn't believe me. I wouldn't be able to assuage her guilt. Only she could do that.

"You didn't tell Ash," I said suddenly.

She looked at me. "No. I didn't. But how did you—"

"Because she was just as confused about your behavior as I was," I admitted. "She didn't understand why you wanted another baby, and she didn't understand why you left in the middle of the night. You face your problems, Barrett. You're strong, but you ran. I understand guilt eating you alive. But you should've shared it with me."

"I should have." Barrett winced.

"Do you not trust me? After all this time?"

"No. God, no. I just—Christ, do you ever feel like you just need a moment. Several moments? To clear your head, so that when you do explain yourself, you're not making more of a mess?"

"You made a bigger mess by leaving. By making us all worry about you."

She paused, the silence heavy between us.

"I am sorry for that. For causing unnecessary worry. Are you upset, Flynn? About losing the baby?" she asked finally.

"Upset? No, I don't think I am. It happened so long ago, Barrett. I didn't even know."

She opened her mouth like she was going to protest, but I quickly covered her lips with my hand. "Let me speak. Another bairn would've been…well, another adventure, for sure. But the miscarriage happened *to* you, Barrett. This feels… I don't know, like I'm somehow removed from it and not just because of the time that's passed." I lifted my hand to let her speak.

She swallowed. "You don't grieve this loss of what could've been?"

"Grieve? Aye, but more for you and your sadness." I clenched my jaw. "You shouldn't have grieved alone. If there's anything to be upset about, it's that. Woman, you're never alone—and if you feel like you are alone, it's because you choose to feel that way, but that doesn't make it true. What more do I have to do to prove to you that I'm here, that I'm not going anywhere?"

She looked around. "Here. In Dolinsky's home. Yeah, it's official. I really don't deserve you."

"Why do you say that? Look what you've done for me. For the lads. For our family. The sacrifices you've made."

"What sacrifices?" she asked.

"Your career. You would've gotten your PhD and had a full teaching load long ago if it weren't for your family."

"And gone home to that same small apartment night after night, if I wasn't falling asleep at my desk," she said with a wry smile. "I don't miss that life, Flynn. I really don't."

"I'm glad to hear it."

Her smile dimmed. "Does this change things for you? About adopting?"

"I don't know," I said with a sigh.

She nodded. "I meant what I said though. I won't pressure you into anything. I've had a lot of time to think about things, even though admitting them to myself took a while." She paused. "Speaking of bairns, ours are way too smart for their own good. When I called Moira to check in with them, Hawk immediately asked if we were fighting. I told them we weren't. Hawk didn't sound like he believed me. He's definitely your son."

I smiled, feeling inordinately pleased with myself. "We should call them. Together. We should do it soon, considering the time change. They'll be going to bed soon."

"We might want to find some clothes first," she suggested. "Did you pack a bag?"

"A small one. It's in the car."

She sat up, the blanket dropping from her body. Barrett looked around the room, her expression resolved.

"I don't think I need to come back here," she said quietly.

"No?"

Barrett looked at me. "No. This place is a tie to the past. I don't want to live in the past anymore. I want to move forward, Flynn."

I took her hand and laced my fingers through hers.

"Let's get dressed and call our boys. I need to hear their voices."

We got back into our clothes and then settled on the couch. I removed my cellphone from my pocket and dialed my aunt's number.

"They're not here," Moira said. "Colleen took them for the day."

"She already has three of her own children to look after," Barrett said with a laugh.

Moira chuckled. "I'd never tell you your children are a handful, but—"

"Why do you think we have three nannies?" I asked.

"Fair point. Hold on, James wants to say hello."

There was some shuffling and then a moment later, my uncle's face appeared on the screen. "Are you spending Christmas with us?"

I looked at Barrett.

"Not this year," Barrett said. "We do promise a family visit soon, though."

"We'll take it," James said. "It really has been wonderful having the boys here. They're growing so fast."

"They are," Barrett murmured. "Thank you for watching them."

"Anytime. The invitation always extends to the both of you," Moira said. "We want to see more of you."

I grinned at Barrett.

"You could always come to Scotland, you know," Barrett said. "But I realize your children live close to you, so holidays at your house makes sense."

"Only because we've been doing it this way for so long," James said. "Maybe next year I can convince Moira to spend Christmas at your castle."

Moira piped up, "There he goes, blaming things on

me, when really he just wants to drink his whiskey on Christmas Eve and get to bed early."

"Let's call this a stalemate," I said. "Or we'll never get off the phone. We're flying out tomorrow. We'll call again in the morning and tell them we're coming."

"Sounds good, lad," James said.

"Bye," Barrett said.

I hung up the phone and tossed it aside. I leaned back against the couch and Barrett cuddled into my embrace.

"I forget sometimes," she said.

"Forget what?"

"That I have a beautiful life." She looked up at me, her eyes glistening with love and emotion. "Thank you."

"For?"

She smiled. "Everything."

Chapter 12
BARRETT

WE TOOK our private jet and landed in Belfast and then drove to James and Moira's home outside the city. Their yellow house had a picturesque postcard appeal and smoke from the stone chimney puffed into the sky before dissipating. It was a winter wonderland, as if a painter had brushed a dream into existence.

The front door of the house opened, and my three perfect, exuberant, and heathenish children ran outside. Before Flynn had even parked the car, I was unlatching my seatbelt and opening the door. I barely made it two steps toward them before I was engulfed by tiny arms.

"Mam!" Iain cried, wrapping himself around one of my legs.

Hawk spoke in rapid fire Gaelic, his face a perfect mirror of Flynn's as he looked up at me.

Quiet, sensitive Noah stared at me with something akin to understanding. Only six-years-old, and he saw more than a boy his age should be able to see.

Flynn shut his car door, and my children let go of me to run to their father. I turned just in time to see him squat down to greet them. Due to their excitement, they knocked him to the ground, causing him to laugh as he squeezed them with all his might.

I smiled, tears stinging my eyes. Flynn met my gaze and his expression softened. He whispered something to the children, and they immediately crawled off him and ran back toward me.

Hawk latched onto one of my hands and Noah took the other. Iain skipped ahead.

"I'm being herded, aren't I?" I asked with a laugh.

"Why didn't you tell us you were coming?" Hawk asked.

"We thought about it, but then we realized we wanted to surprise you," I replied.

The late afternoon sun failed to penetrate the cold Irish winter and the back of my neck quickly grew chilly. I hadn't bothered to put on a coat before getting out of the car.

"Aunt Moira!" Hawk called out when we stepped through the front door.

Flynn closed the door behind him and slid his boots along the rug in the foyer, dusting off the snow before it began to melt. Moira came out of the kitchen, wiping her hands on a dishrag.

Her smile was warm and genuine. "You're just in time. A loaf of soda bread just came out of the oven."

"Let me guess. There's warm honey butter, too," Flynn said, moving toward his aunt and kissing her cheek.

"I know my audience. And if I want you to stay for a few hours before you take my grand-nephews home—"

"Guilt. You're good with the guilt." I smiled. "Is there Irish whiskey, too?"

Moira nodded. "We'll sit by the fire. Make yourselves comfortable."

I let Hawk and Noah pull me to the den and I sat down in a big, plush blue chair. I scooted over and patted the spot next to me. Iain immediately took it and then Noah settled himself on my lap.

Hawk clearly was too old to be a mama's boy. Suddenly, a vision of him walking across the stage at his university graduation assaulted me. I got lost in the moment picturing him looking deceptively solemn and then sticking out his tongue at the last moment.

I smiled as I gazed with tenderness at my eldest who was running a hand though his mop of dark hair. He plopped his bottom on a cushion in front of the fireplace and Flynn took the spot next to him.

"What trouble have the three of you been getting into?" Flynn asked. His cobalt blue eyes looked at each of his sons. Hawk, feigning innocence, didn't squirm at all. That one would become an iron vault, I had no doubt about it. Iain was a picture of guilt and deception. Noah's gaze darted to his brother's before coming back to rest on his father.

"Out with it," Flynn demanded.

"It was Brandon's fault," Iain blurted out. "It was his idea."

"What was his idea?" I asked.

Hawk sighed. "He was the one that said Aunt Moira was scared of spiders. And he took us to a shop in Belfast and we bought fake spiders and placed them all around the kitchen, in drawers, everywhere, and the next morning when she came downstairs she…"

"She what?" I demanded.

"Screamed," Noah said. "*A lot.*"

Iain nodded. "And then Uncle James ran into the kitchen to see why she was making a fuss."

"That wasn't nice of you," I said.

"But they got even with us," Hawk retorted.

"Did they?" Flynn asked, his lips twitching with amusement. "What did they do?"

"Toads," Iain said. "Lots of them. In our beds."

"Kilmartins don't get mad, they get even," James said as he entered the den.

Flynn rose and held out his hand to his uncle. James grasped it and then pulled Flynn into an embrace.

"So, we don't need to punish them for their rotten prank." I smirked.

James released Flynn and then came over to me. When I patted Noah to get up, James waved him down and then leaned over to kiss my cheek. "No. I think they've learned their lesson."

"And Brandon?" I asked.

"He'll get his just reward." James winked and took a seat on the couch. "Hate to break this to you, Barrett, but your sons are tiny little versions of Flynn."

"I'm aware," I said with an arch of a brow at my husband. "I suppose I'll keep them, since I'm rather fond of their father."

"Thank you, hen," Flynn said dryly.

Moira entered the den with a tray laden with Irish soda bread, honey butter, and a plate of cookies.

Iain hopped up and immediately went to the coffee table where Moira set down the tray.

"Don't worry, Mam," Hawk said with a grin that was all trouble. "Even though you're a girl, we'll keep you too."

Chapter 13

BARRETT

"Home sweet home," I breathed as I stepped into our expansive foyer.

I was bone weary, but the trip had been worth it. Moira and James had attempted to coerce us into staying the night, but I wanted to sleep in my own bed. Thank goodness the tension between Flynn and I had disappeared. It would've been hell trying to keep it a secret from the boys, along with everyone else.

Flynn stepped close to me and leaned down, brushing his lips against mine. Hawk made a gagging noise in the background.

"Okay, ruffians," I said when I finally pulled away from Flynn. "Baths first, then bedtime."

"Awwww, Mam," Iain whined.

"I'm not dirty," Hawk protested. "I had a bath yesterday."

Flynn flicked Hawk's lobe. "Then why are your ears covered in dirt?"

Hawk rubbed the tender spot and then shrugged and smiled.

"Baths," I repeated.

"Listen to your mother. And the sooner you take a bath," Flynn said, "the sooner you go to sleep. Tomorrow, we're going with Uncle Duncan to cut down our Christmas tree."

"Will you let me swing the axe?" Hawk asked eagerly.

I shot Flynn a look.

"We'll see," he lied.

Iain muttered, "I know what that means."

"Upstairs, the lot of you." Flynn said. "I'm right behind you."

The boys tore up the stairs, disappearing from sight.

"When the boys are done with their baths, what do you say we have a bath of our own in our master tub? It fits us both."

I leaned against his chest. "I'm so tired. Rain check?"

"Aye," he agreed. "Tomorrow night. After I get home from chopping down our Christmas tree, you can scrub my back."

"My very own Scottish Paul Bunyan."

"Who?"

"He's a—never mind."

He kissed me again and then let me go. "You might want to call Ash and tell her you're back safe and sound."

"Doesn't she already know?" I arched a brow. "Haven't you texted Duncan?"

"Aye, they know. But she'll want to hear your voice."

"I'll send her a quick text and tell her I'll call tomorrow. I'm wiped, and starving."

"Good thing we have a refrigerator stuffed with food." He kissed the end of my nose. "I'm sure you'll find something you like."

"I'm opening a bottle of wine," I said as I heard yelling from upstairs. I looked in the direction of the staircase. "All hail King Flynn, Master of Children, Commander of Baths."

"Yeah, yeah. I'm on my way."

He lightly smacked my behind and then took the stairs two at a time. I watched him run out of sight after our little heathens and thought about how lucky I was to have them.

I loved them so much my heart ached.

I reached into my back pocket and pulled out my cell phone. I shot off a quick text to Ash. My plan was to catch up with her the following day while the boys were doing manly things and come clean with her and tell her about the miscarriage.

She replied: *Glad you're home. I'm going to hug your face when I see you. And swat you for terrifying us all.*

I smiled. She'd forgive me in time. Once I explained what had been going on I was sure she would understand. She was Ash, and I was Barrett, and we were as close as two people could be, and I knew we would get through it.

I kicked off my boots before tromping to the kitchen and then dialed a number on my favorites list.

"You're a stone-cold bitch," Sasha said in Russian.

"Then I'm in the best of company, because you're a stone-cold bastard," I replied in the same tongue and same droll tone.

He let out a low chuckle. "You worried the hell out of your husband. So much so that he called *me*."

"Yeah, I know. I'm not proud of it."

"Are you still there? At his place?"

"No. We're home now."

"How are you?" he asked. "Really."

I inhaled a shaky breath. "I'm okay."

"Yeah?"

"Yeah." I paused. "I'm not going back to Dolinsky's."

"No?"

"I don't need it anymore."

"Are you sure about that?" he asked.

"Yes." I cleared my throat. "Yes," I said again, my voice stronger this time. "I'm sure. It's time to let him go."

"I'll never let it go," he voiced. "I'll carry the guilt with me until I die."

"How Russian of you," I said with a teasing laugh. "Sometimes I think I've got some of that in me."

"The pain and misery that's part of our blood?"

I snorted. "I think it's why Russians can create such beautiful music and art. Nothing but deep sadness can fuel the creation of such beauty."

"I don't know how not to be tortured," he said.

"Practice?"

"*Da*, maybe." He paused. "He wasn't Igor in the end. Not the man I remembered. Not the man I'd have taken a bullet for."

"But it doesn't ease your burden knowing that, does it?"

"No. No, it doesn't." He fell silent for so long I wondered if he was still on the phone, but I heard his breathing and knew he was still with me. "We're bound, you and I. By him. By his ghost. Sometimes it's like he's walking next to me. I wish my daughter could've met him. Met the man he used to be."

"If he was still alive, Flynn would be dead, you never would've met Quinn, your daughter wouldn't exist, and you and I would be something else entirely."

"Oh, yes. I'm convinced now more than ever that you're actually Russian."

I let out a soft chuckle. "Kiss Helena for me."

"I will." He sighed. "Your husband..."

"What about him?"

"Is he going to try to end my life the next time he sees me?"

"It's a possibility."

"Hmm. Well, if he does try to kill me, ask him to make it quick, *da*?"

"*Da*," I repeated.

"Goodbye, Barrett. I'm glad you're home safe."

"Goodbye, Sasha. Thank you for keeping my confidence."

We hung up, and I set my phone aside. I opened the bottle of wine and poured two glasses to let them breathe. I rummaged through the refrigerator and found a dish of venison and potatoes. I grabbed two plates and was just about to scoop out two hefty servings when Flynn walked into the kitchen. His white shirt sleeves were rolled up to the elbows and he looked casual and relaxed.

"The boys are in bed, just waiting on their Mam to wish them good night."

I held out the serving spoon to him. "I'll be back in a few minutes."

He took the utensil from me, but just as I was about to move past him, his hand went to my hip to halt my movement. "I never stop wanting you, Barrett."

I smiled and kissed his strong jaw. "You know what we haven't done in a long time?"

"What?"

I gestured with my chin to the large window. During the day, I had an unencumbered view of Dornoch Firth. "You haven't fucked me against that glass in far too long."

"When you have three bairns, nannies, friends, and staff that come in and out constantly, it makes it complicated."

"No excuses, Flynn Campbell."

He laughed and then got to doling out our food. I headed down the hallway and took the long flight of stairs slowly. My knee was giving me trouble and I knew I'd have to baby it later with ice and anti-inflammatory medications.

I went to see the twins first. Two single beds were along opposite sides of the room. Noah's wall showed the solar system and countless stars. Iain's had a fire-breathing dragon swooping down on a knight with a scarred shield and broken sword in the fight for his life.

The lamps on the bedside tables next to their beds glowed warm amber. I pulled the covers up to Iain's chin—he liked to pretend he was in a cocoon. I kissed his head and brushed a hand across his damp hair.

"Did you brush your teeth?" I asked.

He nodded.

"Prove it," I commanded.

He opened his mouth and blew out a breath.

"Minty fresh." I smiled down at him. I then went to Noah who was staring up at the ceiling.

"What are you thinking about?" I asked him, pulling up the covers but not tucking him in tightly. He slept with abandon and hated feeling trapped.

"I'm wondering what's up there."

"Up where?"

"Heaven."

I sat down on the side of his bed. "All your wishes and dreams just waiting to come to you."

"If I wish for something hard enough, will it come true?"

"Yes," I said. Now was not the time for the truth. That sometimes, no matter how you wished, things didn't always turn out the way you wanted.

Noah closed his eyes, like he was about to go to sleep.

He breathed deeply for a few moments and then he opened his eyes to look at me.

I smiled. "What did you wish for, Noah?"

"I'm not telling or it won't come true."

"Sweet dreams." I leaned over and kissed his forehead.

I rose and turned off their lights and then quietly crept from the room, closing the door behind me. I went to tuck in Hawk. He was in bed, his lamp dim, the covers pulled up to his chin. His eyes were closed like he was already asleep.

Frowning, I sniffed the air.

"Are you sure you took a bath?"

He didn't open his eyes when he replied, "Aye."

I held in a grin. He sounded just like Flynn. "Then why does it smell like a farm animal in here?"

In the low light, I saw a massive lump under the covers next to Hawk suddenly move, and then Betty's face popped out. She bleated in my direction.

"Gavin Malcolm Campbell," I began. "You know she's not allowed upstairs, and certainly not in your bed."

"I missed her."

"How did you get her up here past your father?"

"I'm not telling." His eyes were beseeching. "Please, Mam? She loves sleeping on my bed and I don't have nightmares when she's with me."

I'd killed men and used my feminine wiles on others to get what I needed. I was cunning and ruthless when necessary, and completely immune to the emotions or manipulation of men. Except the ones I'd birthed, and the one I'd married.

"Okay, just for tonight," I stated, knowing I was about to set a precedent and that Hawk's room was going to smell like sheep for the foreseeable future. "But when she poops and pees in this room, you're cleaning it up."

"She paws at the door when she has to go out," he said. "She wakes me up and I let her outside."

"So, then this isn't the first time she's slept in your room, is it?" I demanded.

He yawned.

"Hawk."

"No." He sighed. "This isn't the first time."

"The nannies," I said in realization. "They've been covering for you, getting rid of the smell, haven't they?"

"Don't be mad at them."

"I'm not mad. I'm impressed." My first born was going to leave a trail of broken hearts across Scotland. I just knew it. He was only seven years old and already he had grown women wrapped around his little finger, willing to risk their jobs to keep him happy.

I scratched Betty's head and she leaned into my touch. After she'd had enough, she settled down at Hawk's back, nuzzling her face against the covers. I kissed Hawk's forehead and couldn't help the smile that stretched across my face.

I closed the door and then quietly trekked downstairs. Flynn was already half-way done with his meal.

"Sorry I didn't wait for you," he said. "What took you so long?"

"Your son snuck a sheep up to his bedroom and I had to pretend to be upset about it."

"I told you that sheep would be nothing but trouble."

"Then you go up and put a stop to it. Hawk says Betty keeps his nightmares at bay."

He took a sip of his wine. "Do you ever think—"

"That Hawk is smarter and more manipulative than all of us, and he deigns to let us take care of him? Yeah. I do."

"Okay," I said pouring boiling water into two mugs. "Let's hear it."

"Hear what?" Ash asked.

"How I ran off like a teenager and didn't tell anyone." I stirred in honey and then plopped a tea bag into each of the cups and then brought them to the kitchen table.

Her children were napping upstairs, and we had the baby monitor turned up so we could keep an ear out. Our husbands and my boys were in the process of finding our Christmas trees. A Campbell-Buchanan tradition.

"No. I'm not going to give you shit about running away like a teenager. You needed to get your head screwed on straight. So, did you? Get it screwed on straight?"

"I think so," I replied.

"I won't berate you, but I'll fully admit I'm curious as hell about what made you run. It wasn't just about the anniversary of Igor's death, was it?"

I looked at her in shock.

She snorted. "Please. I know it was more than just that. I mean, that's an issue all by itself. But what compounded it? The wanting of another baby?"

I finally told her about my miscarriage and the guilt I had been experiencing since it happened.

"So his vasectomy failed," she said.

I nodded. "I've been on birth control to prevent it from happening again."

Ash was silent for a long time and then she said, "You've been keeping that to yourself all this time. Why?"

I shrugged. "I don't know, Ash. I couldn't even think about it without the guilt clawing at me. So I didn't want to talk about it." I peered at her. "Do you still think about your own miscarriage?"

She nodded. "Yes. From time to time. In an abstract way. It's hard to envision things differently. Malcolm and

Wee Duncan wouldn't be here if not for the miscarriage, you know?"

"I know," I murmured.

"That makes me think…do you ever wonder what our lives would've looked like if we'd wound up with different men?"

I thought of her children upstairs. I thought of mine.

"I can't even imagine something so different."

"Then let it go," she said quietly. "Let the guilt go. You can't control everything, Barrett. Even though I know you try to."

"It gets me in trouble—trying to control everything."

"Yep. It's not healthy. Don't shut us out because you think you have to control everything, including your own emotions."

I pondered her words. I hadn't just been shutting Flynn out, I had been shutting out Ash, too. "I'm sorry."

"How did Flynn take the news about the miscarriage?"

"He was supportive. I never expected him to be anything else. But it's strange. It happened years ago, but it still feels fresh in my mind."

"I wonder, if you'd shared it with Flynn when it happened, do you still think you would feel this way and feel the need to flee?"

"I don't know. I know I needed the time to myself. In a different place. Alone."

"You sure about that? Or did you need Flynn to come after you and prove he wasn't going to leave, no matter what crazy stunt you pull?"

"I wonder if I'll ever not be a head-case."

"Doubtful."

"Thanks," I said in a dry tone.

She rolled her eyes. "I just mean, you're Barrett. And

you've lived through a lot. More than most people by a long shot."

I shook my head. "I think we need a girls' weekend."

"More like a girls' month," she said with a grin.

"You, me, and Quinn. What do you say?"

"I say Quinn and I have babies attached to our breasts. We're not going anywhere for a while."

"Damn," I said. "I wanted to go topless in St. Tropez."

"You really think we can do the topless thing? We've breastfed children for years."

"No one cares," I pointed out. "I guess we've entered that phase."

"What phase?"

"That phase of 'we're no longer in college and hot as fuck'."

"Speak for yourself. I'm still hot as fuck."

"Yeah, you are." I grinned. "The proof that your husband still wants you is resting right upstairs."

"You look like a weight has been lifted off your shoulders."

"I feel lighter." I lifted the mug of tea to my lips. "I feel a change coming."

"Do you?"

"Yes. I don't know what it's going to look like or what it'll be, but I feel it."

The cry of a baby blasted through the monitor.

Ash groaned. "I *just* got comfortable."

"I've been there," I said with a laugh.

Another cry echoed through the kitchen.

I set my mug down and stood up. "I'm a whiz at changing diapers and cuddling infants."

"You're so lucky your children are already potty trained. I can't wait to get there."

"Treasure these moments, Ash. They're gone far too quickly."

"I wish Ramsey were here," I said, looking at Ash and Duncan's perfectly decorated tree. "Christmas doesn't feel the same without him."

Duncan nodded. "Agreed."

"Why would he want to stay in Dallas when he could be here with us?" Ash asked.

Flynn raised a brow. "Let's see... He can be here, surrounded by happily married couples with a brood of very loud bairns, or he can stay in Dallas where he was crowned Dallas' Most Eligible Bachelor. My guess is he's drowning in—"

"Please don't say it," I begged.

Flynn merely grinned.

"Besides, he doesn't need a title to make him desirable to women," I pointed out.

"Oh, he gets plenty of women, just not the right ones," Ash said.

"Anyone need an eggnog refill?" Duncan asked, rising from his spot on the couch.

"I'm good," I said.

"I'll have a top off," Flynn stated.

"Ash?" Duncan looked at his wife, who shook her head.

Duncan took our glasses to the liquor cart in the corner. He added a splash of rum, filled the cups with homemade eggnog, and then dashed cinnamon on top.

The den was cheery with the Christmas tree and roaring fire. The children had been put to bed hours ago. They'd been allowed to open one present, with the promise that the following morning would bring many more.

Now it was just the adults sitting and enjoying the peace of a quiet house. The week leading up to Christmas was usually hectic, but this year had been different. It was low key without any fanfare. It was by tacit agreement that it stay that way.

Duncan handed off our drinks and took his seat again. "I'm worried about Ramsey. Our phone conversations are brief, vague, and he hardly ever makes time to fly home for a visit these days." He looked at Flynn. "Has he said anything to you?"

Flynn shook his head. "It's the same when I speak to him."

"You guys are so clueless," I remarked.

"What's that, hen?" Flynn demanded.

"He's tired of living in both your shadows," I said with a roll of my eyes. "It's so obvious."

"You don't think this has anything to do with Jane?" Ash asked.

"I think he's seeking solace in strangers when it comes to Jane," I said, taking a sip of eggnog.

"It's been years," Ash pointed out. "And he's still not over it?"

"He's over her, I think. But she betrayed him. Now he has trust issues where women are concerned. It'll take a very special woman to get him to open up again," I said. "Besides, have you seen Ramsey? There's no way he's settling down any time soon."

"Like a stag in rut," Duncan muttered. "And all too happy to keep living that life."

I raised my brows at Duncan's tone and discreetly looked at Ash. A frown marred her forehead.

The trill of Flynn's phone diverted our attention. Flynn dug his cell out of his pocket. He pressed a button and put it to his ear. "Cormac?" He paused for a long while and then said, "Shite. I'm on my way."

He hung up.

"What happened?" I asked.

Flynn rubbed the back of his neck. "Donal and Maisie Henderson were in a bad car accident a few days ago."

"Oh, that's awful," Ash murmured. "Didn't Donal just start working at the distillery?"

"Aye," Flynn said.

"Is it bad?" I asked.

Flynn nodded. "Donal died on impact. Maisie was rushed to emergency surgery when they brought her in, but she just went in again. She's hemorrhaging."

"Maisie's pregnant," Ash said. "What happened to the baby?"

"Delivered by C-Section," Flynn replied.

Duncan took Ash's hand and gave it a hearty squeeze. "I met Donal briefly. Good man."

"Indeed," Flynn said with a shake of his head.

"Wait, why did the hospital call Cormac?" I asked.

"He was listed as Donal's emergency contact," Flynn said. He stood, setting his eggnog on the coffee table. "Cormac asked me to come."

I nodded. "I'll go with you."

"You don't have to, love." Flynn touched my cheek. "I could be a while."

"I'm going," I said. I looked at Ash and Duncan. "You mind? The boys—"

"Go," Duncan waved us toward the door.

"Thanks."

Flynn shook Duncan's hand and then we walked to the front room to gather our coats.

Angus usually drove us, but he was in Wales visiting his sister for the holidays. And since we were spending

Christmas at Ash and Duncan's, we hadn't planned on needing Angus anyway.

"Take it slow," I said once we were buckled into the car.

"Aye, hen."

We arrived at the hospital half an hour later. Cormac, the master distiller for the SINNERS distillery, was in the waiting room. He stood up when he saw us, his hand outstretched to Flynn. His hair was the color of burnished honey, and his blue eyes were somber.

"Barrett," he greeted, brushing a kiss to my cheek.

"Any news?" Flynn asked.

"Maisie's still in surgery. That's all I know right now."

"What about the baby?" I asked.

"A little girl," Cormac said. "Healthy."

I let out a sigh. "One piece of good news, then."

"Nothing to do but wait," Cormac said. "And hope Maisie makes it."

"So, we wait," I repeated.

And pray.

"Can I get you anything? Coffee? Tea?" Cormac asked.

I shook my head. "I'm fine. Thank you."

The three of us took our seats and fell silent. I grasped Flynn's hand and he linked his fingers through mine.

"They don't have any family," Cormac said. "Both of them met in the system. Somehow, they made it out. Damn shame to have gone through that adversity and then have it come to this. In a hospital on Christmas Eve of all times, fighting for your life and losing the man you love."

I leaned close to Flynn and whispered, "I'm going to the restroom."

He nodded, squeezed my hand, and then let it go. I got up and walked out of the waiting room, searching for the loo. I found it and locked myself in. I doused my cheeks with some cool water, wanting to revive and refresh myself.

The dinner Ash's personal chef had cooked for us sat like a lump in my belly as I reflected on life. I had Flynn. We were both healthy and safe. Our children were asleep, protected by our family. They would wake the following morning to cheer and presents, and love.

Donal was dead.

His wife… Their child…

I couldn't stop thinking about what Maisie was about to wake up to, if she was lucky enough to live—raising their child on her own while grieving the loss of her husband.

Donal's death was an earthquake to my soul. His life had been cut tragically short before he'd even gotten a chance to truly live, and I realized that Flynn and I had everything Donal would never have.

I needed Flynn to put his arms around me. I felt like I was being emotionally dragged over the coals right as I'd begun to heal. Then I wondered, did wounds ever truly heal? Or were we all destined to wear our scars, hoping to find the means to conceal them?

Flynn wasn't in the waiting room when I returned, and neither was Cormac. I wandered around the hospital, walking aimlessly, reflecting on all the things hospitals made you think about. Birth, death, the life in between and the randomness of it all. God, and the general existential crisis that death brought about which always culminated in the general question of *what the hell was this all truly about?*

I found Flynn standing outside the nursery, peering through the glass at the tiny infants swaddled in pink and blue blankets, resting in bassinets.

"Hey," I said softly.

He lifted his arm and wrapped it around me, pulling me into his side. "We forget."

"What do we forget?"

"How small babies are when they're just born."

"They grow so fast. You blink, and time just slips by."

I rested my head against his chest.

"Maisie died."

My heart pounded and tears welled in my eyes.

"Maisie and Donal named us the baby's legal guardians because neither of them had family."

"Oh, wow," I murmured, my head whirling.

"You wanted a baby."

"Yes," I croaked.

He turned me to face him and cradled my cheeks in his palms. "This one needs a good home. Let's make her part of our family."

I blinked. "Are you sure about this?"

"I'm sure."

"Why? Why have you changed your mind?"

"I haven't changed my mind at all, hen." He smiled. "It's my heart that's changed."

"Such a beautiful heart," I whispered, tears filling my eyes.

Chapter 14

FLYNN

"HEN," I said. "We have to get going."

"Five more minutes," Barrett responded.

We were in a private hospital room and Barrett was holding our new daughter, gazing down at her with an enraptured expression on her face.

"We need to get home before the boys wake up if we want to surprise them."

She chuckled softly and stroked the sleeping baby's cheek. "Are you sure there won't be any trouble with the hospital?"

"Positive. Everything's been arranged."

Barrett sighed. "You're okay with her name?"

"More than okay," I assured her. "I love it."

Barrett placed our daughter in the carrier that Cormac had found for us. She secured a blanket with bright yellow ducks around her, tucking her in to make sure she was warm and comfortable.

It was nearly six in the morning by the time we were on our way back to Ash and Duncan's.

"We're the craziest two people in the world," Barrett said with a laugh.

I chuckled. "Why? Because we make decisions quickly? Once we know what we want, we make it happen."

"She's beautiful, isn't she, Flynn?"

"Aye. A bonnie wee lass."

"Do you think the boys will take to her?" she asked with concern on her face as she looked at me.

"I think they'll adore her," I predicted.

She fell silent for a moment and then sniggered. "I just had a vision of her going out on her first date, her three brothers standing behind her as her date comes to the door."

"How old was she in this vision," I asked.

"Thirty," Barrett jested with a teasing grin. "And she was in a tower and had long golden hair."

I shot her a disgruntled look. "Two can play that game. I know how you'll be the moment Hawk brings home the girl he's going to marry. You're going to lose your shite."

"I *never* over-react. It's not in my nature."

I snorted. "What about the time—"

"Let's not do this," she said. "Let's just enjoy the moment."

The weather had cleared but the sky was still gray as I pulled into the driveway. The baby was still fast asleep, and I wondered if that boded well for our future.

I parked the car and then Barrett unlatched her seatbelt. She got out and then opened the back door, unstrapped the carrier, and pulled it out.

"Do you think anyone's awake yet?" Barrett asked as we trekked to the front door.

I removed my keys from my trouser pocket. "I guess we're about to find out."

I pushed open the front door and we stepped into the

warm foyer. I listened for a moment, but there were no sounds of little feet running along wooden floors, no sounds of bairns crying.

Barrett took the baby while I removed my shoes. As I was hanging up my coat, Duncan strolled down the front staircase.

He came to a halt when he saw the sleeping baby in her carrier.

"What the ever-loving fuck?" Duncan whispered.

"Is Ash awake yet?" I asked.

Duncan shook his head. "She was up with Wee Duncan most of the night."

The three of us went into the den. Barrett sat down on the couch and settled the carrier near her. I took the seat next to Barrett while Duncan continued to stand.

Barrett quickly explained what had happened to Donal and Maisie and how we'd been named the baby's guardians.

"We're her family now," I stated.

Duncan continued to peer at our new daughter and then he let out a soft chuckle. "Well, I'll be damned."

A door slammed upstairs, causing the baby to jolt awake. Her cry was almost immediate. Barrett quickly reached into the carrier to pick her up, pulling her toward her chest to soothe her.

A few minutes later, Hawk, Noah, and Iain ran into the den, wearing matching Campbell tartan pajamas.

"What's that?" Hawk asked, pointing to the baby.

"Er, Santa brought her," Barrett said.

"It's a *her*?" Iain asked as he inched closer.

"Aye," I said. "You have a sister now."

"A sister," Hawk repeated. "I didn't ask for a sister for Christmas."

Duncan smothered his laugh. I shot him a glare. He

raised his hands and got up off the couch. "I'm guessing the door slam woke Carys and Malcolm. I better check on them."

He left the den, giving our family privacy. I gestured to the boys. They came, reluctantly, but their curiosity quickly overpowered their hesitation.

"She's going to need protecting," Barrett said, pinning Hawk, Noah, and Iain with a piercing stare.

"How are babies born?" Hawk asked.

"I want to know too," Iain said.

"Stork, cabbage patch, or the truth?" Barrett asked with a look at me.

They were too young for the truth, so I interjected, "The baby needed a family, and she found us."

"She's really small," Hawk said.

"Can I see her?" Iain asked.

"Easy, now," I said. "She's fragile."

"What's her name?" Noah asked.

"Piper," Barrett replied.

Noah looked from Piper to Barrett and then grinned. "You were right, Mam."

"What was I right about, love?" Barrett asked.

"You told me if I wished hard enough, my dream would come true."

"You wished for a sister?" I asked him.

He nodded.

I met my wife's gaze. Her hazel eyes were glassy with tears, and she didn't bother trying to hide them, not even when one rolled down her cheek.

The front door opened, turning our attention. I frowned in confusion.

"Ho, ho, ho! Merry Christmas," Ramsey boomed as he appeared in the doorway of the den. "Holy shite. That's a baby!"

Chapter 15
BARRETT

"You have such a way with words, Ramsey Buchanan," I said with a wry grin. "Like a Roman poet. And might I remind you about little ears being present?"

"Holy shite, holy shite, holy shite!" Hawk chanted.

"Holy shite, holy shite, holy shite!" Iain mimicked his older brother.

I glared at Ramsey. "Now look what you've done."

Piper started to fret again. While I was busy trying to mollify her, the boys skipped a circle around Ramsey crying out *holy shite* like an incantation.

"Boys, enough," Flynn boomed. "This is why we call them heathens."

"You mean the Great and Ominous Flynn Campbell can't even control his own offspring?" Ramsey asked. "Priceless."

"What's priceless?" Ash asked as she appeared in the den, carrying Wee Duncan. Not so wee Duncan loomed behind her with Malcolm to his shoulder. Carys had her entire hand wrapped around Duncan's finger, but she squealed and let go of her father when she saw Ramsey.

"There's my princess," Ramsey said, grinning at his niece. He held out his arms to her and she ran toward him.

The boys, thankfully, ceased their actions as Carys ran toward her uncle, who promptly scooped her up into his arms.

"I'm glad you're here," Ash said, Wee Duncan against her hip. She moved further into the room and brushed her cheek against Ramsey's in greeting. "Way to give us a surprise, though. You didn't even let it slip you were coming."

"Last minute idea," Ramsey said as he wrestled his arm underneath Carys, making his forearm a little shelf for her behind. "The idea of spending Christmas in a penthouse hotel room with nothing but a bottle of scotch and a naked—"

"Ramsey," Ash and I intoned at the same time.

He grinned.

"As happy as I am to see Ramsey, I need to see the newest edition to the Campbell clan. Duncan told me she's gorgeous," Ash stated.

"And your newest goddaughter," I said with a smile.

Ash ambled over to the couch and plopped down next to me, setting Wee Duncan on her lap. She bounced him up and down even as she peered at a recently soothed Piper. "She's perfect, of course."

"What? No shock or disbelief that we came home with a baby?" I asked.

"I'm not sure there's anything you can do that will surprise me. We've been friends for too long at this point."

"Mam," Hawk whined. "It's Christmas morning. Can we open our presents now?"

Flynn answered, "Go ahead."

The boys ran to the Christmas tree and ripped into their gifts like lions on a fresh kill.

"Cool!" Hawk shrieked as he peered into a large box and pulled out bagpipes.

Noah and Iain were equally as excited by the mini-Viking costumes Hadrian and Sterling had sent.

"Mam? Can I take Piper to school with me for show and tell?" Hawk asked.

I shot Flynn a look and then said, "We'll see."

"Who's hungry?" Ash asked.

"Me," three little voices chimed in unison.

"Da!" Carys yelled. "I'm hungry!"

"Oh good, Carys is joining in the fray," Ash said with an eyeroll at Duncan.

"I blame the Campbell children," Duncan stated, switching Malcolm to his other side.

"Hey," I said, feigning offence.

"You know he's right," Flynn added.

I didn't want to relinquish Piper. "How are we supposed to do this?" I asked.

Ramsey set Carys down and then rolled up his sleeves. "Lads, I need your help."

I raised my brows. "*You're* going to cook?"

"I have more to offer than just a pretty face, Barrett." He scooped up Noah and carried him upside down out of the den and toward the kitchen. Iain and Hawk skipped after him.

"Thank God. I *so* didn't want to cook this morning," Ash said.

"You never want to cook," Duncan said with amusement.

I was glad Ramsey was here, and now he was throwing himself into cooking with the boys, almost as though he didn't want to remain in the same room with the adults.

Piper instinctively nuzzled against me. "Someone's

hungry," I announced, having to shelve my thoughts about Ramsey for the time being.

"We have formula. You're welcome to it," Ash said.

"Thanks." I looked at Flynn. "We really weren't prepared to bring home a newborn."

"Luckily we still have the boys' baby furniture in the attic," Flynn said. "Won't be hard to find it."

"Hawk! No!" Ramsey yelled.

The four of us looked at each other and then we were up out of our seats. As I entered the kitchen, my jaw dropped open. Noah was covered in flour. Hawk and Iain were squared off at opposite ends of the kitchen table, arms pulled back and just about to throw eggs at one another. Both of their tartan pajama tops were already sporting egg yolk. Hawk ran a hand over his forehead, pushing back his hair.

"What the hell?" Flynn demanded, pinning each boy with a stare.

"He started it," Noah muttered.

"He, who?" Flynn asked.

"He, *me*." Ramsey said as he raised a spatula in the air.

"My kitchen is a mess," Ash moaned, brushing her cheek against Wee Duncan's dark hair.

"You're nothing but a big child," I said to Ramsey as I stepped over a concoction of eggs, flour, and milk that should've become biscuits or pancakes.

"Are you going to ground me?" Ramsey asked. "Please, please, please ground me. I like it when you get all Queen B."

"Flynn, take the baby," I commanded.

Flynn immediately lifted Piper from my arms. I kept my gaze on Ramsey as I stalked toward him. Everyone was silent, staring at me.

I picked up an egg out of the carton and glanced at it. Then I looked at Ramsey and in one swift movement, I cracked it over his head. Yolk and shell dribbled down his hair, coating the sides of his face.

He grinned. "Game on, Barrett. Game on."

Chapter 16
SASHA

QUINN ATTEMPTED to get out of bed, but I grasped her wrist and pulled her back down to the mattress. And then I rolled on top of her and pinned her beneath my body, smiling down at her beauty. "Where do you think you're going?"

"Some of us need hydration to live," she remarked dryly.

I reluctantly released her, though it physically pained me to do it. Before she climbed from our bed, she clasped the back of my head, hauled me toward her, and placed her plump lips on mine, easing her tongue into my mouth.

Every fiber of my being lit with desire.

"I've got plans for you," I said, watching her gracefully prowl around the room in a pink satin robe that concealed creamy Irish skin from my hungry gaze.

"You had plans for me earlier," she reminded me with a cheeky grin. "And those all went to hell."

"You know I can't think straight, let alone talk straight, when you grasp my—"

She let out a laugh.

"You did it on purpose. Every time I bring it up, you distract and deflect. Or you blame it on Helena."

"Speaking of Helena, she's going to be up from her nap soon."

"Quinn…"

She sighed and I patted the spot on the bed next to me.

"If I come back over there, I'll get distracted and you clearly want to have a discussion about something serious."

"Quinn," I said, lowering my voice. "Come here, *myshka*."

Her eyes shone like liquid emeralds as she came to me, finally sitting down on the bed. I rolled to my side and propped an elbow underneath my head.

Quinn's gaze roved over my face, lingering on my scars.

"You don't want to marry an ugly man," I said lightly. "That's what this is about."

She glared at me. "You're not ugly. I've never thought you were ugly. You know that."

She was right. It had been my own self-loathing that I'd been projecting. Even years later, I couldn't battle it back. I still avoided mirrors when I could. It was easier that way.

"The fire burned more than your face, Sasha," she said quietly.

"Are you talking about my heart?" I asked with a wry twist of my lips.

She pulled her knees up to her chest and set her chin on her kneecaps. "You're not who you used to be."

"Neither are you," I pointed out.

She looked away from me to stare out the window of the cottage bedroom. That morning—Christmas morning —we'd bundled up Helena and walked along the shore. Then we'd returned to the quiet home and exchanged a few gifts by the tree. After putting Helena down for a nap, I'd dragged Quinn to bed and kept her there. Now, it was late afternoon, the sunlight was dying, and our time with one another would soon be interrupted by Helena waking from her nap.

"The fire nearly took everything from us," she said, her brow wrinkling.

"But it didn't."

She looked from me to the door, and I knew she was thinking of Helena. The fire had set things in motion that couldn't be undone. It had led us here. Without it, Helena would never have come to be. And I had no regrets about her birth. My heart claimed her as mine, and we would see to it that she would never know the truth about her paternity.

"Why won't you marry me?" I asked.

Quinn was silent for a long moment and then she took a deep shuddering breath. "I want to marry you. I want to marry you more than anything in the world."

"Then why won't you set a date? You've put my ego through the shredder denying me the way you have."

She sent me a look. "You have a healthy ego, Sasha Petrovich. I have no doubt it's still intact."

"*Myshka*," I murmured. "Explain it to me."

"Every time I look at a wedding dress, I picture Ori." She kept her eyes on mine. "Every time I visualize marrying you, standing up on an altar surrounded by friends and…and family—"

Her voice broke. Quinn didn't have any family left. Both her parents and her brother were gone. And she'd been married before.

That was my fault, too.

"I know you want a real wedding, Sasha," she said, wiping the corners of her eyes where tears had begun to escape. "I don't want to deny you that, but I…"

"A wedding is a formality. I want to celebrate our

union with the people we've made our family. *Da.* But I'd never put my desires over any pain they might cause you."

"I hate him," she said softly. "For ruining a day that was supposed to be ours."

I reached out and gently cradled her cheek. "Hate me instead. I'm the one to blame. I left you. You were vulnerable and fragile and hurting, and he preyed on you. If I hadn't left—"

"I know why you had to leave. You needed to. I needed you to also, I just didn't realize it at the time." She sighed. "I had to learn how to stand alone. I'd never had to be strong before. I had my father, who gave me everything. His money cleared any and every path. Whatever I wanted, it was given. Sports cars, beautiful clothes, vacations in Europe or island paradises. I was a spoiled brat. And then you came along."

"And then I came along," I repeated.

Quinn smiled. "And you showed me what it meant to be a woman."

And because babies have impeccable timing when it comes to interrupting poignant moments, Helena let out a belting scream that could be heard even without a baby monitor.

I chuckled softly and got out of bed. I pulled on a pair of gray sweats and then followed Quinn to the nursery.

I scooped Helena from her crib, put her to my shoulder to soothe her, and then walked to the changing table. I changed her diaper quickly and then handed her off to Quinn, who'd already sat down in the comfortable padded rocking chair in the corner of the room. She opened her robe and put Helena to her breast.

"I could be convinced to have a party," she said after a long while.

"Could you?" I asked as I leaned against the crib.

She nodded. "With good food and cocktails. Conversation with friends. Maybe a band. But I'm not wearing white and I'm not saying my vows in front of other people."

"Quinn," I began, "I have your vow every morning when I wake up next to you. If you want a party instead of a formal wedding, we'll have a party."

Her smile was slow and full of warmth.

A cell phone in the other room rang.

I arched a brow. "I'm guessing that's Barrett and the clan calling to wish us a Merry Christmas."

"Answer it," she said. "And tell her our happy news."

Chapter 17
QUINN

Sasha took the baby from me and left the nursery. I headed to the bedroom and quickly threw on a pair of lounge pants and a sweater before going to the living room. I came up behind Sasha who was seated on the couch with a phone in his hand and a video chat open.

"Hi, Quinn," Barrett greeted with a wide smile.

I smiled back. "Merry Christmas, Barrett."

"Merry Christmas. Let's spend it together in person next year."

"We'd like that," I said, speaking for both Sasha and I.

"It would be so much more convenient to spend holidays together if you just lived here. Are you sure I can't convince you guys to move to Scotland?" she asked.

"The weather is too dreary," Sasha said.

"*You* think the weather is too dreary? You. The Russian."

I smiled to the camera. "The Russian won't admit it, but he's become fond of walks on the beach and sunshine."

"Not the monotony of such an easy life, though," Sasha stated. "I need a change."

Barrett paused. "Are you guys moving back to New York?"

"At some point," I said. "No time frame, though. But speaking of time frames..." I trailed off when Flynn appeared on the screen holding something in his arms that was swaddled in a gray blanket.

"Petrovich," Flynn said.

"Campbell," Sasha replied in the same droll tone.

But then Flynn grinned.

"What do you have there?" I asked.

Flynn cleared his throat and gently pushed aside the blanket just as Barrett angled the phone down.

"That's a baby," Sasha stated.

"Well spotted," Barrett said with a huge grin. "This is Piper. We just adopted her."

Tears of joy filled my eyes. "She's *lovely*."

"How did that happen?" Sasha asked. "*When* did that happen?"

"Early this morning," Flynn said. He then launched into the story of how Piper had come into their lives.

"Now Helena will have a friend close to her age," Barrett said, her eyes darting from mine to Sasha's. "They can grow up together. *If* you move to Scotland."

"You're really pushing for that," Sasha said.

"I have this dream of all of us living close to each other, our collective gaggle of children running wild together," Barrett replied.

"Nice dream," I said.

Sasha looked at me over his shoulder. "You'd really want to live in Scotland?"

"I'd consider it," I said.

Out of the corner of my eye, I saw Barrett and Flynn exchange a look.

Sasha turned his attention back to them. "Congratulations on your newest addition to the family." With his free hand, he reached over his shoulder to me.

I clasped it.

"Quinn and I have some good news, too."

"You're pregnant," Barrett announced.

I laughed. "No."

"Damn," Barrett said. She peered at Sasha. "What's wrong with you?"

"Wrong with me?" Sasha repeated. "Nothing. I'm trying every moment of every day to get Quinn—"

"Anyway," I interrupted, not wanting to go down the rabbit hole about the expansion of our family. It would happen in time, like anything else.

I heard the shouting of three young boys with far too much energy as they entered the room and a moment later their faces appeared on screen. They said their hellos and then zoomed around the room with wild abandon.

"Ramsey gave them sugar, I know he did," Barrett said to Flynn.

"Wait, Ramsey is there?" I said in surprise.

"Aye. He showed up this morning and within an hour he caused a food fight. Ash and Duncan's kitchen is a mess."

"Sounds like we missed a good time," I said.

"Next year," Barrett vowed again.

"Next year." Sasha nodded. "If Flynn promises not to end my life the moment I step foot on your property."

"I guess you'll have to wait and see." Flynn scratched his jaw.

Helena started fussing and Piper heard it over the phone and began to cry.

"Tell Ash, Duncan and Ramsey we said Merry Christmas," I said.

"Will do. Talk soon, yeah?" Barrett said.

"Yep."

"Love you," she said.

"Love you back," I replied.

Sasha pressed a button, and the screen went black and even though he tried to soothe Helena, he wasn't having much luck. He handed her off to me. I put her to my shoulder, and she stuck her head in the crook of my neck and began to calm down.

"Magic touch," he said with a wry smile.

"For now. She prefers you at night," I pointed out. "Wow, they have another baby."

"She looks happy, doesn't she?"

"She does." I nodded.

The anniversary of Igor Dolinsky's death this year had caused a lot of turmoil. It weighed heavily on both Sasha and Barrett. Flynn and I were outsiders and only knew what they chose to share with us. Sasha had told me about owning Dolinsky's house and that Barrett had free run of the place. It was strange, and I wasn't sure I understood the reason for the secrecy, but then again, I wasn't a part of it. Their relationship had always been unusual, and it was something I'd long ago accepted.

I was glad Barrett was back in Scotland with her family. She seemed deliriously happy, and now that they had a new baby, they could focus on the future and stop living in the past.

Barrett did things in her own way, and so did I. It was one of the many reasons we understood one another. It reminded me that at one point in time we'd been engaged in an emotional war, with Sasha between us.

And yet after all of that she'd become like a sister to me. I could call her in the middle of the night, and she'd answer. If I needed her, I had no doubt at all that she'd fly to me immediately, wherever I was.

There was a reason Barrett was Helena's godmother. If anything happened to Sasha and me…

"Did you mean it?" Sasha asked.

I took the spot on the couch next to him. Helena was warm in my arms and seemed comfortable as she snuggled against me. "Mean what?"

"About living in Scotland?"

"We can't live in Scotland," I protested. "Not with what you're involved in. You have to be close to the coast.

"That's not what I asked."

I paused for a moment and really pondered his question. "I do feel like we're left out of things, being over here in the States and them being so far away. But that's not a reason to move to Scotland, even if we could."

He scratched his jaw, the sound of his fingers rasping against his stubble. "We should move to Scotland," Sasha said.

My head whipped around from staring at a wall, and I met his gaze. "What?"

He nodded. "You clearly have no desire to move to New York, and to be frank, neither do I."

"You just said you needed a city and were bored with life here."

"*Da*, I'm bored with life *here*."

"But how can you run things in New York and Boston if we live in Scotland?"

He looked amused. "The same way I've been doing it while we've been here. Dimitri handles New York. We have men in Boston. I didn't come back because I wanted to take the reins again. I knew what I was giving up when I walked away. I came back because of you."

"A man like you can't just walk away from all that," I insisted despite his heartfelt statement.

He shrugged.

"What?" I demanded. "What's that shrug about?"

"Flynn changed his life. He's no longer involved in the day-to-day operations of running The Rex in New York. He stepped back into the shadows, and when he needs to be somewhere, he just goes. Why own a private jet and have a pilot on standby if you never travel?"

"Flynn is still co-leader of the SINS," I pointed out. "He lives in Scotland for that reason."

"Flynn could turn it over to Duncan and take his wife and children and move back to New York at any time. Or even live somewhere else if he wanted. The point I'm trying to make is that things don't have to look the way they used to. In what world would I have ever thought I'd do business with the Scots? In what world would I ever have thought I'd be marrying a beautiful Irish lass. But back to our discussion…"

"You don't want to live in Scotland. You said so yourself—the weather, remember?"

"The weather there isn't that terrible," he mused.

"Holy shit. *You're* the one who wants to move to Scotland! Why the hell didn't you say so?" I demanded.

"I didn't want you to think—"

"That you were doing it to be close to Barrett." I sighed.

"I've killed for you, Quinn."

"You've killed for her, too," I pointed out.

He looked at the baby snuggled in my arms. "One day, I'll probably have to kill for Helena. It seems that's what I do…kill men for the women I love." He paused for a moment and then said, "You love me, but you don't fully trust me."

"That's not true. I do trust you."

"You know there's nothing romantic with Barrett, and there hasn't been since I met you."

"I know."

"You make things about Barrett because you don't want to say what's really in your heart. You don't want to hurt me. Tell me what you really need to tell me, Quinn."

Chapter 18

SASHA

"Let me put Helena in her crib," Quinn said. "Then we can talk."

Talk.

I wasn't going to like this.

Not one bit.

But hearing what she had to say, no matter how brutal or how emotional, would be my cross to bear. Anything she had to tell me, I'd deal with it.

When she came back from putting Helena down, Quinn took a seat on the couch next to me. She stared me in the eyes and said flatly, "I wish you hadn't killed him."

Bile rose in my throat, but I mashed it down like I did with everything else.

"You still love Ori," I accused.

She shook her head. "*No*. It's not about love. It's about hate. I hate him, Sasha. I never should've asked you to get your hands dirty. I should've been the one to end his life. Then I'd know…"

"Know what?" I asked.

"That I was strong enough to do it. He took so much from me. From us. He gave me Helena, yes. But at what cost? I feel so weak, Sasha."

Guilt swamped me. "I'd left. You'd lost your father, our son... Grief impairs our judgement."

"I know," she murmured, her beautiful face scrunched up in an expression of pain and anguish. "God, it's all such a blur. I hate him. I hate him so much. I hate that he made me feel weak and needy. I hate that I wasn't the one to kill him. I hate that it fell to you."

"That's not who you are, Quinn. You're not a killer. My hands are stained with blood, and I have no regrets about the lives I've taken. I have no regrets about killing Ori for you. For us. For Helena."

"You didn't think I was strong enough to kill him then. You *still* don't think I'm strong enough, do you?"

"This isn't about strength. Strength has nothing to do with it."

"Barrett has killed more than once. She's not just survived it, she's thrived in the world she created for herself," she pointed out.

"It depends how you look at it, I suppose. Besides, Barrett ran away on the anniversary of Igor's death. She hasn't escaped the trauma; she just manages her darkness. Sometimes she embraces it. But once you kill, you can't go back. Thinking and doing are not the same." I sighed. "I don't want you to have to live with guilt or regrets. I don't want you to become a killer. I don't want you to become like us."

"Maybe *I* want to become like the two of you. Maybe *I* want to open that door and see what's on the other side. Right now, it feels like I'm being refused entrance to a private club because I'm not good enough."

"You don't want in this club. Trust me."

"This is just another thing you and Barrett share. You're bound to each other in a way I can never be. And your relationship is beautiful. I used to be jealous, but I'm not anymore because I know you love me. And I know that she loves me like a sister, and I love her the same way. But, Sasha, this is about control. I don't feel like I have control."

"Control over what?"

"Life. Circumstances. Everything. I hate being at the mercy of stronger people than me."

"And you think killing Ori would've made you feel differently?"

"Yes. Without a doubt."

"There are different ways of being strong. You don't have to be a killer to be strong. You don't have to be like Barrett."

"I admire the hell out of that woman. I picture her when she's older as this gray-haired, bad ass matriarch that still commands everyone like they're a part of her personal legion. But what about me, Sasha? Why do I feel like I live in the shadows of everyone around me?"

"Why do you put yourself there?" I fired back.

"A damn fine question." She paused. "I want to take control of my life. I want to choose the course of the river, not just feel like I'm being swept away in it." She raked a hand through her tangled hair. "I need something from you."

"Anything."

"I want you to teach me."

"Teach you what?"

She pinned me to the spot with a stare I knew was deadly serious. She was filled with resolve, and I worried what she might ask.

"Teach me how to kill."

"No," I said flatly.

She shrugged. "Fine. I'll ask Barrett to teach me."

I scrubbed a hand over my face. "That's not a good idea, Quinn."

"That's not for you to decide," she said, her tone stony. Her expression hardened further. "I've been a princess my entire life, Sasha. Teach me to become a queen. I'm ready."

I sighed a long, drawn-out exhale. "You know I can't deny you."

"I planned on that," she said with a slight smile.

"Training and doing are not the same," I stated. "I'll show you what you need to know, but I pray you'll never have to use it."

She clenched her fists in her lap. "I think I finally get it."

"Get what?"

"Why men need a good brawl sometimes."

I smirked. "It's what comes *after* the brawl that I look forward to."

She beamed and her eyes slid down my naked chest. "Yeah. The *after* is always pleasurable."

Chapter 19

BARRETT

I LOOKED DOWN at the baby sleeping against me. I hadn't been able to put Piper down yet since we were in the early stages of bonding. I wasn't her blood, and I didn't want to do anything to interrupt her attaching to me. I felt her curl into my body; she was a comfortable weight against my chest. "We should've gone home. Taken the boys and given you your space back."

Ash waved her hand. "We've destroyed your peace often enough, what with our brood."

"You've never had a food fight in my kitchen."

"Truth. I'll send you the cleaning bill."

"Why? You can afford it," I said with a grin.

"Also truth."

The children had been bathed and put to bed more than an hour ago. The men had congregated in the private study where they were drinking, smoking cigars, and talking about all the things men talked about when they were alone.

Ash and I had taken over the den, giving them privacy, but the truth was we enjoyed being alone, too. There were some things you could say to another woman that you never wanted to share in mixed company.

"Strange," I murmured, taking a sip of my scotch.

"What's strange?" she asked.

"I was just thinking about the luxury I've grown accustomed to even though I know where the money comes from. I mean, Flynn has earned his wealth through illegal dealings. It's blood money."

"Not just Flynn," she pointed out. "You, too. You're involved now. Hell, you call some of the most dangerous criminals in the world your best friends and confidants."

"Aside from Sasha, who is my best friend and confidant?" I asked with a raise of my brows.

She gave me a sneaky smile. "I know you keep in contact with Mateo."

"Business, only."

"The man sends you Christmas flower bouquets every year."

I rolled my eyes. "And I give them away every year."

"Angelo Moretti sends you wine and the world's finest limoncello, hoping you'll throw Flynn overboard for him. How did you ever manage to get the leader of The White Company to fall in love with you, anyway?"

"Can't tell you," I said. "I've been sworn to secrecy."

"Hmmm."

The only other person who knew what went on between me and Angelo Moretti was Sasha, and that knowledge would follow him to his grave.

"I only want my husband. Now and forever," I promised.

"My brother's marriage failed because of you."

"No. You don't get to blame me for that," I protested. "Jack's a work-a-holic."

"I still think you're a succubus."

I stole a hand across Piper's back. "I can go upstairs at any moment and leave you to enjoy your scotch alone, you know. I don't actually *need* your company."

"What's it like?" she prodded.

"What?" I asked.

"Having so many men in love with you?"

"Oh, stop. You've had your fair share of men in love with you, too," I pointed out.

"True," she allowed. "But country club investment bankers aren't the same as men who actually control criminal domains."

"I don't think of it that way, Ash. I just—I don't know. I treat them like men instead of the movers and shakers they are. They're all so used to having women fawn all over them. They don't turn my head. I'm immune. So, they try even harder to sweep me off my feet."

"Femme Fatale. Truly, I'm impressed."

"Do you miss those days, Ash?" I asked quietly. "When you were a free agent, and no one had any claims on you?"

"Sometimes," she admitted. "Not that I'd trade what I have with Duncan and our family for those days, but that feeling of being unencumbered, of walking into a room and having all eyes on you…"

"You can still have that," I said.

"I guess. But being a mom, I don't know, sometimes I feel invisible to the opposite sex. And it's nice when you get the validation from a man that isn't your husband. It's truth in a way that can't be faked. They're either attracted to you, or they aren't." She took a sip of her drink. "You wouldn't really know what that's like."

"I wouldn't?"

"No. We just established that. Everyone wants you."

"How do you walk into a room," I asked.

"What do you mean?"

"I mean, do you walk in like you own it? Do you dress like you want to be looked at? Or do you do things to hide?"

She paused, clearly weighing my words. "My clothes. I'm wearing a lot of black these days."

"There's nothing wrong with black."

"It's slimming," she said flatly. "And I feel like no matter how much I strive to get back to my old body, it doesn't want to go back the way it was."

"You've had three children."

"So have you. You look fantastic."

"You look fantastic too," I said.

"Are you lying?"

"No. Are you the same size you were in college? No. But you don't have to strive for that either."

She touched her blonde hair that she'd cut into a long bob. It was a great hairstyle on her and framed her face well, but she'd left it long enough to be able to pull it back into a ponytail.

"I feel frumpy," she finally admitted. "Here in Scotland, I'm not the socialite I once was. And somewhere along the way I got used to dressing down. I used to be the woman who put on makeup to go to the gym."

"I remember." I smiled at the memory. "You don't dress down. You just dress differently."

"Barrett, stop trying to make excuses for me. You don't dress down ever in public, and you kept your hair long."

I clamped my mouth shut.

"Say it," she commanded.

"Say what?"

"Say whatever it is that's on your mind."

"I'm not the person to give marriage advice, ever," I pointed out. "I'm not the ideal partner."

"You're not traditional. You don't just stand in Flynn's

shadows and let him call all the shots. That doesn't mean you're not ideal."

"Are we really doing this? Not being honest with each other?" I asked in amusement.

She sighed. "I'm asking you to be honest. Even if it hurts my feelings."

"You put the kids first," I said. "And you put Duncan second."

"What does that have to do with how I dress, or my hair cut?"

"You've done what's easy and convenient, not what's best for your marriage."

"So, I need to glam it up?"

"I don't think it would hurt."

She nodded. "You're right. I've been putting the mom thing first, instead of the wife thing. I need to change that pronto."

"It's just something to be aware of," I said. "And now that you are, you can do something about it."

"Thanks. Thanks for being honest."

"Happy to help," I said. "But honesty is a dangerous game…"

After a moment of quiet, she asked, "What now?"

I looked at her. "What do you mean what now?"

"I mean, what's next? You got your baby. What's the next thing you can't live without?"

"I have everything I want."

"Hmmm," she replied.

"Hmmm? What does that mean?"

"You'll want something else. I don't know what it'll be, but you'll want it anyway. I don't even mean that as a strike against you. It's the human condition."

"The human condition: I breathe therefore I want?"

"Yeah, sounds about right." She took another sip of her drink.

"I sometimes think life is nothing more than a series of transitions. Everything is calm and happy for a while, but that just means there's another storm brewing."

"Take your doomsday-ness and shelve it," Ash joked.

"Not doomsday," I protested. "But when has anything gone according to plan?"

"That's a different question though, isn't it?"

"Life is either a series of emotional pitfalls or actual catastrophic events. Very rarely do any of us just get to sit and *be*."

"Why are we talking about this?" she demanded. "Don't you worry that talking about it will bring it about? Like summoning a ghost?"

A hazy film seemed to appear over my eyes. I blinked a couple of times, clearing it away and my focus returned. I was exhausted. I hadn't slept in hours. I knew when my head hit the pillow, I'd fall asleep almost immediately, and I also knew I'd only have a few hours before I'd be reawakened by Piper's needs. But once a mother, always a mother. I hadn't truly slept long or deep since Hawk's birth. Sleep was the price you paid for motherhood.

"You're allowed to be happy, Barrett," she said when I didn't reply. "You have everything you want."

"Then why do I have a vision of a large hand flipping the edge of a chessboard, sending the pieces clattering to the floor?"

"Clearly you don't trust it to last."

"Probably," I agreed. "In the grand scheme of the cosmic universe, we're just pieces being maneuvered until we no longer have any use."

"Jeez. Morbid much?"

"Sorry. But it is sort of terrifying. We're all healthy.

We're all young. We're all alive. That won't always be the case. I'm sorry. I don't mean to sound so gloomy, but everything is perfect, and you're right, I'm scared it won't last."

She tapped the side of her crystal glass. "I've been thinking a lot about Malcolm recently."

"Have you?"

"Yeah. It feels... I don't know. We lost him so suddenly, so tragically. It's been years now, but...this was *his* home. He raised Duncan and Ramsey in this house. And Flynn when he was a teen. And now, Duncan and I are raising our own family here. It's just weird, you know? The cycle of life."

"The cycle of death."

"Gloomy, indeed," she said with a wry smile. "We're quite a pair."

"We are."

She paused for a moment. "You never talk about your parents."

"I don't," I agreed.

"Do you miss them?"

"Of course I miss them. I just...can't think about them."

"Why?"

"If I think of them, I'll think of my brother, and he needs to stay in the steel box I put him in."

"That makes sense." She nodded. "I'm not sure I would've survived if I'd been through what you've been through."

"What have I been through?" I asked with a laugh.

"What *haven't* you been through?" she countered. "My parents are still alive, but I don't particularly care for them. Yours are gone. My brother is still alive, and I adore him. Your brother is deceased and... I mean you get that what you've been through isn't normal, right? You've been through so much—"

"Let's not do this," I suggested. "Let's not put things in columns just to see what the tally will be for each of us. We're both happily married, we're here to watch our children grow, we've created a family, Ash. A family that was chosen. Blood doesn't matter like people think it does."

Piper let out a little noise, but otherwise didn't stir.

"We have the most important things in life: love and health. What else is there?" I asked.

"Nothing," she agreed. "Nothing at all."

Chapter 20

RAMSEY

"I DON'T KNOW how either of you do it," I said, leaning back against a black leather couch and crossing a leg over the other. "I'm exhausted watching you. Bairns, bairns, and more bairns."

Flynn and Duncan exchanged a look. "I guess that means you don't feel the inclination anytime soon?" my brother asked, arching a dark eyebrow.

"Subtle, brother, real subtle."

Duncan's laugh was booming, and he sounded just like our father. I felt a sharp pain in my chest, which I effectively ignored.

"We could sit here and regale you with tales of fatherhood," Flynn replied good naturedly. "But I doubt it will change your mind. If anything, it might convince you to remain a womanizing bastard for all eternity."

"Says the man who was also a womanizer in his heyday," I pointed out.

Flynn went to the liquor cart. "Ah, the good ole days."

"Right." I shook my head. "You wouldn't exchange what you have with Barrett for my life, would you?"

He poured us three glasses of scotch. "I've already had your life. I enjoyed it when I lived it. Now I enjoy other things."

"The same woman every night," I stated. "Sounds dreary. Even if Barrett has enough personalities to keep you entertained."

"Do *not* let my wife hear you say that or she'll have your bollocks for it," Flynn said as he walked over to me and handed me a drink. He clinked his glass against mine and then gave Duncan his.

"Why does she need mine, when she already has yours?" I taunted.

Flynn's smile was slow as he looked at me. "Ramsey Buchanan, I never thought I'd live to see the day…"

"What day is that?" Duncan asked.

"The day that Ramsey is jealous, and tired of the endless parade of women that run through his life."

"I'm not tired of that," I lied.

"Aye, you are," Flynn said with a chuckle. He took a seat next to Duncan on the other part of the leather couch.

"You look weary," Duncan said.

"Of course I'm weary. Between my sisters-in-law and the flock of nieces and nephews, it's a wonder any of you find any sort of peace."

"Well, Ash and Barrett are in the den. The bairns are bathed and asleep," Flynn pointed out. "We have all the peace we could want."

"This is rare," Duncan said. "The three of us together in the same room."

I finally took a drink of scotch, enjoying the peaty burn as it slid down my throat.

We were silent for a moment and then Flynn said, "You look tired, lad."

I grinned. No doubt it looked feral instead of the usual

charming veneer I portrayed. "An all-night fuck fest before getting on a plane will do that to a man."

"Who is she?" Duncan asked.

I shrugged. "No one important. Don't even remember her name."

Duncan and Flynn exchanged another look.

"Stop that," I snapped. "You both had your fun. Let me have mine."

"Doesn't look very fun," Duncan murmured.

I slammed back the rest of my drink and then set the glass down on the Biedermeier coffee table before standing up and stalking from the room.

At least they hadn't brought up Jane.

Thinking of Jane made anger simmer through my veins. Fucking and drinking were the only two things that obliterated her from my mind.

Demon woman.

I would never fall I love again.

Never.

Chapter 21
BARRETT

THE DOOR to the guest bedroom opened and my vivid dream disappeared like a wisp of smoke in the wind. Flynn came in, grimacing. "Sorry. I didn't realize you were asleep."

I looked down at Piper, who was snoozing on my chest. "Dozing," I said. "I was trying to wait up for you so we could give Piper her first bath."

"It's past midnight," he remarked.

"And her schedule is already good and screwed."

"Hmm. Valid point. I'll run the bath water." He leaned over and pressed a kissed to my forehead and then my lips.

"I had the strangest dream just now," I remarked as I sat up slowly.

"You can tell me about it while we bathe her."

Flynn disappeared into the ensuite bathroom while I shifted Piper to my other shoulder.

He hadn't shut the door to the bedroom, and I went to close it.

But there on the threshold, standing in the doorway, was the ghost of Igor Dolinsky.

"She's beautiful," Igor said.

I instinctively clutched Piper tighter to me.

"Barrett!" Flynn called. "The bath is nearly ready."

"Coming," I called back, hoping my voice hadn't betrayed my phony calm.

Why was Igor Dolinsky's ghost still hanging about?

I'd exorcised him. I'd let him go. I was never returning to his house. I was moving forward with my life.

Why was my past determined to cripple my future?

I'm tired. Of course!

Sheer exhaustion wreaked havoc on a person's mental state, I knew that. I hadn't slept in far too many hours. We hadn't prepared to go to the hospital and come home with a newborn.

I let out a sigh of relief, realizing how simple it was. As soon as I slept for a few hours, my hallucination of Igor would no longer plague me.

I brought Piper into the bathroom. Flynn was kneeling at the tub with his hand in the bathwater. I quickly divested Piper of her clothes, and then my husband and I gave our daughter her first bath.

"It's strange," I said as I handed the squeaky-clean infant to Flynn. He wrapped her in a soft towel and brought her to his chest.

"What's strange?" he asked.

"Everything feels new all over again."

"I know," he agreed. "With Hawk, everything was new. By the time the twins came around we were seasoned. But with Piper…I'm not sure I know what to do with a girl. Aside from locking her in a tower until she's thirty."

"Knowing you, you'll teach her how to pick a lock, so shutting her away in a tower might be for naught."

Flynn walked into the bedroom, and I followed at a

slower pace. Igor was still hovering around the doorway, watching me with a dark, penetrating gaze. I ignored him.

Flynn put Piper in a fresh diaper and then slid her into a onesie that Wee Duncan had long since grown out of.

I went to the door and locked it for good measure.

"Don't want the lads to be able to come in?" Flynn asked in amusement.

He gently set Piper in a bassinet we'd borrowed from Ash and Duncan.

"I want us to have some privacy," I said, batting my lashes at him.

"Hen, do you even have the energy to seduce me?" Flynn teased.

"Honestly? No."

"Thank God. I'm exhausted," he said with a dry laugh.

"Flynn Campbell," I said, slowly removing my clothes but leaving my tank top and lace underwear on. "Are you getting old?"

His eyes dipped down my body as I revealed skin. "Not getting old, love. I'm just human. I have the same weaknesses as anyone else." He peeled off his sweater and tossed it onto the chair in the corner.

I climbed into bed, my eyes dipping shut despite my desire to stay awake a little bit longer. I groaned when my head nestled against the plush pillow. "You don't have the same weaknesses as anyone else. Do you know that when we first met, I was in complete and utter awe of you?"

He flipped on the lamp and then went over to the switch and killed the main light in the room. "And now? Has your awe for me completely disappeared due to years of cohabitation and child rearing?"

I sniggered.

Flynn quickly dropped his trousers and then got into

bed next to me. He took me into his arms, and I tangled my bare legs with his.

His hand skated down my leg and settled on the curve of my butt. "I'll never forget seeing you for the first time, walking into the restaurant to meet with your shithead of a brother, only to find you there. You captured my attention immediately. And then when you casually said you wished you'd ordered scotch instead of red wine, I knew I was done for."

I laughed softly. "You did not."

"No? You don't believe me?"

"The great and mighty Flynn Campbell, falling for a woman because she wanted single malt scotch? No, I don't buy it."

"Fine. It wasn't just that you wanted single malt scotch. It was your sweet and glorious arse, too. I watched you walk to the loo and had to stop myself from following you."

A thrill of desire shot straight to my core.

"What would've happened if you'd followed me to the loo?"

He caressed up and down my skin, sliding beneath the black lace panties I wore to gently cup the attribute he'd just mentioned.

"I would've locked the door, told you to bend over and grip the counter, and then I would've fucked you from behind. I would've fucked you so deep, so raw, you would've begged for more."

"I was so hot for you; I would've let you."

He chuckled. "Maybe. I doubt it sometimes though. You led me on a merry chase."

"Me? You were the one acting like an emotional yoyo."

"I wasn't sure I could trust you. I wasn't sure you'd

decide to stay once you knew the truth about who I was and what I was involved in."

"It was your eyes," I joked. "I was a sucker for those blue eyes of yours."

I rubbed my toes up and down his calf and let my hand wander across the bare expanse of his chest. His vision of what he'd wanted to do when we'd met all those years ago caused desire to flare in my blood and heat my body.

Slowly, I pulled away from him.

"Where are you going?" he demanded.

I slipped from the bed. "You didn't think you could paint that dirty little vision in my mind and then fail to make it come true, did you?"

No sooner had I thrown down the gauntlet then I saw him throw off the comforter and all but jump out of bed.

Grinning, I backed up toward the bathroom with Flynn stalking naked toward me. His eyes drank me in. "You've got to stay quiet, so you don't wake Piper," he warned.

"Me, stay quiet? You're the one who comes with a lusty groan."

"Lusty groan?" He grinned.

I entered the bathroom and hit the switch, illuminating the way. "I think I read that term in a romance novel once."

He quietly shut the door behind him and then stalked toward me to clasp my hips. We were face to face and Flynn leaned down to capture my lips with his. His tongue thrust into my mouth, pillaging and taking, dominating me in the way that I needed and loved.

We were dynamite.

When I was in his arms, I was Barrett Campbell. A woman he owned, and never stopped wanting.

My hands plowed through his hair, and I pressed closer.

Flynn pulled his mouth from mine and opened his eyes. They were dark, glittering with desire and command.

"Turn around, Barrett."

A shiver of excitement danced down my spine as I obeyed.

"Grip the counter, and don't move."

I grasped the granite and looked at our reflection in the mirror. My cheeks were already flushed, and my lips were plump from his kiss.

Flynn stood behind me and for a long moment, he didn't move to touch me. Then he skimmed his fingertips lightly up the sides of my hips to rest on them. He kept his left hand on my hip, but with his right hand, he slowly cupped the heat of me.

I closed my eyes and swallowed my groan.

He played with me, toying and teasing, not giving me what I wanted.

"Flynn," I begged.

His head dropped and he bit the sensitive skin where my shoulder met my neck. "What do you want, Barrett?"

"Your fingers. Inside me."

There was no shame, no hiding from this man. Not after all we'd been through. Not after all our years together. In the bedroom, we both had only one goal: satisfaction—no matter how.

He slid his hand into my panties, finding me wet for him. But even though I had no shame in begging, Flynn wouldn't give in until he was good and ready.

His fingers danced around the apex of my thighs, dragging through the folds of my body, making me even more slick. I would welcome him when he decided it was time.

Flynn pressed himself against me. He was as hard as a steel rod at my back.

He slipped one finger deep inside me, causing me to shudder. He stilled, refusing to stroke me into climax. I ground against him, willing to do the job myself.

With one quick movement he removed his finger and then jerked me around to face him.

"Get on your knees," he commanded. "Now."

This hadn't been part of my fantasy vision, but I loved it anyway.

I sank to my knees.

He took himself in hand and stroked himself. "Open."

Flynn guided himself inside my mouth until he hit the back of my throat. I nearly gagged, but I took more of him. I took all that he offered.

I grasped the base of his shaft, squeezing while I sucked him deep.

He let out a low groan and I smiled in satisfaction.

I grabbed his thighs, so I had something to hold onto as I pleasured him.

Abruptly, he pulled away, and then his hands were on my elbows, helping me stand. He whirled me quickly and pushed at the small of my back, silently commanding I bend over.

He worked my lace panties down my legs, and I stepped out of them. He spread me wide and then he impaled me.

Pleasure ignited inside me. He slammed into me again and again, almost like he didn't care about my gratification. But his ruthlessness spurred me on. I was wet and primed, and when he slipped his hand around to the seam of my legs and ground his fingers against me, I came hard and fast.

I clenched around him as he continued to thrust into

me. Gripping my hip hard enough to leave a bruise, he plunged once more and then stilled.

He rested his cheek in the spot between my shoulder blades and stayed there as our breathing returned to normal. Finally, he pulled out of me.

When I stood up, he leaned down to kiss me on the lips. "It keeps getting better, doesn't it?"

I grinned. "Damn right it does."

He laughed softly and then took a few moments to clean himself. He went back to bed and gave me a few minutes of privacy. I adjusted the straps of my tank top, shaking my head at the fact that I'd left it on. There was something sensual about being partially clothed while being intimate with your husband.

After cleaning up, I turned off the light of the bathroom and went back into the bedroom. Flynn was already settled in bed, his arm tucked underneath his head, the lamp light on low. "Your daughter slept through our entire interlude."

"Glad to hear that." I tip-toed over to the bassinet to check on her, but she was sound asleep with one of her arms over her head, her tiny fist clenched. "I swear she's already bigger."

"I don't doubt it."

I trekked back to bed and climbed in next to Flynn, sated and sleepy.

When my eyes were half closed, I saw something move in the corner of the room. My eyes snapped open.

Igor was standing at the mantle of the gas fireplace as it blazed with heat. He lifted his hands and began to slow clap.

I swallowed and then glanced at Flynn. He was already asleep.

Chapter 22
BARRETT

THE SOUND of the doorbell woke Piper who began to cry. Flynn handed her to me, and when I put her to my shoulder, she nuzzled into my neck. I crooned to her, ignoring Igor, who stood in the corner of the nursery.

"Tony didn't call to let us know we had a guest arriving," Flynn said.

"Then it's someone on the guest list," I replied. I wrinkled my nose. "She needs changing. I'll take care of it and meet you down there."

"You sure? I don't mind," he said.

The doorbell rang again.

"Go," I insisted. "I've got Piper."

Flynn nodded and headed to the door. At the last second, he turned and looked at me. "Hen? The nursery?"

I smiled. "You did good. It's perfect. Better than anything I could've envisioned."

He flashed a satisfied grin and then left the room, closing the door behind him. I couldn't hear his fading footsteps over Piper's cries.

I went to the changing table and placed Piper on top.

Flynn had thought of everything, of course. There were diapers and wipes, and our favorite cream for diaper rashes, the one we'd used on the boys.

"I want you, Barrett," Igor said simply.

"What are you doing here?" I hissed at Igor. "This was a private family moment and you spoiled it."

He was wearing a three-piece black suit, his dark hair combed off his forehead. His hands were shoved into his trouser pockets.

"You can't have me," I snapped. "I don't belong to you."

"I beg to differ," he said. "I've owned you since I first laid eyes on you."

I took off Piper's soiled diaper and pitched it into the bin. I cleaned her bottom and had her in a new diaper in less than a minute.

"You do that so well, Barrett," Igor said.

"And to think I never wanted children."

"You were born to be a mother."

"Now I know for sure you're a figment of my imagination." I said as I rolled my eyes. "I am not maternal."

Knowing Flynn, he'd already made sure Piper had clothes for me to change her into after cleaning her up. I picked up Piper and settled her against my shoulder and then opened the top drawer of the changing table that doubled as a dresser.

Yup, full of baby girl onesies. Pink, yellow, green. Every other color of the rainbow.

My husband thought of everything. He always did.

I quickly slipped Piper into a onesie that fit her and then lifted her into my arms, cuddling her against my shoulder.

When I headed toward the door, Igor moved from the corner of the room and began to follow me.

"Stop," I commanded. "You're done. You don't get to do this."

He cocked his head to the side. "*Da*, I do. I want you."

"This is unbelievable," I muttered. "I don't know if I should talk to a shrink or a priest. I'll talk to both if it means getting rid of you for good."

"You can't get rid of me. I'm inside you. There is no purging me."

I opened the door and stalked out into the hallway. I heard voices before I'd even made it down the stairs. When I walked into the den, my mouth gaped.

"What are you guys doing here?" I asked in surprise.

Sasha grinned. "Quinn didn't want to start the new year in the States."

I frowned as I looked at Quinn, who sat on the couch with Helena in her lap. "I don't get it."

"We're moving to Scotland," she announced.

My eyes widened in shock. "You are?"

Igor stole my attention as he moved through the den and headed toward the liquor cart. He picked up a bottle of *Krasnyy* vodka and poured himself a shot. He downed it in one swallow.

"Hen?"

I looked at Flynn. "Hmm?"

He was peering at me, his brow furrowed. "Did you hear what Quinn said?"

"Yeah, I heard," I said, my smile quickly blooming across my face. "They're moving to Scotland."

Flynn shook his head. "After that."

"No, sorry, I missed it." I turned my attention to Quinn. "What did you say?"

"I asked if we could crash with you while we castle hunt," Quinn said with a rueful grin.

"I said it was fine," Flynn announced. "There's just one thing we need to settle first."

"*Da.*" Sasha nodded.

Flynn clenched his fist and slugged Sasha across the jaw. Quinn's breath hitched, but otherwise there wasn't a sound in the room.

"Welcome to Scotland," Igor muttered.

"I deserved that," Sasha said, gingerly touching his face.

I looked at Flynn who wasn't staring at Sasha, but at me.

"It's done. I forgive you," Flynn proclaimed. His eyes slid from me to Sasha and held out his hand to him.

Sasha took it.

Quinn glanced at me from the confines of the couch, her eyebrows raised nearly to her hairline.

I shrugged and then went to properly greet Sasha with a hug. Then I sat down next to Quinn.

"We're really not putting you out?" Quinn asked, pitching her voice lower. She looked at me and then to Sasha who was already engaged in conversation with Flynn as if no violence had occurred. They took the chairs by the fireplace. Two masculine men; rulers of dynasties and creators of legacies that would last centuries.

Igor poured himself another shot of vodka, and I heard the sound of the bottle as he set it back down on the cart.

"No, you're not putting us out. Not at all," I assured her. I attempted to ignore Igor's presence, but he dominated my attention.

"We didn't call and let you know we were coming." She bit her lip and brushed a finger down Helena's cheek.

"Never call," I stated. "I'm glad you guys just showed

up. How did you get Tony not to call ahead and let us know you were at the gates?"

"He was in on the surprise," Sasha stated.

Quinn glanced at Piper. "Now I get to see this little beauty in person. Can you believe it? We have daughters. It's a pity they're not closer in age."

"That only matters when they're young and the age difference is more obvious. But I think if they grow up together, the age thing won't matter."

"Two peas in a pod, I hope."

"They'll be best friends," I assured her. "They'll keep each other's confidences, gush about boys—"

"But never fight over the same one," Quinn interrupted.

"No, they won't. They'll be way too enlightened to do that," I agreed.

"Sleep overs," Quinn added. "Almost every weekend."

Quinn painted a beautiful picture that could only occur if we lived in close proximity. "What made you decide to move to Scotland? You both mentioned it, but I didn't think you were seriously considering it."

"She's jealous of your relationship with Sasha, you know," Igor called out. "She's never gotten over how close the two of you are."

If that was the case, then why would she bring her fiancé and I closer together?

Igor raised his eyebrow and I realized he'd heard my retort because he was inside my head.

"Family," Quinn said easily. "I've been hiding in Martha's Vineyard for longer than I care to admit. It was safe and comfortable there, but I didn't realize how removed from everything I was until we spoke on the phone the other day and I just…missed it all. The craziness and energy of family, the connection. I want Helena to grow up here. Is that okay?"

"Is that okay?" I repeated. "More than okay! This makes me so happy I can't even tell you. Are you sure I didn't badger you into it?" I shuffled Piper to my other shoulder.

"No," she assured me with a smile.

Igor's stare pinned me to my seat. "Your husband will not be happy that the man who'd gladly take his place is planning to move a stone's throw away from you."

"Hell," I muttered.

"What was that?" Quinn asked, leaning forward as if to hear me better.

"Nothing," I said hastily. "Flynn surprised me with a nursery for Piper—all brand-new furniture. But we still have the baby furniture from Hawk and the twins in the attic. Flynn and Sasha can move it down into one of the guest rooms on the other side of the castle. I would say we could give you the baby furniture Ash and Duncan use for their kids when they're here, but—"

"Better to leave it where it is, since it's still needed," Quinn said.

I nodded. "My thoughts exactly."

Quinn chuckled. "Helena is going through a screaming in the middle of the night phase."

"Oh, is she? You've conveniently left that information out when you asked to stay." I smiled, letting her know it was all in jest. "Not that it matters. We have a newborn, and Ash and Duncan stay here frequently enough that I'm well versed in sleepless nights."

"You sound like you're happy that you get to do it all over again," Quinn commented.

"I am. I don't know why, but I am."

"Where are the boys?" Quinn asked. "They haven't come down to investigate who showed up at their house."

"They're used to the revolving door of guests. Besides, they're probably making a fort in the playroom while watching a movie."

"Ah. Little boys and their forts."

"Are you hungry? Mrs. Aducci made something this morning that smelled fantastic when we got home, though I haven't had time to rummage through the refrigerator and figure out what it is."

"I could eat," Quinn said. "Sasha? Are you hungry?"

He paused in conversation with Flynn and shook his head.

"Flynn?" I asked.

"No, I'm fine. Thank you." He smiled, the corners of his eyes crinkling.

Igor glowered. "No one asked me if *I* was hungry."

"Flynn?" I asked, trying to hear myself think over one very annoying and stubborn Russian ghost. "Will you and Sasha head up to the attic and get Hawk's old crib?"

Flynn looked at Sasha and slapped him on the back. "What do you think, old man? Are you up to the task? It's heavy and solid furniture."

"Who are you calling *old man*?" Sasha demanded, shooting Quinn a flirtatious wink. "I'm in better shape than you."

"Prove it," Flynn goaded.

"Oh, I'll prove it all right. Let's go."

The two of them continued to rib one another as they left the den.

Quinn grinned at me. "Things are all right between them."

"Thank goodness." I sighed in relief. "Are they good between us?"

"What do you mean? Why wouldn't they be?"

"Quinn," I began. "Igor's house."

"What about it? That has nothing to do with me."

"It didn't bother you that he didn't tell you about it until he had to?"

"I'm long past the point of thinking your secrets with Sasha mean anything more than deep abiding affection and loyalty. We're good, Barrett. Truly."

"She's lying," Igor said.

Shut up, ghost.

Chapter 23
SASHA

I WATCHED Barrett all through an afternoon meal that was too early to be dinner and too late to be lunch. Even though she laughed, there was a strain around her mouth, as if her smile was being summoned from deep within her, but it was neither sincere nor joyful.

I knew Barrett like the back of my hand. And the crinkles at the corners of her eyes when she laughed at something Hawk said were staged. In a random, unguarded moment, I saw a flash of panic streak across her face before she hastily buried it.

I studied them together, her and Flynn. His hand went to the leg of her chair, and he pulled her closer to him. Even after all the strife they'd been through, it hadn't broken them.

"Will you show me your sword?" Hawk asked me.

Flynn raised his brows at me and smirked. "Good luck."

"I didn't bring my katana," I told him.

Hawk leveled me with a look that told me I'd fallen down a tier in his estimation of the man he thought I was.

Quinn laughed and set her hand on my thigh, giving it a hearty squeeze. I knew what she said with that touch. She understood without me having to say a word. I loved Helena; she was the daughter of my heart. But there was something about having a son. I was a man who yearned for a legacy.

I thought of the child Quinn and I had lost.

Ciaran.

I wish I'd been there for Quinn when she'd buried him.

Barrett and Flynn had everything they'd ever wanted. They should've been happy.

They weren't.

At least, Barrett wasn't. I wanted to speak to her alone, but it wasn't my place. Flynn had tolerated me early on, but now we were friends. I respected him, admired him. And I would not come between him and his wife again.

A cry blasted through the baby monitor. Quinn and Barrett exchanged a look.

"I suppose we should both go," Barrett said. "Doesn't matter whose baby is crying. The other one will wake soon."

Quinn rose from her chair. "You're right about that." She looked at me and smiled, and then ran a hand down my scarred cheek. "I'll be back in a bit."

"Mam, can we be excused?" Iain begged.

"Yes," Barrett said, ruffling her son's hair. "I appreciate how nicely you asked me."

"More flies with honey," Iain quipped.

Barrett shook her head. "I stand no chance against your charm, Iain Willoughby Campbell."

"Mam," Iain whined. "No middle naming me, please!"

The boys rushed from the table and out of the room.

"You've got your hands full with that one," Quinn stated.

"I've got my hands full with all of them," Barrett said fondly. "Let's go tend to the wee lassies."

"Your affected Scottish brogue is terrible," Quinn said with a laugh as she and Barrett left.

"Leave the dishes. Someone will take care of it," Flynn said to me. "Let's have a drink."

I followed Flynn out of the kitchen. I thought he was going to the den, but he surprised me when he entered the study. I closed the door behind me.

A black and white stone chess set rested in the corner of the room near the gas fireplace, which wasn't currently on. Flynn pressed a button on the mantle and the synthetic logs were suddenly aflame.

"You sure you don't mind us being here?" I asked.

"No, not at all. Scotch or vodka?"

"Scotch."

I sat down on one of the black leather couches and stretched out my legs.

Flynn plucked a crystal decanter from the antique liquor cart and poured two glasses. He walked with them to the leather sofa, handed me one, and then took the seat across the coffee table.

Only in the last few years had Flynn and I developed a relationship independent of his wife. We were bonded in ways that normal people weren't.

"Have you decided how you're going to live in Scotland and run the business?" Flynn asked.

"Dimitri is more than capable of handling the day-to-day in New York. He did it before," I reminded him.

"Aye."

"I'm still mulling over what to do about Boston. The Irish and the Russians aren't meshing the way I expected them to, even though I'm engaged to Quinn. I think a co-leader situation is necessary. It will force them to work together and bridge the divide."

"It could work," Flynn said.

"It works with you and Duncan."

"Aye, but we're brothers. It's different."

"There will always be growing pains," I said. "I've ensured both sides that neither is losing territory, but everyone is still uneasy about this new venture."

"They don't trust your word?" Flynn asked.

"No."

"You might have to show them," he replied.

I sighed. "*Da.* Violence. It seems to be the only way to get them to listen."

"It has to come from you. Not Dimitri." He paused. "You'll get bored here."

"I don't think so."

"You were bored in Martha's Vineyard."

"That was different."

"Was it?"

"Quinn needed time there. Away from…everything. Moving to Scotland is not the same."

"You're making your job harder by moving even farther away," he pointed out. "It would be easier if you moved back to New York. Hell, even Boston."

"Then it'll be harder." I shrugged. "I'm still the one the old men in Russia want to do business with. When they heard I was back in the leadership position, they made it clear that they'd prefer to speak to me when it came to negotiations."

"So you're not walking away."

"No."

"You walked away once."

"And came back," I stated.

"For Quinn, aye?"

"For Quinn," I agreed. "But once a king always a king, *da*? Too much blood has been spilled. I've paid a hefty price for my position. So I'll lead from Scotland. I have men I trust. I won't be seen as weak."

We drank for a few moments, letting silence fill the room.

"Would you do anything differently?" I asked him. "Knowing what you know now?"

He paused and stared into his glass, like a scribe studying ancient scrolls. "I would still make all the same choices."

"No regrets, then."

"None." He looked at me. "Even if my choices come home to roost."

Chapter 24
BARRETT

"I THINK you're the prettiest girl in the world," Hawk said as he snuggled down into his bed.

I grinned. "Nice try, kiddo. It's bedtime, and it's been a long day."

"Not for me."

"You're younger and have more energy," I stated.

"Why can't Betty sleep with me tonight?"

"Because we have enough pandemonium going on and I don't want a sheep roaming the hallways. Someone will think this house is haunted."

His eyes widened with eagerness. "Haunted? Like with ghosts? How do you find ghosts? Do they find you? Can you talk to them?"

I held in a sigh. It was my own fault for stirring his curiosity. "I'm sure most houses in Scotland have ghosts because of all the history here. Ghosts generally find you, if you're open to them, and yes, you can talk to them."

"Are they friendly?"

"Some of them."

"How do you get rid of them? The mean ones?"

"You tell them to go to the other side. You tell them that you release them, and that they should move on from this world to the one they are supposed to be in and be happy."

Hawk's brow furrowed like he was seriously pondering what I was telling him. He wasn't a kid you could distract with another topic until he was satisfied with the answers he received. He was relentless in his pursuit of knowledge. Perhaps he'd follow in my footsteps and become a historian, I mused.

"Do you want to hear a story tonight?" I asked him, hoping like hell he took the bait.

"Aye."

"What kind of story do you want to hear?"

"How did you meet Da?"

I smiled, looking into my son's earnest blue eyes. I knew he was delaying going to sleep, but I was helpless to resist his charm. And maybe I was feeling nostalgic.

"How did I meet your father," I repeated. "I worked for him in New York. You know the hotel we stay in when we're in New York?"

Hawk nodded.

"I was a waitress in the restaurant." I wasn't very well going to tell my seven-year-old son that I'd been a cocktail waitress in a burlesque club and that my deceased brother had owed Flynn a debt and had made a shady introduction between us.

I never wanted Hawk to know the truth, even when he was older.

"Did he take you out to nice dinners? I'm going to take my wife out to nice dinners," Hawk informed me.

"Yes, he took me to nice dinners. I think you'll make a very good husband one day if you've already got that on your mind."

"There's a girl in my class. Her name is Lennox. Can I have her over and show her my fort?"

My heart twinged. He was already discovering the opposite sex. The teenage years were going to be hell.

"I'll call her mother," I promised.

Hawk's eyes began to close. "I love you, Mam."

"I love you, too." Tears pricked my eyes as I ran my hand across his hair. I got up off the bed and turned off the bedside lamp before padding to the door past Igor's solemn form.

I hated that Igor's ghost dogged my heels, and that he'd witnessed such a special moment between me and my son. But I ignored him and refused to address him as I passed. He'd get the hint sooner or later that he wasn't welcome, and he'd leave.

Unfortunately, he slipped into the twins' room behind me. He went to the wall with all the black and white photos of me and the twins when they were newborns. Lacey had taken them, and she'd captured the true essence of motherhood.

"Beautiful," he said gruffly.

A part of me wanted to throw myself in front of them so he couldn't see me in such a vulnerable state. The pictures were far too personal.

Turning away from Igor, I went to Iain first, who was already asleep. I brushed my lips across his forehead, but he didn't stir.

Noah was still awake, staring up at the ceiling like it contained all the secrets of the universe.

"What are you thinking about?" I whispered.

"Piper."

I sat down on the bed next to him. "Yeah? What about Piper?"

"I'm happy she's here. It feels right."

I smiled at my beautiful, thoughtful son.

"She needs a pony, though."

A wide grin stretched across my face. "She won't be able to ride for a few more years."

Noah nodded. "Iain, Hawk, and I already have horses. It's not fair that she doesn't have one."

"She'll have one," I promised.

I wondered if Piper would be a natural born equestrian. Would she want to show? It was too far ahead into the future for me to be thinking that.

I kissed Noah's forehead. "Good night."

He rolled over onto his side and closed his eyes. "Good night, Mam."

I flipped off the main light and then left Noah and Iain's room, closing the door behind me. I passed Piper's nursery and because I couldn't help myself, went to look in on her.

I wondered what babies dreamed of. Did they know fear or panic the way adults did? Did the world's ugliness infect their dreamscapes, or were they spared the imprinting of horrors until they were older?

"You're philosophical tonight," Igor commented. "Unusually so."

I ignored him. I did not engage, or even look in his direction. Instead, I stared down at my sleeping daughter, wondering if I'd ever slept so peacefully.

It had been a long day. With the arrival of Sasha and Quinn, getting them settled, not knowing Piper's routine yet, I was ready for bed.

Quinn had gone to sleep hours ago due to jet lag, but Sasha had remained awake, and he and Flynn had been solidly imbibing in the study.

The bedroom was a welcome and quiet haven. I dropped down face first onto the bed and conked out.

I stirred when I felt Flynn settle down on the bed next to me. I turned my head and stared at my husband. My handsome, wonderful husband.

"Sorry," he whispered, his eyes slightly glassy. "Did I wake you?"

"Kind of," I said. "It's okay, though."

"You fell asleep with the light on. You must've been tired."

"Must've been. How much scotch did you and Sasha drink?" I demanded.

"A fair bit." He grinned and finally dropped down onto the bed next to me, pulling me close.

"I'm worried about Iain," I said.

"Iain? Why are you worried about the lad?" He rolled over onto his back and gently patted his chest. I nuzzled against him and pressed my cheek to his shirt.

"Hawk is the eldest. He's a natural leader. Noah is quiet, but sure of himself. Iain is sandwiched between two strong, yet different personalities and I worry he's going to be living in Hawk's shadow and that he'll always try to emulate his older brother."

Flynn stroked a hand down my back. "Awareness is key. We'll keep an eye out. We should carve out some time with him, alone. We don't want him lost in the shuffle of Quinn and Sasha being here, along with introducing Piper into the family mix."

I smiled. "This is why you're the father of my children."

Chapter 25

QUINN

"No," I said. "I don't like that. How do *you* like that?"

"What do you mean how do I like that?" Sasha asked. "It's a castle, and you want a castle."

"It was *once* a castle. Now it's a ruin. And it's an hour away from Barrett and Flynn. Besides, we can't stay here for months on end while it's being restored. We need something now."

"Why move to a country with so much history just to buy something new?" he asked in confusion. "I think it would be the adventure of a lifetime to restore a six-hundred-year-old castle like this to its former glory. This property even has a moat, Quinn. We could have a literal moat."

"You're off your rocker."

"Barrett and Flynn wouldn't mind if we stayed with them for a while. They have enough space."

I shook my head. "We took them by surprise when we showed up here unannounced. They're good sports, but they need to be able to get back to their lives."

"It's only been a few days, Quinn."

"A few days…that could turn into weeks. Months if we buy a ruin."

"I'd never let it come to that," Sasha said. "We'll buy a townhome and stay in that while we have the castle remodeled."

"Fine. It's not just about staying with them for months on end. You're talking about putting in plumbing, wiring a ruin for electrical, and rebuilding stone walls. Stone walls, Sasha! All because of a moat? Can't we just move into a place that's already been modernized?"

"Where's your sense of adventure?"

"I want to be settled," I admitted. "I want stability. I want something that's already beautiful. I don't want potential; I want the end result already."

"I can understand that," he said. "I just thought it would be an experience."

"It would be," I admitted. "But it would take so much time."

"So, we'll throw money at the problem." He shrugged. "I can have it done for you in a few months."

I sighed. "This is important to you, isn't it?"

"I want to give you something, Quinn. Something beautiful, and something that will last. I want you to walk from room to room and decorate it in your style. I want enough bedrooms that we can have five children if we want them."

"Five," I murmured. "Oh my."

He grinned. "Just one would be fine though. Helena's enough if you feel that way."

"You want more children, don't you? I saw how you looked at Hawk. You want a boy."

"I wouldn't say no to a boy."

"Fathers and sons." I nodded. "I understand. We can try for a boy next."

"Can we try right now?" he teased.

"Here? In Flynn's study?"

"The rug looks soft." His blue eyes twinkled with devilment.

He'd be up for a good time. He always was.

Sasha continued, "What do you think? You want to make love on a Persian rug? Helena just went down for her nap. We have some time."

"What if someone walks into the room while I'm naked on the floor?"

"I'm willing to take the risk if you are."

"Another reason I want our own space." I paused, my brow furrowing.

"What?" he demanded.

"Nothing."

"Not nothing. There's something on your mind that has nothing to do with people potentially walking in on us while we're naked. So what is it?"

I bit my lip and then asked, "Have you noticed…"

"What?"

"Anything weird about Barrett's behavior recently?"

"You noticed it too."

I nodded. "She seems…jumpy."

"I was going to say troubled."

"Troubled?" I repeated. "How do you mean?"

Sasha shook his head. "I don't know. She just—she stares at me, but I don't think she sees me. She laughs but it sounds hollow, like her mind is somewhere else."

"She looks thinner. Her cheekbones…" I stroked a finger across one of my own. "Has she said anything to you?"

"Why would she say anything to me?"

"Because you're Sasha, and she's Barrett."

EMMA SLATE

"No. She hasn't divulged anything to me." He rubbed his chin.

"You haven't asked?"

"No."

"Why not?"

"Because I've overstepped my bounds already with her. This is for Flynn to handle."

"And is he? Handling it?"

"I don't know."

"What do you mean *you don't know*? You guys drink and talk almost every night in the study. What do you talk about?"

"Business." He arched a brow. "You could ask her."

"I could," I agreed.

"But you won't."

"No, I won't. She needs time to open up about whatever is bothering her."

"I concur with you on that," he said. "Pushing her to talk has never worked, and she might run again if she feels trapped."

I weighed his words and nodded. "Do you know why I really don't want to go through the process of restoring a castle?"

"Why?"

"Because I want to marry you." I looked him in the eyes. "I want to plan our party and celebrate with our friends. I want to have more babies with you. I'm tired of waiting, Sasha. There's always some roadblock popping up between us. No more."

His smile was slow, beautiful. And when his smile turned into a wicked grin, my heart galloped in excitement.

"I'll tell you what," he said. "You plan the party. I'll find us our home."

160

I let out a sigh of relief. "Would it bother you if I didn't wear white for our private ceremony?"

"*Myshka*," he began, "you could wear a towel and I wouldn't care. All I want is for you to marry me. I'm tearing your wedding dress off of you on our wedding night anyway. It doesn't matter what color it is."

My eyes went hazy with the vision he painted.

"Now I have your attention," he said with a smirk. "Helena's still asleep. What do you say we have our own nap?"

"You mean a naked nap?" I teased.

He arched a brow. "Is there any other kind?"

Chapter 26

SASHA

I CREPT from the guest room, not wishing to disturb Quinn who had fallen asleep. Late afternoon sun painted the wooden floor in bright rays as I closed the door behind me. It had been raining off and on since we'd arrived a few days prior, but there was a break in the weather, and I decided to venture outside to walk around the estate grounds.

The house was far quieter than it should've been. I assumed that meant the Campbell boys were burning off energy that was inherent in youth.

I passed their playroom. Empty. I trekked down the staircase, and headed for the kitchen, wanting to grab a drink.

I paused when I heard Barrett on the phone with someone.

"No, I'm not having this discussion with you again. It's over. We're done. *I'm* done. I'm not doing this with you any longer."

Her words filled my chest with ice.

Was Barrett having an affair?

No. I didn't believe it. Couldn't believe it. She wouldn't do that to Flynn. To her family.

But what the hell? What other explanation could there be?

I debated for all of five seconds before marching into the kitchen, wanting to catch her in the act of talking to her lover on the phone. Instead, I caught her gripping the counter, her head bent and her breathing harsh and rapid.

"Barrett?" I asked.

She whirled, putting a hand to her heart. Her hazel eyes were unnaturally wide in her pale face. Her cheekbones were stark and bony. Now I knew the truth; her sleeplessness and lack of focus was more than just adjusting to a new baby.

Barrett was haunted by the guilt of her affair.

"Where are the boys?" I asked.

"Boys," she repeated. "With Barnabas. There's a new litter of puppies. Angus drove them over there."

"And Flynn?"

Her brow furrowed. "At Duncan's. Ramsey's leaving tomorrow and heading back to the States."

"Do you want to put Piper into a sling and take a walk with me. I could use some fresh air."

She shook her head. "No, I—Piper just got to sleep, and I don't want to move her."

"Come sit outside with me," I commanded.

Barrett looked like she was about to argue.

"Get your jacket," I urged bluntly. "Meet me on the patio."

I didn't give her a choice in denying me. I went outside before she could respond. The sunlight was nothing more than an illusion of warmth at this hour, so I turned on the heating lamps since the temperature had started to drop. I sat down and stretched out my legs underneath the table.

The sliding glass door opened and then shut. Barrett appeared and set the baby monitor on the table before taking a seat next to me.

She wore one of Flynn's peacoats and it swallowed her. Her auburn braid was tucked into the collar of the jacket, and she hunched down into it as if it would offer her some protection against me.

I was instantly enraged.

I thought I knew her.

I knew nothing.

"Who is he?" I asked, my voice soft, careful.

She frowned. "He who?"

"The man you've been having an affair with?"

Her eyes widened. "I'm not having an affair."

"Don't bullshit me," I snapped. "I heard you on the phone, talking to your lover."

She clamped her mouth shut and her lips went white with anger.

"You're not going to tell me?"

"It's none of your business."

"None of my—you were having a conversation out in the open, Barrett. What if it hadn't been me who walked in on you? What if it had been Quinn? Or your husband?"

"You don't understand," she whispered. She turned her face away. In that moment, she reminded me of one of those classic paintings, of a woman with mystery hidden in her eyes, and secrets buried within her lips.

"Make me understand," I beseeched.

"I can't."

"Can't? Or won't?"

"My own husband wouldn't understand." She looked at me, her eyes tormented. "Why would I tell you and not him?"

"I understand you in ways he can't," I began. "So, explain it to me."

She pondered my statement for a moment and looked like she was about to unveil everything she was holding in when Piper's cry echoed through the baby monitor.

Without a word, Barrett rose and went to tend to her daughter.

Chapter 27

BARRETT

I'D NEVER BEEN MORE grateful for a crying child. Seeing to Piper's needs allowed me to escape Sasha's penetrating gaze.

I wished he didn't know me so well.

I wished I'd thought to keep my mouth shut while people were staying with us.

I wished I'd been able to keep the fact that I was going insane on lockdown.

Instead, I'd allowed Igor's ghost to get the better of me. Even now, he followed me up the stairs into Piper's nursery. She was howling like a banshee. Her tiny fists were clenched, and her mouth was open in ravenous hunger. I scooped her up and placed her at my shoulder, crooning Gaelic endearments into the warm skin of her head.

"Why didn't you tell him?" Igor asked.

I set Piper on the changing table and got to work. "Because he wouldn't understand."

"If anyone can understand, it will be Sasha. I am the link that binds you together."

"You are the noose around my neck," I muttered. "How many times do I have to tell you to go away?"

"I can't go away. I can't leave you alone."

I slathered cream onto Piper's bottom and then put her into a clean diaper. "You won't be happy until I ruin everything in my life."

"It's not about *my* happiness, Barrett. It's about yours."

"I am happy."

"Are you?"

"Yes," I snapped. "I'm more in love with my husband now than when we met. We have three beautiful boys, and now we have a baby girl to spoil too. My life is perfect. My life is charmed. Why the hell are you ruining it?"

"Why are you ruining your own life?"

I looked at him. "I'm not self-sabotaging if that's what you're getting at."

There was a soft rap against the nursery door, and I instantly quelled my one-sided conversation with a ghost.

The door opened and Quinn popped her head in. "Hey," she said softly.

"Hey."

"Have you seen Sasha?"

"Downstairs," I said, forcing a smile. "Is Helena awake?"

"Not yet." She frowned.

"What's wrong?" I picked up Piper and cradled her in my arms.

"Nothing. He just—we were—never mind." She shook her head. "Heading downstairs?"

I nodded.

Helena's epic cry shattered through the baby monitor Quinn was holding. She sighed. "I'll be down in a few minutes."

I smiled. "Take your time." I walked downstairs with Piper

and heard the front door open. Just as I got to the first floor, the boys ran inside, and they were covered head to toe in mud.

"Stop!" I commanded before they could take another step forward and ruin the Persian rug that graced the front hallway.

I sniffed. "That's not mud."

"Iain slipped in a pile of sheep poop," Noah explained. "And then when we started laughing at him, he pulled us down in it with him."

"Oh, God, the car—" I wrinkled my nose at the potent aroma.

"Don't worry. Angus made us sit on a towel," Hawk explained. "And we drove home with the windows down. Still smells a bit though."

I sighed, wishing Flynn was home to help me with the boys. They were a handful on a good day. A wonderful, exhausting handful. I couldn't wait for the nannies to return from holiday.

"All right, lads. Out of those clothes—leave them on the front steps. Then head upstairs and take your baths."

Piper was fussing and needed to be fed, but I had three boys who would not scrub themselves to my satisfaction without me present.

I went out to the patio, ensuring Piper was nestled against me and wrapped in a wool blanket for warmth. Sasha was still sitting alone.

"I need help with Piper."

He stared at me for a long moment and then said, "What do you need help with?"

"She needs a bottle, and the boys need baths. I can't be in two places at once."

"Why do they need baths?"

"They fell in sheep poop."

His lips twitched like he wanted to smile but he refrained. Sasha stood. "I'll feed Piper."

It took four rounds of scrubbing and draining the water before the boys were squeaky clean. After the boys were settled and snacking in their theater playroom and watching a movie, I went to find Sasha, bracing myself for the interrogation that had been interrupted.

I didn't know what to say to him. A part of me was concerned that he'd tell Flynn what he'd overheard. I wasn't sure he'd keep my confidence again, not after the Dolinsky house secret.

I walked into the den and found Quinn sitting on a floral couch, looking through a magazine. Helena was playing on the floor at her feet, but she was occupying herself.

"Hey," I greeted.

"Hey," she said. "Just so you're aware, Sasha put me on Piper duty. He left after he gave her a bottle and a burp. She's asleep in the bassinet and I opened a bottle of red. Hope that's okay?"

"My house is your house," I said. "Thanks for watching her. Where did Sasha go?"

I went to the liquor cart and poured myself a glass of wine.

"No idea. He just said he was going for a drive. I hope Flynn doesn't mind, but he took the Aston Martin."

"As long as it's not the Shelby Cobra. That one was a gift from Hadrian and he's quite possessive about it."

"Yeah, we were warned." Quinn smiled.

I held in my sigh of relief about getting a bit more time before facing Sasha.

Quinn's phone chimed. She looked at the screen and quickly unlocked it. A frown marred her forehead.

"What is it?" I asked, taking my glass of wine and sitting down on the couch next to her.

"Sasha," she began. She glanced at me, eyes wide. "He bought a house."

"Are you serious?"

She nodded. "Wow, he really took what I had to say to heart."

"What did you say to him?"

"He asked if I wanted to restore a Scottish castle."

"That's a massive undertaking…" I raised my eyebrows.

"Massive, indeed. I told him I wasn't going to restore a castle, because I wanted to focus on our lives. I don't have the bandwidth to handle months of construction and the delays that inevitably come with it. We just changed everything by moving to Scotland. I want to settle down, watch Helena grow, expand our family. He said he'd take care of finding us our home and I would take care of the wedding."

"Wedding? What wedding? Have you guys finally set a date?" I asked in excitement.

"Not an official date," she said. "We want to have a private ceremony, but then celebrate with our friends by having a party. I didn't want a big fanfare."

"Sounds fun."

"No push back?"

"Not from me. It's your day. Do what you want." I gestured to the phone. "So the house?"

"He already made them an offer and they accepted. He didn't even show me!"

"Well, you did sort of give him free reign to take care of it as he saw fit," I pointed out.

"I just didn't expect it this soon," she said. "He told me he was going for a drive to clear his head, but now I know he was going to look at this house. Do you think he bought the first one he saw?"

"It looks that way, doesn't it? Did he send you photos at least?" I asked.

"A few," she admitted. "Here, look at them."

Quinn handed me her phone and I scrolled through the photos. "Huh."

"What?" she demanded.

"It looks nice. Better than nice. Sprawling and more than enough space to keep horses if that's what you want."

"It has a lake," Quinn stated with a shake of her head.

"What's wrong with a lake?" I asked in confusion.

"Nothing. There's nothing wrong with a lake. There's nothing wrong with the house."

"Then…"

"It's one thing to say *I'll take care of it*. It's another not to involve me at all."

I let out a laugh. "Well, that's what happens when you give men like ours no parameters. You told him to take care of it and that's exactly what he did. You have no one to blame but yourself."

"You're right," she agreed with a grumble. "I know you're right."

"Besides, he moved here because of you, because you wanted this."

She was silent for a moment and then she said, "I think he moved here for you, too."

I stilled. "What do you mean by that?"

"He missed you. He's happier when he gets to see you."

"You're not worried, are you?" I boldly met her eyes. "About my relationship with Sasha—"

"Oh God, no," she hastened to assure me. "I've long put that to rest."

"Have you?" I pressed.

"Have *you*?" she fired back.

"I have. I just want to make sure you have too. You're perfect for him. You're exactly what he needs and continues to need. I'm not right for him. I never was. It's always been Flynn. It'll *always* be Flynn."

She nodded slowly. "You don't have to convince me, Barrett. I believe you." She paused and took a sip of her wine and then said, "Do you think there will ever be a time in our lives where we don't have this discussion?"

"Yes. Starting now."

"Now?"

"Now," I affirmed. "This is the last time it needs to be discussed. Agreed?"

"Agreed."

We clinked our glasses together and exchanged smiles.

The front door opened, and I immediately heard the unmistakable sounds of a mother trying to corral a young child.

Frowning, I looked at Quinn and then got up to see what was going on. She followed me.

Ash was attempting to coerce Carys through the front door while maneuvering the double stroller.

"What are you doing here?" I asked, picking up Carys and making Ash's job easier.

"My house has been overrun with testosterone," she said. "Sasha showed up and is now in the billiards room with the others, drinking, smoking, and playing cards. The sun hasn't even set yet. I expect them to party long into the night and into the wee hours of the morning."

"When did we marry eighteenth century dukes?" I asked.

"Hell if I know," Ash muttered. "They're carousing. Like, in epic fashion."

"I'm inclined to blame Ramsey," I said. "He's a bad influence."

"The worst," Ash agreed.

"Ash, you look like you could use a glass of wine," Quinn said.

"Several. I could use *several* glasses of wine," Ash stated.

"You've come to the right place." I smirked. "I've got you covered."

"Just one little problem," Quinn said.

"Which is?" I asked, raising my brows.

Quinn lifted the glass of wine to her lips. "Three of us, eight children, no nannies or husbands. We have to stay marginally sober."

Chapter 28
FLYNN

"Read 'em and weep boys," Ramsey drawled, setting his cards down on the table. "Full house."

Duncan groaned. "I've been on a losing streak all night." He threw his hand face down with annoyance and then took a sip of his scotch.

"I'm on a hot streak." Ramsey grinned, eyes glassy. We'd been steadily drinking and gambling for hours, and a heavy cloud of cigar smoke hung in the billiards room.

Sasha had arrived late that afternoon and had been unusually quiet. I knew he enjoyed Duncan and Ramsey's company, but he looked pensive, often staring into his glass of vodka—which I knew meant only one thing: something was weighing heavily on his mind.

"You're on a hot streak because you've been bluffing," Duncan accused, but he didn't sound annoyed. If anything, he sounded proud of his younger brother.

Sasha set his cards down. "You called my bluff. I've got nothing."

Ramsey shot me an impudent grin. "And you, Flynn Campbell? Master and Commander?"

I laid my cards down one by one to reveal a royal flush of hearts.

Ramsey cursed. "I don't fucking believe this! How the hell did you beat me?"

I grinned and leaned back in the heavy antique chair. "I know your tells when you're bluffing. You're easy to read."

"Like hell I'm easy to read," Ramsey quipped.

Duncan's laugh boomed across the room. "He's got you there, lad."

"This is bull shite," Ramsey muttered.

"Don't like the heat? Get out of the kitchen." I smirked.

Duncan's phone chimed and he reached into his trouser pocket. After a moment, he set it down on the table.

"Everything good?" I asked him.

"Aye. A hen night at your house, apparently." He grinned. "Our women can't get too crazy since they have the brood."

"I'm going to catch hell," I said in amusement. "Our poker night was impromptu, and now they have to wrangle eight children between the three of them. Thank Christ the nannies return tomorrow."

I'd only meant to have dinner with Ramsey and Duncan, but then Sasha had shown up, and we'd decided to make a night of it.

Ramsey, Duncan and I were in pleasant moods despite how much liquor we'd consumed. But with every glass Sasha drank, he became more and more morose. I blamed the Russian in him.

"I need some air," Sasha announced, pushing back from the table. He placed his cigar between his lips, grabbed his glass of vodka, and then marched from the room.

"I want a woman," Ramsey muttered. "Do you think Ash would be upset if I invited—"

"Aye, she'd be upset." Duncan frowned. "Furthermore, I'd be upset too. I know the kind of women you'd call to distract you. Those kind of women are not welcome in this house."

Ramsey sighed. "Fine. I'll respect your wishes." He stood. "I gotta piss."

He stalked from the room, leaving me alone with Duncan.

"Let's hope he passes out before he forgets that I told him no and calls one of them," Duncan remarked.

"You sound old. And prudish."

He grumbled. "Aye, I know."

"Especially considering *you* used to do the same thing."

"That's different," he stated. "This is my home. My children play on these floors."

"Do you miss the debauchery of our youth, Duncan?" I asked with a winsome grin.

"Honestly? Sometimes." He peered around the billiard room that looked the same as it had when we were young lads. It hadn't really changed since Malcolm used it as a place to discuss SINS business with his captains.

"What do you miss about it?" I inquired.

"The hunt," he said. "Late nights on the streets, the adrenaline rushing through my blood, the fighting and the fucking." He fell silent. "I love my wife. I love my children. But sometimes I feel like I'm in captivity."

"Restless."

"It's more than that." He ran a hand down his face. He had a few days' worth of whiskers, and for the first time in a long time Duncan looked more than tired—he looked weathered and beaten. "I know I'm lucky to be alive. I could've died the night Da did. Should've, maybe. But what am I doing, Flynn? Is this really living?"

"We're family men now," I told him. "What do you think would happen if we try and live now like we did when we were younger? We took foolish risks and had only the *illusion* of invincibility. Do you want to leave Ash a widow? Do you want to leave your children fatherless?"

"Of course not," he said automatically. "I just— nothing gets my blood pumping anymore, Flynn."

"We've come a long way from picking the lock on Malcolm's liquor cabinet and drinking all his best scotch straight from the bottle," I remarked.

"We have money and power. We have strong, beautiful wives. We have children that will carry on our legacies, and still it's not enough," Duncan said quietly.

"What *is* enough?" I asked slowly. "We want for nothing, so what is this elusive *thing* that's tugging at your soul?"

"If I had the answer, do you think I'd be putting away a bottle of SINNERS with you and letting you win at poker?"

"Duncan," I began.

He sighed. "It's not about wanting another woman. Or even wanting another life. But I yearn for something I can't name." He paused his speech and gathered the cards. He began to shuffle them.

"I still pick up the phone to call him," I said after a while.

He didn't even pretend not to know who I was talking about. "Same. What do you think Da would tell me?"

"He'd tell you that you were being an ungrateful arsewipe who suffers from what all wealthy men suffer from—extreme boredom."

"I think I'd like to run with the bulls in Pamplona."

"Why not hike Everest?" I taunted.

"Maybe I will."

"Have fun." I saluted him in a mocking fashion.

"Don't be so cavalier," he snapped. "Do you have everything you've ever wanted? Is this how you envisioned your life? Don't lie to me—and don't lie to yourself."

"We're not talking about me," I said, my voice low. "But before you do anything stupid, perhaps you should talk to Ash."

"And tell her what? That I love her? That it's not her or our marriage, or our children? How do I even explain something like this to her?"

"Is this you facing your mortality? Are you afraid this is the rest of your life?"

"Aye," he said quietly.

"So, do something about it. Shake it up. Roll the dice." I gestured to the billiards room. "You're living in your late father's home. Just because you inherited his estate and his things doesn't mean you inherited his life, Duncan. If you're unhappy, change your life."

"Change it," he repeated. "Like it's so simple."

"That's just it. It *is* simple. *You're* the problem. Do you know how many people blow up their lives and run off to marry someone else and start a new family, only to realize the problem wasn't external?"

"I'm not leaving Ash or the children," Duncan growled.

"Glad to hear it."

"Have you never thought of leaving Barrett?" he pushed back.

"Again, this isn't about me," I repeated.

"Enough said."

"What the hell does *that* mean?"

"It means you thought of leaving Barrett at some point."

"*Never*," I stated, my tone emphatic.

"Never?" He raised his brows. "Not even after her time with Dolinsky?"

"Not even then," I admitted. "She didn't return to me the same woman. That wasn't her fault. It was mine."

"Are you saying… Wait, you didn't stay with her out of guilt, did you?"

"No. It wasn't guilt. Not at all. But she chose me. The moment she raised the pistol and killed him she chose me. What kind of man would I have been to walk away from her?"

"The kind that believes in self-preservation." Duncan threw back the rest of his drink. "She's put you through hell."

"There has never been a more loyal, brave or resourceful woman, and I'm proud to call her my wife," I said, my tone darkening. "Do not put your shite on me, brother."

Duncan rose, and without a word, prowled from the room.

I sat back in my chair, letting Duncan's words claw their way deep into the marrow of my bones.

I hadn't ever thought of leaving Barrett, but when she'd come back to me after Dolinsky, I had seen the truth in her eyes.

She'd considered leaving me.

So, I'd done the only thing to ensure she stayed with me.

I got her pregnant on purpose.

Chapter 29
BARRETT

The children were asleep, and I was far too sober for my liking. I'd switched to tea after one glass of wine, knowing that Piper would be awake several times in the coming hours.

"I say we leave the kids with the husbands and skip off to somewhere tropical," Ash muttered.

"I support this endeavor, fully," Quinn murmured. She was laying on the rug in front of the gas fireplace absorbing the warmth like an alligator in the sun. She wiggled her blue argyle clad feet and groaned in pleasure. "This fire is sinful."

"Yeah, just ask her how many times she and Flynn have had sex in front of it," Ash said with a grin.

"Hush, you." I laughed. "I thought you only had one glass of wine, too."

"I did. But it was enough to loosen my tongue."

"We should go to bed before this devolves further," I suggested.

Quinn pulled herself up and rose. "Good plan."

"I doubt I have the energy to even climb the stairs," Ash commented.

"Come on, I'll help you," I said with a smile. "You'll be more comfortable in a bed."

She sighed. "Does anyone else feel like a busted, worn-out hag?"

"I'll admit to the worn-out part, but I do not claim hag status," I remarked.

"Ditto," Quinn said with a chuckle.

I turned off the fireplace and was ready to head upstairs when my phone chimed with a text.

"Flynn?" Ash asked.

"Yup," I replied.

"Dick pic?" Ash's grin was wicked.

I chuckled. "He's not the dick pic type. More like, I'll fly across the country and show it to you in person, type."

"That's a good type." Quinn giggled. Her cheeks were rosy, and she bit her lip. "I miss Sasha, but I'm glad to have had a girls' night."

"You miss Sasha?" Ash snorted. "He's not that far away. You'll see him tomorrow."

"You don't miss Duncan?" Quinn asked.

We began to walk up the stairs and Ash pitched her voice low so as not to wake one of the children. "I think distance from your husband is a good idea sometimes."

Husbands and wives annoyed one another, it was inevitable. And there were times that I didn't know how to be honest with Flynn about what I was going through, but he was my everything.

Ash's words gave me pause as we arrived at the guest room she and Duncan always slept in when they stayed over.

"Night," she said quickly, slipping into the room and closing the door.

Quinn glanced at me. "Was that…"

"Weird." I nodded. "Yeah. I'm too tired to march in there and ask her what the hell is wrong."

"Give her time," Quinn said. "I think she wants space."

"Why is it always this way?" I asked.

"What way?"

"We're all always going through *something*. Is there ever going to be a time of peace and serenity when nothing is wrong with one of us?"

Quinn looked at me for a long moment and I mentally smacked my forehead for being too honest.

I wondered if she'd call me on it and ask me what I meant outright. But she surprised me when she said, "Yes, there will be a time of peace and serenity when nothing is wrong."

"When will that be?"

She gave me a side hug and then released me. "When we're all dead."

"God, could you be more Russian by association?"

Quinn smiled and shrugged. "Night, Barrett."

"Night, Quinn."

She disappeared around the corner as she headed to the opposite wing of our home. I checked in on Piper to see how she was doing. Moonlight dribbled through the half open blinds in her room, illuminating the edge of the crib.

One day soon I'd look at her and she'd no longer be a newborn, but a baby. And then one day she'd grow from baby to toddler.

I shut down that line of thought, lamenting the inevitable passage of time that no one could escape.

My phone vibrated and I quickly but quietly left the nursery, shutting the door behind me.

"Love," I greeted, the phone to my ear. "Shouldn't you be smoking cigars and drinking scotch instead of talking to your wife?"

"I've done the smoking and the drinking. I also missed my wife, and I wanted to hear her voice."

Warmth curled through me at his words.

"How are the bairns?" he asked.

"Everyone is good. We're fine," I assured him. "We're able to handle the children without the nannies present."

He chuckled. "Hawk could test the patience of a saint."

"Hmm. I'm no saint."

"No, hen, you're not."

I could hear the smile in his voice.

"You should get back to your night," I said. "All too soon, you'll be back in the thick of the craziness. Enjoy your male bonding time while you can."

He didn't reply with banter. Instead, he fell silent.

"What's going on, Flynn? Are you okay?"

"Me? I'm fine."

"Then what's—"

"It's them."

"Them who? Our children? I told you they were fine."

"Not the bairns. *Them*. Duncan, Ramsey. Even Sasha."

My blood chilled at the mention of Sasha's name.

"What do you mean?" I asked, attempting to keep my tone casual.

"Poker and drinks devolved into existential, philosophical conversation."

I frowned. "Meaning what, exactly?"

"Where are you now?" he asked.

"Our bedroom."

"So, you're alone?"

"Yes."

"Something's going on with Duncan," he admitted. "Something deep. Something at a core level that I'm having trouble comprehending. He's profoundly unhappy."

"With who? Ash?"

"He said it wasn't about Ash, or even the bairns. He just has this…malaise."

I debated for a few second before saying, "Ash was being weird too."

"Was she? How?"

"She said something right before she went to bed. I didn't go after her and demand she explain more. It just seems… I don't know. Like she's lost in her life somehow."

"They have everything they could ever want," Flynn pointed out. "I just don't understand why they're not happy. Especially if it has nothing to do with their marriage."

"They have everything, huh? They're in love. They have a family. Maybe they're afraid it can be taken away from them."

"It's possible. It's definitely possible that's all it is."

"You think it's more."

"Aye, I think it's more." He paused for a moment and then said, "I've been thinking a lot about you. And about those first few weeks when you worked in the burlesque club. I'd come into the club under the guise of watching the show, but really it was to watch you. You moved like you'd been born to it. And the cigar girl outfit you wore… God, woman, there were nights I went up to my penthouse, took myself in hand and thought of you bent over with your nylons around your ankles, your skirt flipped up. You made me ache. You still make me ache."

"I never stop wanting you, Flynn. Never. Not after all these years, not after four babies. Not after all that life has thrown at us."

"Promise me you're happy," he said suddenly. "I couldn't take it, Barrett. If I thought you were unhappy."

And with those words, he split open my heart and almost made me weep.

"I'm happy," I promised, my throat thick with emotion. "I swear it. We have Piper. We have the boys. We have each other." It was the truth. I was happy. I had everything I wanted, but it was smudged with darkness.

Igor's ghost still haunted me though I'd let him go.

"What about you?" I asked. "Are *you* happy?"

"Aye," he murmured. "The happiest I've ever been."

"And Sasha?" I prodded. "What's going on with him?"

"I got the feeling he was mulling over something disturbing."

"Interesting."

"You don't have any idea what it's about?"

"No," I lied, feeling more than a twinge of guilt. "What about Ramsey? How is he?"

"Restless. Despite what he says, I think he's sick of the endless parade of women. None of them have managed to hold his interest long-term."

"What's the definition of insanity? Doing the same thing over and over and expecting different results?"

"One day, there will be a woman who crosses his path, one he can't live without, and one he will do anything to possess."

A flash of jealousy pierced my soul. There was something about having the horizon of possibilities in front of you that was lost when things were set in stone after a marriage.

"It will be fun to watch. I can't wait to meet her. Whoever she is."

Flynn let out a long sigh. "She'll have to be strong enough in her own right not to let him tread all over her."

"I can't imagine Ramsey winding up with a milquetoast."

"He won't," Flynn predicted. "She'll have some fire. And what she doesn't know, she'll learn from you."

"About how to handle a strong-willed Scotsman?"

"You do have years of practice, hen."

I laughed. "I do, indeed."

"I'll try and be home by dawn."

We hung up and I set my phone down on the night-stand. I went into the bathroom to brush my teeth and wash my face. When I climbed into bed, I made sure to sprawl diagonally and buried my head into Flynn's pillow.

Everything will be all right.

Chapter 30
FLYNN

After I hung up the phone with Barrett, I went in search of Sasha. I assumed Ramsey was down for the count. I knew Duncan was brooding because he'd locked himself in the study, no doubt to think about life and all the choices he'd made that had led him here. I just hoped he didn't call his wife in the middle of the night to tell her nothing and everything was wrong.

Honesty was not always the best policy when it came to women. It made me think of my own decisions where Barrett was concerned.

When she'd returned from Dolinsky, she hadn't been on birth control. It had run out. I didn't remind her about it. Instead, I'd used the lapse to my advantage. It had been calculated, for sure. She'd be livid if she found out what I'd done to ensure she never left me. Barrett had claimed she didn't want to be a mother. At the time, I'd believed her, and I knew she had the capacity to be a rolling stone. If we hadn't had children to bind us together, I often wondered if the pressure of the SINS would've done us in. If Igor Dolinsky's memory would've been enough to tear us apart.

A woman could leave a husband far more easily than she could leave her children.

Was it manipulative? What I'd done?

Absolutely.

If I could go back and do it all over again?

I'd have made the same decision.

Barrett was a hair-trigger. Aye, she was loyal, and she loved fiercely, but she also had an innate survival instinct within her. She would detonate her entire life if she thought she had to in order to protect herself.

I stepped outside to the terrace and stood underneath the overhang of the balcony. It had rained earlier, and the stone walkway was slick. The air was chilly, and it cooled my blood and calmed the thoughts in my head.

Sasha stared across the lawn of Duncan's home, hands in his pockets. There was enough light from the house that I could see one side of his face, the side that wasn't scarred.

"Can I join you? Or would you prefer to be alone?" I asked.

"You can join me," he said. "I was just admiring the landscaping."

"Are you having buyer's remorse?" I asked him with a grin.

"Not at all. I made the right decision, even if Quinn is upset with me." He smiled. "She can be as upset as she wants, but she'll be glad once she's moved in and redecorating."

"You didn't have to run out and buy the first place you liked. You could've waited a few weeks, maybe adjusted to the time change completely. We would've been glad to have you stay for a while."

"I appreciate that," he said. "But when you see the right thing, you just know it."

I approved of men who knew what they wanted and went out and got it. Sasha was one of those men.

"I'm ready to go home. You?"

Sasha nodded. "I'm too drunk to drive your Aston Martin back to your house."

"Leave the car. Angus can drive us back."

I texted Duncan to let him know we were leaving, but I didn't get a reply. I assumed that meant he'd passed out on the leather couch in his study.

Thirty minutes later, I crawled in bed next to Barrett and stole a hand across her back.

She inhaled a sharp breath. "Flynn?"

Her voice was husky with sleep. I chuckled softly. "Who else would it be, hen?"

Barrett draped herself across me and pressed her face to the crook of my neck. "I'm so glad you're home."

I hugged her tightly.

Piper's cry came through the baby monitor.

"I'll handle it. You go back to sleep."

"You sure?"

"Aye."

The scotch had long ago run its course and I was clear headed. I could tend to our infant daughter, and from the sound of it, Barrett was exhausted. Better to let her sleep.

"Thank you," she whispered, lifting herself off me and collapsing back into the pillow.

I went and tended to Piper. She was squalling, her tiny fists clenched in anger. I quickly picked her up and placed her to my shoulder to soothe her for a moment before changing her. After I cleaned her up, I took her downstairs to the kitchen to make her a bottle.

The sun was just starting to creep up when I made it back to bed. Barrett was asleep, but she was having a fitful dream. She was on her back, her hands were grasping the headboard, and she was moaning.

Grinning, I stripped out of my clothes and crawled in next to her.

There was no point in letting Barrett's dream stay a dream.

I was about to make it a reality.

Chapter 31
SASHA

THE DOOR OPENED and Barrett appeared with Piper.

"Sasha," she said in surprise. "What are you doing here?"

"Can I come in?"

She didn't move and I half-expected her to slam the door in my face, but finally, she stepped back and allowed me to enter. A look of weary caution spread across her features.

"The house is quiet," I commented.

"The boys are still at school. Mrs. Aducci just left, and Flynn is in London."

"I know Flynn is in London." I nodded. "So, we have complete privacy."

She blanched. "I guess we do."

Piper let out a milky burp, stealing Barrett's attention from me. She smiled and gently patted Piper's back.

"We need to talk," I announced.

She reluctantly looked at me. "Why?"

"Why? What do you mean *why*? I can't get it out of my mind, Barrett. I've been going over and over it, and nothing is adding up. Every time we're surrounded by friends and family, you purposely avoid me. You've been ignoring my calls. I want an answer."

"Is this why you stopped by unannounced?"

"*Da*," I said without a hint of remorse.

"It doesn't concern you," she said quietly.

"Like hell it doesn't. You're battling. I know what you look like when something is weighing on you. Even now, you look thin and haggard, and the sparkle has left your eyes. Tell me what's going on. Let me help you."

She swayed ever so slightly on her feet. "Sasha?"

"*Da?*"

"Take Piper. *Now.*"

She all but thrust her daughter at me. No sooner had I brought Piper to my chest than Barrett collapsed onto the Persian rug of the foyer.

I watched in horror as she began to twitch and gasp as foam appeared at the corners of her mouth. I rushed into the den so I could set Piper down in her bassinet, but it wasn't in its usual place, so I placed her gently on the rug in front of the unlit fireplace and rushed back to Barrett's side.

She was no longer seizing when I returned, but I rolled her onto her side and cradled her head in my lap. My heart thundered in my ears.

Color returned to her cheeks and a moment later, she opened her eyes and blinked a few times. She caught her breath and then asked, "What happened?"

"I think you had a seizure," I said, panic slicing through me.

"A seizure," she repeated. "Where's Piper?"

"She's on the rug in the den. I'm calling an ambulance," I commanded.

"Don't. I'm fine."

"*Fine?* You just had a seizure. What if you'd been alone? What if you'd been alone holding Piper?"

"I don't want an ambulance here," she said quietly. "I don't want anyone to know. I'm scared, Sasha. I'm so fucking scared."

I cradled her in my arms like she cradled Piper. And then I rocked her back and forth, crooning words of comfort in Russian.

"No one can know about this," she said. "Not Flynn, not Quinn. No one. Not until I find out what is happening to me. Promise me, Sasha. Promise me you'll be my confidante."

"Barrett—"

"Promise me," she insisted, her voice filled with terror.

"I promise," I heard myself say. "But you're going to the hospital. Right now."

Barrett refused to go to the local hospital, concerned that doctors and nurses in town might recognize her. It took a long time, but we drove all the way to Inverness with Piper in the back seat. I'd suggested calling one of the nannies to come and watch Piper, but Barrett hadn't wanted to leave her daughter. She was too emotional after what had happened at the house, and there was no reason to fight it.

She hadn't called Flynn, and I hadn't pressed her to do it, knowing what the outcome would've been. She would've shut down, and I wouldn't be here now with her. At least she hadn't fought me when I suggested taking my car.

My knuckles were white as I clenched the wheel, trying desperately to stay within the speed limit.

Barrett touched the window that was dotted with fat

raindrops, tracing the glass like she could feel the water on her skin.

"I'm not having an affair," she said, shattering the silence between us. The windshield wipers swished with rapid force. "I've been having…hallucinations."

"What kind of hallucinations?" I prodded.

She paused, and I wasn't sure she was even going to say anything more, but she said softly. "Igor. I've been hallucinating Igor as though he is real. They aren't memories, Sasha. They aren't daydreams. I see him everywhere I go. I can't escape it."

My breath caught in my throat.

"At first, I thought it was just guilt. I thought I hadn't put him and my past behind me. Now, I know that's not true. Something is wrong, Sasha."

Understanding flashed in my brain. "That's who you were talking to in the kitchen…"

She nodded.

"You haven't been having an affair," I repeated.

Barrett shook her head and looked at me. "I went to the doctor today and she's running some tests."

"You have to tell Flynn."

"Tell him what?" I asked.

"Tell him everything you told me. He has to know."

She looked out the window again and leaned her forehead against the glass. "I won't tell him. Not until I know how bad it is."

"Why?" I demanded. "You should call him. He's the one who should be here with you, not me."

"I've put him through so much, Sasha. I have to protect him."

"You don't have to protect Flynn. Let him be here for you."

"You're here for me. Right now, that's what I need."

"She's beautiful."

I absently patted Piper's back, the woman's words flowing in one ear and out the other. "Sorry," I said after a moment, looking at the elderly lady who sat in the hospital waiting room a few chairs down. "Did you say something?"

The woman's dimples appeared when she smiled. "Your daughter. She's beautiful."

"Oh," I began. "She's not—I mean, thank you."

She picked up her knitting needles. "You're not from here, are you?"

Barrett had been admitted to the hospital and was in the process of having an MRI. I was in no mood to be polite, let alone engage in idle conversation, but cutting down an elderly woman wouldn't help my mood.

"No, I'm not from here," I said.

"I was born and raised not five miles from here. So was my husband. He's having surgery for his gallstones."

"I wish him a quick recovery."

My phone pinged. I reached into my jacket pocket and extracted it. It was a text from Quinn, asking me if I had plans to be home for dinner.

I didn't know what to say. I'd told her I had to run out for a bit, but that had been hours ago, and I hadn't mentioned I was going to see Barrett.

But I had to protect Barrett and her secret.

So, I lied to my fiancée.

"Mr. Campbell?" a nurse called from the doorway.

"Dear, is that you?" the elderly woman prodded after I failed to respond.

It took me a moment to realize they were both speaking to me, and they thought I was Barrett's husband.

What else were they to think? I had a baby in my arms, and I'd been the one to check Barrett in.

What a mindfuck.

I looked up from my phone to see a blonde nurse in light blue scrubs standing in the doorway of the waiting room.

"Your wife is back in her room. You can see her now." Her smile was genuine and full of warmth.

"Thank you," I said, not bothering to correct her about who Barrett was to me.

I gently set Piper into her carrier and grabbed the diaper bag.

"Have a good one," the elderly woman called to me.

"You too."

I followed the nurse down the hallway. She stopped outside a closed door and gestured to it. "She's just inside. Do you need anything else?"

"No. Thank you."

"The doctor will be by in a bit to talk to you." The nurse looked down at Piper. "What an angel."

I pushed open the door and walked into the hospital room. Barrett sat on the edge of the bed, dressed in a hospital gown. A plastic bracelet was cinched around her slim wrist. She was staring at her lap, and it didn't appear as though she'd even heard me enter.

I couldn't imagine what was going through her mind.

"I just spoke to the nurse. She said the doctor will talk to you soon," I said, wanting to fill the silence.

She nodded absently, like she wasn't truly processing what I'd said.

"I have to go to London," she said, finally meeting my gaze. "Tonight."

"You're telling Flynn." It came out like a statement, not a question.

"Yes," she admitted. "You're right, Sasha. He has to know."

"Why do you have to go to London?" I asked her. "Why can't you ask him to come home and have the conversation there?"

"He's finalizing business at The Rex. I know he'd come home right away if I asked him to, but I don't want to have this conversation in our home. With our children running up and down the halls. I don't want to pollute our home with this."

I gently set Piper's carrier next to the chair and took a seat. Barrett looked longingly at her daughter and then clenched her fists, as if to stop herself from reaching for her.

She stared at the ceiling when she said, "It's always something, isn't it?"

"It might be nothing."

Her hazel eyes met mine and her smile was sad. "You don't really believe that, do you? You know something's wrong."

"I don't know a thing."

"What's your intuition telling you?"

"What's yours?" I pushed back.

She was silent for a moment and then she said with finality, "I'm sick."

"Don't get ahead of yourself. You haven't talked to the doctor. You haven't had your scans read. You don't even know what this is."

"It's a brain tumor. It has to be."

"Even if it turns out to be a tumor, not all brain tumors are malignant," I pointed out. "It could be benign. It could be pressing on the part of your brain that makes you hallucinate and have seizures. It could be as simple as shaving your head and having surgery—and in six months, this will just be another memory. A memory in the rearview mirror of life."

She smiled slightly. "I'm pretty vain, Sasha. All I could focus on was the fact that you said I might have to shave my head."

"There's that glimmer of dark humor," I said with a grin.

Piper let out a squawk, turning our attention toward her.

"She's hungry," Barrett said. "Will you hand me the diaper bag?"

Barrett pulled out a clean bottle and a container of baby formula and then leaned over to her side of the bed and pressed the call button.

A few minutes later, the same nurse that had come to tell me Barrett was back from her MRI entered the room. "Do you need something, Mrs. Campbell?"

"Call me Barrett," she said. "And yes. I was wondering if you could fix a bottle for my daughter."

The nurse took the bottle and formula. "Absolutely."

"Thank you."

When Piper was half-way finished with her bottle, the doctor finally made his appearance. He was a tall, lean man with dark hair. Confidence radiated from his brown gaze.

"Mrs. Campbell," he greeted, holding out his hand to Barrett. "I'm Dr. Elmond. Thank you for waiting. I'm sorry it's taken me so long to come and speak with you."

"Do you have the results of my MRI?" she asked bluntly.

"I have the results, but I can't access them. The computer system has a glitch. I do not want to discharge you until I have your results. The hospital is liable if—"

"I'll sign a waiver saying I left against medical advice,"

Barrett interrupted. "You won't be held accountable if anything were to happen."

The doctor clamped his mouth shut, clearly wanting to argue but realizing it was futile. "All right, I'll discharge you, but only into the supervision of another adult." He looked at me and then back to Barrett. "You've had a seizure, and you need to be monitored. When I can access the results of your MRI, I will call you immediately."

"Doc?" Barrett asked, stopping the man in his tracks as he'd been heading for the door. He looked over his shoulder at her. "Should I be worried?"

He paused ever so briefly and then said, "I wouldn't waste the energy. Worry when and if there's something to worry about."

With a nod to me, he left.

"That felt like a non-answer," Barrett muttered. She got off the hospital bed and reached for her clothes that were folded on the wooden nightstand.

I turned my gaze away to give her privacy.

My phone pinged again, but I didn't bother to look at it.

"Shouldn't you get that?" Barrett asked.

"No."

There was a rapid fire of pings and I sighed.

"Let me guess. Quinn?"

"*Da.*"

"What are you going to tell her?"

"Is it safe to look at you?"

"Yes. I'm dressed."

I glanced at Barrett. "I haven't come up with a decent excuse yet. But I respect you and your need to keep this private for however long you need to."

She appeared pensive for a moment. "No one can

know until after I tell Flynn. I hate asking you to keep this a secret from her, but—"

"I'll do it," I assured her. "I'll tell her you've taken me into your confidence and when the time is right, I'll tell her."

"Jesus, more fucking secrets between all of us," she muttered.

The nurse returned with Barrett's discharge papers which she quickly signed. It was early evening by the time we made it back to Dornoch and still the doctor hadn't called.

We entered the house and Barrett was bombarded by her children. They wrapped their arms around her legs, and I watched as she tried not to cry, tried not to let every fear she'd ever had leak out into their lives.

She spoke quietly to the nannies that cared for the boys, asking them to spend the night because she needed to head to London. I handed off Piper's carrier to one of the waiting young women, knowing Piper was in good hands and would want for nothing.

"I need to pack," Barrett said to me. "And then I need to borrow your jet."

Chapter 32
BARRETT

THE BELLMAN STANDING outside the burlesque club shot me a sympathetic smile while his gaze raked over me. I was dressed in a vintage cigar-girl costume, complete with big hair and bright red lips.

"I'm sorry, miss. The club is closed to the public this evening."

I appreciated that he'd called me *miss* and flashed him a flirty smile. "You're new, and you don't recognize me."

"I just started a couple of weeks ago," he said in a posh English accent. It went well with his black and gold uniform.

"Flynn Campbell...he's inside the club?"

"Yes. How do you—"

"Do me a favor," I interrupted. "Tell him Barrett Schaefer is here to see him and let him know I'm wearing a vintage cigar-girl costume."

"I don't know," he hedged. "I don't want to get into trouble. He said not to be disturbed under any circumstances."

"Trust me." I winked. "I'll see to it you get a hefty bonus if you do me this favor."

My words finally swayed him. I watched as he squared his shoulders and then opened the heavy wooden door of the burlesque club. Sounds of big band music momentarily filtered through the lobby, but when the door closed, all was silent again.

There had been no long-lasting effects of the seizure. Aside from a little bit of tiredness and a few sore muscles, I felt fine.

I wasn't, but I wanted to play dress up and make-believe. For just a little while longer.

A few moments later, the young man returned. "Enjoy your evening, Miss Schaefer."

I flashed a saucy grin. "Thank you."

He opened the door for me, and I sauntered inside the burlesque club that looked the same as the one in New York, with only a few minor differences which would appeal more to the English propensity for opulence.

Two young women were performing a song and dance duet, removing satin red gloves, and tossing them into the audience full of Japanese businessmen.

I surveyed the room. Flynn was sitting alone in a booth. He saw me and beckoned with a chin nod. A zing of excitement trekked down my spine. I loved it when we played games.

A waitress came to him and dropped off a drink and then flitted away to serve the patrons who were clearly enjoying the entertainment.

Vaudevillian bulbs lined the stage and illuminated the dancers, but the club itself was dark except for the gas sconces on the walls. The brass band was loud, the drinks were plentiful, and the tone of the room was full of excitement.

Blood pumped through my veins, the boldness of the music transporting my soul to a different time and place.

The song came to an end and the red velvet brocade curtains shut. One of the dancers popped her head out and blew the audience a kiss. Patrons rose to their feet, clapping in exuberance.

I sauntered up to Flynn's table. "You look lonely, Mr. Campbell," I purred. "Might I be able to cheer you up?"

He turned his head and looked up at me. A sensual grin spread across his perfect lips. "You're a sight for sore eyes."

I slid into the booth next to him, grabbed his drink, and took a sip. It wasn't SINNERS. I raised my brows. "Balvenie?"

"Of course."

"Why?"

"Nostalgia." His gaze raked over me, hungry. "What are you doing here, hen? Not that I'm not happy to see you, but I didn't expect you."

"Which is why I came." I leaned over and gently skimmed my lips over his. "I thought we both could use a night away from the bairns. They're safe at home with the nannies. And now you and I can focus on each other."

His hand slid across my thigh, grazing the nylons covering my skin.

I kept my eyes on his, my breath hitching, when his fingers inched upward to slide across the seam of my body.

He stroked me once, twice, and then pressed the bundle of nerves between my thighs.

"Mr. Campbell," a voice came from next to the table.

I jumped, feeling my cheeks flush at nearly being caught in the act.

"Mr. Amano," Flynn greeted, his hand clenching my

thigh to keep me where I was. "Are you enjoying the show?"

The Japanese businessman straightened his black silk tie as he nodded. "Very much, but we are ready to enjoy the other pleasantries your hotel has to offer."

Flynn inclined his head. He gently urged me to stand. Mr. Amano backed up to give me space and I went to the bar to allow Flynn to handle his business accordingly. I wasn't supposed to be here, so I played my role as arm candy for the night. And that meant that for the evening, I wasn't going to behave like Flynn's wife to his clients, even though security and the hotel staff all knew who I was. It was my job to smile, be beautiful and let the men do the talking.

It was thrilling to pretend to be something I wasn't.

Timid.

Controllable.

It kept our relationship fresh and interesting.

I discreetly watched Flynn pull out an ornate gold key and press it into the palm of the businessman. Mr. Amano reached his other hand out to Flynn and gave it a hearty shake and then he called to his companions who were throwing back the rest of their drinks.

The group of businessmen left the burlesque club quickly, no doubt eager to continue their night of debauchery. Not that I blamed them; I had plans of my own.

Waitresses skittered about the room, gathering empty cocktail glasses and setting them on trays. They brought them to the bar and handed them off to the bartenders, who immediately began to wash them.

The lights turned on, effectively ending the dreamy, nostalgic feel of the club. I was back in the real world. Back in reality.

Flynn strode toward me.

"Guess the magic is over, huh?" I said.

"I'm Flynn Campbell. I create magic out of thin air," he said, and then grinned wolfishly.

I smirked back, enjoying his arrogance.

"It looks like I'm free for the rest of the night," he commented.

"Looks like you are."

"We should go up to the penthouse suite immediately."

I leaned close to him and whispered in his ear. "Fuck me in an elevator first."

"You always have the best ideas."

He clasped my hand and dragged me out of the club. The young man in uniform who'd been guarding the burlesque club door raised his brows when I sent him a little wave.

"Another admirer?" Flynn asked in amusement.

"Hardly. I told him he'd get a bonus if he let me in to see you."

"I'll make sure it happens," Flynn assured me.

"He didn't want to let me in. He's doing his job well."

"I put the fear of God in them," Flynn said with a rueful grin. "I didn't want anyone or anything to interrupt this business deal going through."

"I could've interrupted it," I pointed out.

"I didn't have to let you in the club." He winked. "I could've sent a message through Billy to tell you to go to the penthouse and wait for me."

"Hmm, a wife put in her place…"

"Your place is by my side, you know that."

His words warmed me from the inside out.

Flynn pushed the private elevator button that would take us to the penthouse. The carriage arrived and he stuck his keycard into it. As we began our ascent, he pushed me against the wall. Flynn clasped my wrists and threw them over my head and ground his body against mine.

Desire curled in my belly and swirled down to my toes.

"You played a dangerous game, Barrett," he growled, his brogue thickening, along with something else. "Walking into the club, dressed the way you are, knowing I wouldn't be able to concentrate on anything else."

"It's a good thing you wrapped up your business then," I said, nipping at his chin.

"It's a good thing they love prostitutes. Now I get to spend my night with you."

He took my offered lips in a voracious kiss, his tongue thrust into my mouth. His free hand roved underneath my skirt and then delved into my tight nylons before slipping all the way into my panties.

Flynn found me wet and wanting.

"God damn, Barrett. How is it you're always ready for me?"

I gasped as he planted a finger inside me. I quivered, needing more of him, needing to feel his naked skin against mine, needing him to fill me up, so I couldn't think about anything else.

I was on the verge of coming just from his touch. The elevator doors opened, and he removed his fingers from inside me. We stumbled into the penthouse, tearing at each other's clothes like rabid animals. We didn't even make it to the bedroom. We hit the floor and then he was inside me and my back bowed from pleasure and domination. I loved everything about this man, including his ability to make my brain short circuit with sensuality. Sparks of desire shot along my nerves.

I knew he wouldn't be completely satisfied until he had wrung every drop of pleasure from my body. The thought made me want to sob his name and rake his back with my nails.

So, I did.

He rammed and pillaged, he took and he gave. He was familiar but each time felt new.

I clenched around him, taking him so deep.

When Flynn came, he came with a roar.

He gathered me to him and collapsed against me, settling his face in the crook of my neck.

"You're crushing me," I whispered, smiling.

He slid out of me and rolled off.

I gulped air and tried to get my galloping heart under control.

Flynn lay on his back, and he looked over at me. "You should surprise me more often."

I let out a husky laugh. "Yes, I should."

"We didn't even manage to undress all the way."

"I know. You still have your socks on." I giggled. "And your tie."

"What about you?" he demanded. "I was barely able to get your nylons off." He got up and quickly removed the rest of his clothes. "Shower?"

"Definitely," I said. No doubt my makeup was running down my face and my hairline was dotted with sweat. I'd never felt sexier, especially when he looked down at me with a heated, lingering gaze.

He helped me off the floor and then cupped the back of my head. Flynn stared into my eyes for a moment and then gave me a long, drugging kiss that promised more.

"I'm going to check my messages and then I'll meet you in the shower," I said.

"Are you expecting trouble?" he asked.

"No. I expect the nannies to have everything handled, but you never know with our children."

"Duly noted," he said dryly. "I called to say goodnight earlier, and I swore I could hear the gears in Hawk's head whirring with a new idea about how to cause trouble."

"He lives in a constant state of wreaking havoc. I've accepted it at this point."

"You love it. Don't lie."

"I do love it. He's a force to be reckoned with, and at just seven years old, it's impressive. I'm proud of the little monster."

Flynn strolled naked to the bathroom, and it wasn't until the door shut that I went for my purse. When I'd arrived at The Rex hours earlier, the front desk had given me a key to the penthouse suite. There was always one penthouse suite in every Rex Hotel that was empty so that if Flynn and I traveled unexpectedly, we had a room waiting for us.

My phone was at the bottom of my purse, and I dug it out. I had a few missed texts, one from Ash, another from Sasha. I ignored both. Nothing from the nannies.

I had one voicemail from an unknown number.

Terror coiled in my stomach. I'd been waiting for and dreading this phone call.

Ignoring it wasn't going to make it go away.

I had to know.

I pressed the button to listen to the voicemail and put the phone to my ear.

"Mrs. Campbell, this is Dr. Elmond. I've taken a look at your MRI and I need to discuss the results with you in person. Please call me at your earliest convenience." He paused and then when he spoke again, his tone was softer, "Barrett, the sooner the better." He left his personal cell phone number as well as the number to the hospital. And then the voicemail ended.

I lowered the phone and stared at the screen. The

dread that settled in my stomach spread out like a spider web through rest of my body, infecting me with fear, remorse, and finality.

"Barrett," Flynn called. "Get your arse in here! Sometime before I die would be nice!"

I flinched at his words.

I set my phone aside.

After the shower.

I'd tell him after we showered.

Flynn's cell phone rang on the nightstand. I went to look at the screen and saw that Rex Security was calling. It rang a few more times, but then fell silent. A moment later, it started ringing again, along with the hotel phone.

A chill of foreboding swept over me.

I grabbed his cell phone and took it into the bathroom.

"Flynn," I said. "Rex Security is trying to get ahold of you."

He opened the glass door of the shower and stuck his wet head out. I handed him a towel and he used it to wipe his hand dry before taking the phone. He pressed a button and put it to his ear.

"Campbell," he said into his cell. "Aye, I'll be right there." He clicked off and immediately jumped out of the shower.

Fear skated down my spine. "Flynn?"

"A bomb was found on The Fifteenth Floor."

Chapter 33
RAMSEY

THE VISION of the woman on the security camera screens of The Dallas Rex Casino was impossible to ignore. She stood at the roulette wheel in a gold sequined dress. I could only see her profile, but it was enough. More than enough to take in the blade sharp cheekbones and the honey blonde waves of hair begging for my fingers.

And her mouth…Christ, her mouth. Painted red. Made for sin.

Thank God she was blonde. I didn't sleep with brunettes anymore. Brunettes were nothing but trouble.

I strode to the door of the casino security room and opened it. Sounds of conversation and laughter drifted to my ears. A jazz band played in the corner of the room to enhance the casino's ambiance.

Flynn had known what he was doing when he opened the first Rex Hotel in Manhattan so many years ago. It had given every hotel he would own thereafter a blueprint for total success, and now his empire was a well-oiled machine.

I nodded my head in greeting at men and women I

recognized, but I didn't stop to chat. I was a man on a mission.

Even in heels, the woman only came to the spot just below my chin. I sidled up next to her but didn't speak.

She didn't look like she'd seen me; her gaze was riveted to the roulette wheel.

"Place your bets," the croupier announced.

"One hundred thousand on black 24," the woman said, her voice husky and heady.

"All bets are in." The croupier spun the wheel. There was a heightened sense of excitement, a collective holding of breaths as the ball traversed the wheel until it landed with finality.

"Black 13," the dealer announced. "Sorry, miss."

The beautiful woman turned her head and looked at me boldly. Her eyes were the color of sable fur.

"This is all your fault," she said lightly, a slight smile curving her bright red lips.

"My fault?" I repeated.

"Yes. I was on a winning streak until you showed up. You just cost me a hundred grand." Amusement flashed in her eyes as though she didn't care about the money. And by the way she was dressed it was clear that she had it to lose if she wanted. Most of the patrons in the casino were of the same ilk. Occasionally a desperate low-level gambler came in with everything they were able to swindle or steal, hoping to win big. They usually lost bigger. Gambling and emotion didn't mix.

"Can I make it up to you? Let me buy you a drink."

"That better be one hell of a drink," she said with a smokey laugh.

"I guess I'll have to do something else to get into your good graces then." My eyes lowered and roved over her.

She was beautiful and held her composure against my gaze.

"Shall we?" I asked, offering her my arm.

She took it and then we walked toward the elevators.

"Where are you leading me?" she asked.

"Astray."

She laughed again. "Why do I have a feeling that I'm going to lose more than money tonight? Like my clothes, perhaps?"

"I appreciate a woman who can tell it like it is."

I escorted her to the elevator, and once we were in the carriage, I pressed the button for the top floor of the hotel —the Whisky Room.

It was my favorite part of the hotel. Leather couches, dark wooden floors, gas fireplaces, dim lighting. And every wall was made of glass that showcased the Dallas skyline. This room was impressive and imposing.

I was already making plans in my mind to fuck her against one of the windows while she stared at the city below.

"We have the place entirely to ourselves," she noted.

"There was a private party earlier," I explained. I guided her to the bar on the far side of the room. "Pick your poison."

I reluctantly moved away from her so I could tend bar.

"Scotch," she said, not taking her eyes off me. "Neat."

My smile was slow and full of appreciation. "Do you have a scotch preference?"

"Surprise me."

I picked up two rocks glasses and then grasped the bottle of SINNERS. "This is from a small, family-owned distillery. Tell me how you like it." I slid the glass to her.

She picked it up and sniffed it, her delicate nostrils

twitching. She moaned, giving me insight into the noises she was going to make when I made her come.

"Smells divine."

"Tastes better."

She took a sip, swirling it on her tongue before swallowing it.

I reached across the bar and swept my thumb at the corner of her lips my eyes never leaving hers.

"So, what do you think?" I asked.

"About the scotch or you?"

"Both."

"The scotch is perfect. Magic, mist, and peat. I'm still not sure about you."

I grabbed my glass and gestured with my head in the direction of the gas fireplace. While she took a seat on the leather couch, I turned the fireplace on.

"That's one hell of a dress," I said. "I can't wait to take it off you."

She arched a brow. "You're forward."

"So are you."

"You haven't introduced yourself yet," she pointed out. "You're still technically a stranger. My mother would have heart palpitations if she realized I'd left a casino with a complete stranger."

I held out my hand to her. "Ramsey Buchanan. Now when you tell your mother about the devastatingly handsome man who swept you off your feet, she won't have any reason to be concerned."

She grinned and took my offered hand. She didn't let go of my palm right away. "I'm Lex." She skimmed her fingers across my knuckles. "Ramsey. That's not a name I'm going to forget anytime soon."

"It's the name you'll be screaming until you're hoarse."

"You're arrogant."

"You like it."

"I might." She smiled. "Are you just arrogant, or confident because you're competent?"

"Two sides of the same coin."

She let go of my hand and finished off the rest of her drink. She set the glass on the coffee table in front of us and then she leaned over to kiss me, tasting like scotch and filling me with desire.

Lex pulled back just long enough so that she could pluck the glass from my hand and set it aside and then she moved to straddle me. She slid her tongue into my mouth.

My hands wandered up her curves, excitement pounding in my blood at the thought of sinking into her. My fingers traced the sides of her dress, up her ribs. The top was a modern corset, and it drew my eye to her cleavage.

She tugged on my hair, greedy, demanding.

"Get up," I commanded against her mouth.

Lex lifted her head and stared down into my eyes and then she climbed off me.

I stood up and placed my hand at her waist, guiding her toward one of the large glass walls.

"Turn and put your hands on the window," I commanded.

I watched her pulse flutter in the side of her neck and her lips part slightly, but then she obeyed. When she was bent over, like an offering, I sucked in a harsh breath.

My hands glided underneath her gold dress, skimming up smooth skin, searching for the spot between her legs.

She wasn't wearing underwear.

And she was wet.

I played with her flesh, teasing the pearl between her thighs. Soon, I'd have my mouth there. But first—first—I wanted to make her come with just my fingers.

"Ramsey," she moaned, leaning forward and pressing her cheek to the glass.

I let out a throaty laugh as I plunged a finger inside her.

She quivered around me and inhaled a shaky breath.

I pumped in and out of her a few times, swirling and curling my finger inside her.

Lex smacked her palms against the glass. "Yes," she hissed. "*Yes*, Ramsey!"

I skated my thumb across the seam of her body and caused her to yell out her explosive release. She clamped around me, and it was only when she stopped shuddering that I removed my finger.

While she was catching her breath, I reached into my pocket and extracted a condom. I ripped the foil with my teeth and unzipped my trousers. I was hard and aching, ready to dive into her warm, welcoming body.

She removed her palms from the glass and straightened ever so slightly.

"We're not done," I growled. "Not by a long shot."

"No," she agreed, her tone husky. "We're not."

Lex whirled to face me. Her face was flushed, but her eyes, which moments ago had been welcoming and full of desire, were hard and sharp now.

My lips parted in surprise and a gasp of air escaped me as a sharp pain made itself known.

I looked down.

A knife handle protruded from between my ribs, the blade sunk to the hilt.

She yanked it out before I could reach for it and said chillingly, "For Ainsley."

Chapter 34
BARRETT

It was long past dawn, and I hadn't seen Flynn for hours. After news of the bomb, security had immediately evacuated the entire hotel, including the casino, and then sealed off The Fifteenth Floor. The bomb squad had been called along with the local authorities. Once the bomb had been diffused and disposed of properly, we were allowed into the hotel. I was finally back in the penthouse suite, waiting for Flynn to return.

I sat on the couch, sipping cold espresso, contemplating a shower. I was in a bemused state of exhaustion and disbelief.

Who had done this to us? And why?

My phone flashed and vibrated across the coffee table. I almost didn't want to answer it, suspecting Dr. Elmond was attempting to make contact again.

He'd left me three voicemails already. That didn't bode well. But curiosity got the better of me and I picked up my cell. A wave of relief washed through me when I saw Ash's name.

I pressed the answer button and put the phone to my ear. "Hey."

"Hey? All I get is *hey*?" Ash asked.

I rubbed the bridge of my nose. "I'm guessing you heard about what happened."

"Duncan is on the phone with Flynn right now and I'm packing up the children so we can leave Orkney. Duncan told me you're in London…"

"I am. I came to surprise Flynn. You're not coming here, are you?"

"No. Definitely not. I'm headed home with the kids. Duncan is going to London."

"I'm sorry your time in Orkney was cut short. How are you guys?" I asked.

"Who cares about Orkney? That doesn't matter. How are *you*?"

"I'm okay. Still kind of in shock. Thank God no one was hurt."

"Does Flynn have any idea who's behind this?"

"No." I rubbed my hand over my face.

"Tell me what I can do."

"I don't know yet."

"Do you want the kids with me? They can stay here as long as you need."

"That's a big ask, Ash."

"You didn't ask. I offered."

I let out a sigh of relief. "Yes. That would be—yes. I'll text the nannies and tell them to stay with you. I'd never saddle you with all my children without help."

"I appreciate that," she said dryly.

"Seriously, Ash. Tell me about you guys. I need the distraction. Has anything been resolved?"

She paused for a moment and then said, "Let me go out to the balcony." I heard the sliding of a door and a moment later it clicked shut. "There. Now I can speak sort of freely."

"Is it bad?" I asked quietly.

"I don't know. I mean, it's not good. Not right now. There's nothing really *wrong*, Barrett. Duncan couldn't even give me an answer for what was causing all of this. He says he loves me and our children and our life together, but something is missing."

"Something is missing," I repeated. "Like what?"

"Adventure, excitement, youth?"

"Is this just a mid-life crisis?" I asked.

"I don't know what it is. I just know that I can't fix it. He has to do that himself." She paused. "It feels stupid to talk about, especially with what's going on."

"It's not stupid. This is your marriage. Your life."

She fell silent for a moment and then asked, "How did I get here, Barrett?"

I felt tears prick my eyes, but I held back all the emotion that threatened to surge out of me. My own life was in turmoil. I was avoiding calls from my doctor. But I'd have to face it sooner or later. Burying my head in the sand hadn't made the problem go away. It had only exacerbated it.

"How did any of us get here?" I asked. "Listen, I have to go. Thank you for taking the kids for a little while. I'll be in touch and let you know what's going on."

She sighed. "Sounds good. Keep me posted."

"Will do."

I hung up with her and clenched my phone in my hand.

And then I made the call that I was dreading but knew I couldn't put off any longer.

"Hi, this is Barrett Campbell. I'm trying to get hold of Doctor Elm—yes, I'll hold."

As I was hanging up with Dr. Elmond, the elevators opened and Flynn strode into the penthouse suite. He already had a five o'clock shadow across his strong jaw.

He sat down on the couch next to me and without a word, pulled me into his arms. I pressed my face to the crook of his neck and held onto him for dear life.

"What do we do?" I whispered.

He sighed. "I don't know, love. I called Duncan. I sent the jet for him."

"I know, I just talked to Ash."

"Of course you did. I already spoke with Sasha. He's willing to come to London and lend a hand."

"I have his jet," I reminded him.

Flynn nodded. "I've already called the pilot and he's ready and waiting. I want you to take Sasha's jet and fly home. I need you home. Safe."

I didn't bother fighting him. I was scheduled to see Dr. Elmond later that afternoon anyway, and there wasn't anything I could do to help if I stayed.

A part of me wanted to tell Flynn. To blurt it out. But then he'd drop everything to be with me. And I just couldn't burden him with more worry. Not right now.

Nodding slowly, I stood up. "All right, Flynn. I'll go home."

"You'll have to leave through the staff entrance," Flynn said. "The paparazzi is swarming the hotel."

"Lovely," I muttered.

Flynn escorted me down to the lobby and through the door that led to the staff area. We walked past the laundry facilities and one of the kitchens that dealt only with room service. The security agent sitting in a partitioned glass booth waved as we headed outside.

The winter wind blew against my skin, like an ominous harbinger of things to come. I hunched lower in my coat as I waited for the driver to load my suitcase into the trunk.

Flynn turned me toward him, lifted the flaps of my peacoat, and leaned down to kiss me. When he pulled back, his cobalt blue eyes glittered with intensity.

"Keep your phone on," he said. "When I have news, I'll call."

I descended the staircase of the jet and felt rain drops splatter my forehead. The sky was gray, and a storm was imminent.

Scotland weather mirrored my life. Every now and again both Scotland and I had stretches of sun, but it never lasted.

Sasha met me on the air strip. He looked solemn, yet formidable. I was grateful for him. Not just because of what he meant to me, but because he called Flynn a friend. And he was willing to leave his fiancée and baby to help clean up a mess that had nothing to do with him.

"How are you?" he asked when he was standing in front of me.

"You want to have this conversation now? Your pilot is waiting."

"He can wait," Sasha said. "Talk to me."

"About what's going on with The Rex, or me?"

"You. I'll learn everything about The Rex from Flynn."

"I have an appointment with Dr. Elmond later this afternoon. Flynn doesn't know. I was about to tell him. Literally about to tell him, and he got the phone call about the bomb."

"And you didn't tell him about your appointment because he has enough on his plate."

"Don't make it sound like an accusation," I said lightly.

"I know you. That's why you didn't tell him, *da?*"

"Partly," I admitted.

"And the other part?"

"I want to have all the answers before I tell him anything. I want to know what's wrong with me. I want to know my prognosis first. I want to know all the steps in between so I don't have to be another problem he has to fix."

"You're his wife, not one of his hotels. You're not even remotely in the same category."

I swallowed. "I have to do it this way."

He scratched his jaw. "He'll murder me. When he finds out I knew what was going on with you and didn't tell him."

"Then tell him," I threw out. "And cause him more stress."

"Don't put that shit on me, Barrett. I don't agree with this, and you're putting me between you both. Again."

"I know." I sighed. "I'm sorry. I'm just so mixed up about all this."

"Come here."

He pulled me into his embrace.

"Thank you," I mumbled against his coat.

"For what?"

"For being there when I had the seizure." I pulled back to stare up at him.

"That was out of my control. Timing."

"Timing," I said with a nod.

He squeezed my shoulders and then dropped them. "I'll have my phone on. If you need... anything."

"Can I take your driver for the afternoon?" I asked him.

A slow smile crept across his face. "Why not? You've already taken my jet. What's mine is yours, apparently."

Chapter 35
BARRETT

THE NURSE OPENED the door to an office with multiple placards in the center that showed all of Dr. Elmond's degrees and medical licenses. "He's ready for you."

"Thank you," I replied as I stepped into the room. The walls were lined with built-in wood bookshelves filled with medical journals. There were two matching chairs in front of an oak desk. Dr. Elmond rose from his seat, his hand outstretched.

"Mrs. Campbell," he greeted.

"Barrett," I corrected. "You're about to blow my life apart, aren't you? Why stand on formalities?"

I heard the sharp inhale of the nurse behind me.

"Thank you, Lilith." Dr. Elmond looked at the nurse over my shoulder. A moment later, she left the room. "You don't mince words, do you?"

"No. I don't."

He gestured to the chair in front of his desk. I took a seat and folded my cold hands in my lap and waited.

Dr. Elmond didn't return to his chair. Instead, he

leaned against the edge of his desk. "You didn't bring your husband. Wouldn't you like him here for support?"

"No," I said, not bothering to explain that Sasha was my friend, not my husband. There were enough complexities in my life.

"All right," he said softly. He picked up a manila envelope and held it up. "These are your scans." He pulled them out and then flipped them around to show me.

On the left side of my brain was a silver-dollar sized mass lighter in color.

"This is what's causing your seizures," he said, pointing to the blob.

"Seizure," I corrected. "I've only had one."

"So far." He paused. "You have a malignant glioblastoma. It's a very aggressive type of brain tumor, and as it grows, your symptoms will worsen. Let me be very clear about this, we are talking about weeks or at most, a couple of months before it's going to be too late to do anything."

My body temperature suddenly plummeted, and my hands turned icy. "A glioblastoma," I repeated through numb lips.

"Yes. You're going to need surgery to remove it, but due to the placement of the mass, it's unlikely I'll be able to extract the entirety of it. I've been studying the scans and contacted colleagues at the top of my field, and they concur with my assessment."

The room began to spin, and I quickly reached out to grasp the arm of the chair, squeezing the wood with every bit of strength I possessed.

"Barrett?"

I sucked air into my lungs. "Give me a moment. I just need a moment." My heart thumped in my chest, loud and fast. "All right. Tell me the rest."

"You sure? I can wait a little—"

"The rest. Please." I sounded like I was begging.

"There's a balance between how aggressive I can be during surgery. Because I won't be able to extract the entirety of the tumor, you will need radiation and chemotherapy. There are some clinical trials with experimental drug therapies which might be a good option. As I said earlier, we need to proceed quickly."

"You haven't mentioned my prognosis," I said, trying to drown out the roar of blood in my ears.

He fell silent for a moment, his shrewd eyes boring into mine.

"Give it to me straight," I commanded. "I can take it."

Dr. Elmond paused but a moment and then said, "Even with this course of treatment, you're probably looking at twelve to eighteen months."

"Probably?" I reiterated. "What do you mean *probably*?"

"Only twenty five percent of glioblastoma patients live past the year mark after diagnosis and treatment. Only five percent of patients live past the five-year mark. There is no actual cure for glioblastomas. We can only manage them."

Each sentence was a battering ram to my psyche.

"I'm going to be sick," I announced.

Dr. Elmond moved quickly. He grabbed the small plastic trashcan next to his desk and thrust it toward me.

Espresso and bile expelled from my mouth into the bin. My stomach heaved and my throat burned. Tears clouded my eyes as I struggled to get myself under control.

When it was clear that I was done, Dr. Elmond set the trash can aside.

"I'm sorry," I whispered.

"Don't apologize." He handed me a box of tissues from his desk.

I plucked a tissue and wiped my mouth.

"Would you like something to drink? Water? I can have the nurse—"

"No. Thank you." I clenched the tissue in my hand.

He cleared his throat. "Do you need another moment before I continue?"

"There's more?" I croaked.

"Aye, there's more."

I nodded once.

"Your tumor is nestled in the part of your brain that is responsible for what is commonly known as your personality. Removing the tumor might irrevocably change who you are, and who others perceive you to be. The behavior that makes you, *you*, could be entirely different after your surgery."

My lip trembled and then I bit it hard enough to draw blood and to stop myself from falling apart. "If I don't seek treatment? What does it look like for me?"

"Six months. A year at most. You'll have more seizures, and soon migraines, memory loss, and toward the end you're going to need full-time care."

I closed my eyes and felt a pair of hands on my shoulders. They didn't belong to the doctor because he hadn't moved.

I knew who was touching me.

My tumor was manifesting as the ghost who haunted me.

"Barrett?" Dr. Elmond prodded.

I opened my eyes. "If I'd come to you weeks ago, would things be different now?"

"Weeks ago?" Dr. Elmond repeated. "It's hard to say. The glioblastoma would've been smaller. But we can't really know that since we're just now discovering it. We haven't been able to track it over time, so there's no telling."

I nodded slowly. I couldn't go back in time. I hadn't known Igor's ghost was indicative of a medical problem. I thought it had been my guilt.

But now I knew—the tumor had affected my personality. I'd run from Flynn and our family, thinking I'd needed to exorcise Igor's ghost.

I'd engaged in a food fight in Ash's kitchen.

I hadn't been myself for a long time.

The initial panic and fear of the truth was fading for just a moment.

Now I knew.

All I had to do was make a decision.

Because, based on Dr. Elmond's words, there was a high probability I was going to be dead within the year.

I just had to decide how I wanted to leave this world.

I had Boris drop me off at Ash and Duncan's. He said he'd stick around to drive me home and I thanked him with an absent smile.

I had been instructed by Dr. Elmond not to drive myself again for fear that I'd seize and kill someone else on the road.

He'd also instructed me to have supervision while I was around my children. I ensured him I had enough staff and family to help out, but I still hadn't told anyone except Sasha.

How was I supposed to be a mother? I could hug my children, but I couldn't hold Piper. I couldn't feed her or change her or cradle her against my chest in my arms. I couldn't let our hearts beat in unison and listen to her breathe as she slept.

I'd have to tell the family soon. One minute I could be

EMMA SLATE

fine and the next I could be having a seizure. I couldn't hide this any longer.

I used my key and walked into Ash's house.

It was late afternoon, almost evening. I took a moment and breathed in all the smells of her home. I was assaulted with memories. Our college years, when we were young and idealistic. Meeting the men we'd one day marry. The children we had and raised near one another because we were sisters, even though we weren't related by blood.

The house was quiet—too quiet. Ash and I had seven children between the two of us and instead of the sounds of commotion, it was like a ghost town. Furthermore, Ash hadn't yet come to greet me.

"Ash?" I called out when I got to the landing. I hoped they weren't napping. "Where are you?"

When there was no reply, I opened the nursery door, but the crib was empty. Frowning, I continued.

"Ash?" I called again.

"In here," came her muffled reply.

I went to her bedroom and pushed open the door. The curtains were drawn and it was dark, but the light from the hallway gave me enough illumination to see Ash on the bed, a pillow over her face. I turned on the bedside lamp.

"What's wrong?" I asked, sitting down on the side of the bed. "Is it Duncan? Where are the kids?"

She removed the pillow; her eyes were red from crying. "I sent the nannies and the kids to the guest house to watch a movie. I just needed—" She burst into tears and shot up, dragging me into her embrace.

"Ash," I patted her back. "You've got to tell me what's wrong."

"You haven't checked your phone, have you?" she accused, pulling back. "Where the hell have you been? Flynn said you'd left London hours ago."

"Went for a drive to clear my head," I lied. "I must've put my phone on silent by accident."

"You never do anything by accident," she murmured, peering at me. Her hands reached out to grasp mine. "It's Ramsey."

A coil of dread slithered through my belly. "What happened to Ramsey?"

"He was stabbed through the ribs."

"Oh God. Is he—"

"Alive," she whispered. "Barely. He's in the ICU right now, heavily sedated. His lung collapsed and then filled with blood. They said it's life and death at any moment right now. When Duncan heard, he—he flew to Dallas immediately."

I closed my eyes.

"What's happening, Barrett?" she whispered.

I shook my head and opened my eyes to stare at the woman I considered family "I don't know, Ash. I have no idea at all." I rose from her bedside.

"You really shouldn't leave your phone on silent," she admonished.

"I won't let it happen again," I assured her. "I need to hold my children."

She climbed out of bed. "Me too. I just needed a moment to fall apart by myself." Ash hastily wiped her cheeks. "How do I look?"

"You might want to splash some cool water on your face," I suggested.

She sighed. "Gone are the days where I don't look like I've been up all night, or crying, or wearing my emotions on my skin."

Gone are the days of our youth.

While Ash washed her face, I turned on my phone. It pinged with several missed messages and voicemails. I scrolled through them, one by one.

My phone rang and I answered it. "Hey, love."

"Don't *hey love* me," Flynn snapped. "I've been trying to get ahold of you for hours. Where the hell have you been?"

"Went for a drive," I lied. "My phone was on silent."

"Hen," he began. "You can't do that. You can't. Not ever, and especially at a time like this. You know better."

Ash made a gesture that she was going to leave and give me privacy. I nodded.

She closed the door behind her.

"Hen?" Flynn prodded. "I need you to answer me."

Under different circumstances, I would've raised my hackles and put up a fight at his high-handed tone. But there was too much going on and I didn't have it in me.

"I'm sorry," I said, truly contrite.

He sighed. "You scared the shite out of me."

"It won't happen again. I'll be more vigilant."

"This isn't like you, Barrett. You haven't been this absent-minded in a long time."

I thought for sure this was the moment that he'd call me out on my erratic behavior and then I wouldn't be able to hold back what I knew—what I still hadn't quite come to grips with.

"Where are you?" he asked.

"With Ash. She told me about Ramsey. Is he going to…"

"There's no change in his status yet. Duncan is en route to him."

"This is awful," I whispered. "Every bit of it."

"Aye."

"Do you think this is a coincidence?"

"It seems far too coincidental," he said. "But I don't know for sure."

"I hope he wakes up," I said quietly. "We've lost too much the past few years."

"Story of our lives, it seems."

It was on the tip of my tongue to tell him. But I couldn't do it like this. Not while we waited for news about Ramsey. Not over the phone.

"When will you be home?" I asked, wondering if I sounded as weary as I felt.

"Not for a few days. I have to stay here with Sasha and manage the situation. It's going to be a bitch. We're dealing with law enforcement and attorneys. The paparazzi hasn't let up. Not to mention, we still have to find out who the fuck did this, and why."

"I can call Jordan Bennett." She'd replaced her father as our contact within the FBI and we had an amiable relationship. "Maybe she's heard rumblings on her end."

"No," Flynn stated. "I don't trust her."

"You didn't trust her father, either," I reminded him.

"Jordan is nothing like her father. Don Archer proved himself. Jordan hasn't proven herself yet. No, this stays within the family."

"You called Hadrian, didn't you?"

"Aye. Had to call him and tell him about Ramsey."

A headache began to pulse behind my left eye.

Coincidence? Stress?

Or was it the tumor?

"As soon as we have enough information, then we'll make a plan and act accordingly."

"We?" I asked. "You're going to involve me?"

"After all these years together, it would be foolish not to involve you." He paused. "Whoever did this will not get away with it. When I find them, I'll make them suffer before I kill them."

Despite the horrible situation, something inside of me settled. "I know you will, love. I know you will."

Chapter 36

BARRETT

THE HEADACHE WAS BLOOMING into a full-blown migraine. "Love," I gritted out. "I've got to go."

"Kiss the bairns for me," Flynn said.

"I will. I love you."

"Love you, hen," he said, his tone gruff.

We hung up. My vision was spotty, and nausea churned in my belly. I wanted to see my children, but I would be no use to them. And I couldn't let them see me like this.

I stumbled down the staircase and entered the kitchen. Ash was standing at the counter, appearing lost and confused. A glass of red was poured, but it didn't look like it had been touched.

"Hey," she greeted. "Do you want a glass—what's wrong?"

"Migraine." I staggered toward the counter, and I clutched the marble island. "Do you have any of your prescription meds?"

"Yeah, they're upstairs. Come on." She came to my side.

I leaned on her and let her guide me up the stairs. "Fuck, I'm going to throw up."

She got me to a guest bathroom just in time. After puking in Dr. Elmond's office, there was nothing left in my belly. It was mostly dry heaving. I was shaky and sweaty, and it felt like someone had driven a screwdriver into my skull.

Ash put me to bed and then left the room. She returned quickly with a glass of water and a prescription bottle. I downed the pill and half the glass of water before collapsing back against the pillow.

She moved to the window and shut the blinds. The dying sunlight winked out of existence.

"The kids," I whispered.

"I'll make sure they're fed and bathed," she assured me.

My face sank into the pillow as the bedroom door shut, but I wasn't alone.

"Sleep, *moya krasotka,*" Igor whispered. "Just sleep."

I was pulled from my dream slowly, like being gently kissed awake. My mouth was pasty and tasted like iron. I waited to see if there was any lingering pain in my head, but there wasn't. Just a residual fog as if someone had blown smoke into my brain and given it a good stir like a dry martini.

Hunger had me swinging my legs over the side of the bed. I reached for my cell phone on the nightstand to check the time, but it wasn't there.

After ambling my way to the bathroom and quickly doing my business, I washed my hands and then cradled them below the faucet. I drank my fill, greedy and parched.

I wiped my face on the hand towel and then turned off the bathroom light.

The house was quiet as I padded into the hallway. I listened for sounds, but there was nothing.

My stomach was empty, and it rumbled with the demand to be fed. I walked into the kitchen and stopped. Ash was sitting at the kitchen table with her hands clasped around a mug of tea.

"You're awake," I said, glancing at the microwave clock and noticing that it was just past two in the morning.

"Never went to bed. I have too much on my mind."

"Yeah, I understand that."

"How's your head?"

"Better. Thanks. Have you seen my phone? I want to check my messages, see if Flynn called and if there's an update about Ramsey."

"I haven't heard anything yet," Ash stated. "And you left your phone on the kitchen counter. I kept your cell phone on me just in case Flynn called. So he didn't worry if you didn't answer."

My cell phone was resting on the table next to her mug. She picked it up and waved it at me. "You did get a few calls. I let them roll to voicemail."

I walked across the kitchen to her and was about to take my phone when at the last moment, she held it just out of reach.

"Who's Dr. Elmond?"

I paused at her question, not having been prepared for it. "A doctor."

Her eyes pinned me with intensity. "Isn't your primary care physician Dr. Bristow?"

"Yes. But I'm switching doctors," I lied.

She nodded slowly. "Interesting."

"What's interesting about it?" I asked, sounding far testier than I would've liked.

"Well, Dr. Bristow called too. Barrett? Why are you having two different doctors calling you after normal business hours?"

I fell silent, unprepared for the onslaught of her questioning.

"What aren't you telling me? I've known you for years," Ash stated. "You've been acting strange for weeks. Something's going on with you. I want to know what it is, and I want to know *now*."

Chapter 37
RAMSEY

I woke to the sound of beeping machines. My eyes flipped open, and I stared at the ceiling. If the machines hadn't alerted me I was in a hospital, the scent alone would've done it. It smelled like nothing. A blank slate of aroma. Only the faintest trace of sterilization and cleaning chemicals.

"Christ," I muttered.

"That's putting it mildly."

I turned my head. My brother sat in the chair by my bedside. The lamp was on, carving shadows into one side of his face.

"What are you doing here?" I growled.

"What do you mean *what am I doing here*, you eejit? I came as soon as I heard what happened."

I smiled despite the situation. Or maybe it was the morphine in my system making me daft. "I meant, how are you in my room? It's long past visiting hours, aye?"

Duncan arched a brow, and in that moment, he looked exactly like our deceased father. "Aye," he said. "But when you have the Buchanan charm, you can convince the nurses of anything."

"Charm?" I snorted. "Please. I'm the one who got all the Buchanan charm. You paid off the nurses, didn't you?"

"You're a pain in the arse."

"How much," I pressed, a smile spreading across my face.

"I didn't pay them off," Duncan snapped. He exhaled and ran a hand through his dark hair. "But I might've used some very choice words about what would happen if they chose to deny me entrance to your room."

I scrubbed a hand across my chin. Stubble. I hated it. I wanted to shave immediately.

"I'm alive. Who found me after it happened?" I asked.

"Genevieve." Duncan's jaw clenched. "She found you bleeding out on the floor of the Whisky Room."

The Madame of The Fifteenth Floor of the Dallas Rex was cool headed, calculating, and equipped to handle anything that was thrown at her.

"We're all dying to know what the fuck happened."

"A crazy wench tried to kill me. Thank God she didn't go for my bollocks."

"For fuck's sake," Duncan spat. "This isn't a joke. Why can't you take anything seriously?"

"You take everything seriously enough for the both of us," I pointed out.

"You could've died," he shouted, rising from his chair.

"Aye," I agreed. "But I didn't."

He closed his eyes like he was praying for strength. He opened them and stared down at me. "I need more details than that. What happened?"

"Can I get some water first?"

"You're pushing it," he muttered, but damn if he didn't

pour me a glass from the blue plastic pitcher that rested on the nightstand next to the lamp.

Once I had my fill, I leaned back against the pillows. The morphine in my system was keeping me comfortable, but it was also making me tired, and I could tell from the way my body was responding that I had been seriously injured.

"There was a woman in the casino. I took her up to the Whisky Room and we were… well, I don't like to kiss and tell." I flashed my brother a teasing grin, but he didn't smile back. "She pulled a knife out of her gown without me seeing it. Old school style. Like she was some sort of fucking assassin. She stabbed me hard and deep, and I froze for a moment. I was about to grab her, but she darted away from me. I was losing blood fast. She ran out of the room, and I tried to follow, but I passed out."

"I've been telling Flynn we need better security measures in the casinos."

"What would that entail? Frisking our guests? Metal detectors?" I raised my brows. "No better way to piss off the clientele."

"It would be for their own safety."

"Fuck safety. You don't go to an illegal high stakes casino fronted by a hotel empire for safety." My brow furrowed when I studied him. "You go for the thrill of the underground. Of telling the law to go fuck itself. What the hell has happened to you? Did Ash clip your balls and put them in her purse?"

"If you weren't lying in a bed, I'd beat the shite out of you for that," he snapped.

"When I'm healed, I'm ready and willing. You need a good arse kicking."

"*I* need a good arse kicking? I'm not the one lying in a bed because I followed my prick into the pointy end of a knife. All the blood in your body rushed south, leaving you without a working brain it seems."

I arched a brow. "Bitter much?"

"Why would I be bitter?"

"It sounds like you're in desperate need of spicing up your life."

"What are you suggesting?" Duncan's gray gaze glittered like steel.

I stared at him for a long moment and then replied, "Nothing. Nothing at all."

My brother wasn't happy. Hadn't been for a while now.

"Do you have any idea who she was, or why she attacked you?" Duncan asked.

"She said her name was Lex, but I have no idea if that's her real name or not. And when she stabbed me, she said, '*For Ainsley.*'"

"Who's Ainsley?"

"No idea."

Duncan ran a thumb across his cheek and down his jaw. "A bomb was found on The Fifteenth Floor of the London Rex. They evacuated the entire hotel, and the bomb squad was able to diffuse it. No one was hurt."

"Fuck," I muttered.

"Aye," he agreed. "We're going to have a hell of a time fielding this one. Paparazzi have been camped out for hours. What are the chances? A bomb is found at The Rex and you're stabbed on the same day? Do you think they're related?"

"Anything is possible," I admitted. "But this felt… personal."

"You really have no memory of this Ainsley woman?"

I searched my brain but came up blank. I shook my head.

Duncan's phone vibrated in his pocket. "Flynn," he

greeted. "Aye, he's awake." He began to pace across the floor. "We're trying to figure that out." He looked at me, his eyes widening while still talking to Flynn. "No shite. You're serious? God damn it all. I'll be in touch."

He hung up and shoved the cell phone back into his pocket.

"What?" I asked. "Just say it."

"The Manhattan and Boston ports are on fire—Sasha's holdings…"

"Fuck," I muttered. "What the fuck is going on? Now Sasha? I thought whoever was doing this was just coming after the SINS."

My mind was whirling, trying to piece it all together, but it was too murky.

"Where's my phone?" I asked. "I need to call Genevieve."

Chapter 38
BARRETT

"Sit," Ash stated. "Now."

I wanted nothing more than to run from the room. To hide from my best friend. By telling her the truth, I'd be forced to confront the reality of my brain tumor. Not just confront it, but to make a choice.

Surgery or no surgery.

Short life, or even shorter life.

And then I had to face the possibility that even if the surgery was successful, I might not be the same person when it was over.

It was a lose-lose situation any way you cut it.

Cut.

What was the difference? Now or later, I was going to die, and soon. What were a few months' worth if I wasn't going to be myself? If I didn't have the surgery, my symptoms would worsen, but I'd still be me. My children would still know me. If I had the surgery, there was a chance my personality would change. And there was a high probability that I wouldn't even make it past the year mark anyway.

The result would be the same.

I'd be six feet under, and Flynn would be standing with our children at my grave.

Next to Malcolm.

I sat slowly and placed my hands on the table. With a deep breath, I said, "I have a brain tumor."

Ash looked at me for a moment, her eyes widening, and then she let out a cackle. "Good one."

I frowned. "Good one what?"

"A brain tumor." She snorted. "You've got a sick sense of humor. Come on. Tell me what's really happening. Two doctors are calling you. You're discussing fertility options, aren't you?"

"Why on earth would you leap to that conclusion?" I demanded. "I just adopted Piper and my family is complete."

A reflection of worry appeared in her blue eyes. "I don't know, I was just—"

"Ash," I said quietly. "I'm being serious."

"It's true then? You really have a brain tumor?"

I nodded. "I went to see Dr. Bristow because I was having…unusual symptoms."

Her breath hitched. "What kind of symptoms?"

"Hallucinations. Vivid ones." I bent my head and looked away. "About Igor."

"Igor."

"Yeah." I sighed. "One sign of a brain tumor is hallucinations. Another is irrational behavior that's out of character. But no one thought it was odd when I ran away to his home in Vermont."

"We all thought the anniversary of his death was just too much for you," she admitted. "Guilt."

"I thought it was guilt too." I met her gaze. "The food

fight in your kitchen? I don't behave that way. That's not *me*."

She exhaled and it was shaky. "I thought it was relief. You know, like you'd let go of all the Igor stuff and you were feeling lighthearted."

I nodded. "Yeah, I thought that too," I swallowed. "After my doctor's appointment, I had a seizure. It was just after I'd gotten home. Sasha was there. He—he took me to the hospital." I swallowed, blocking out the horror of almost dropping my infant daughter.

"I had an MRI, and yesterday I met with Dr. Elmond to go over the results. He's a neurosurgeon at the top of his field. He's world-renowned, Ash." I got up from the table and began to pace because the idea of sitting still was unacceptable.

How long would I have use of my limbs?

"It's not good, Ash."

"*How* not good?"

"It's an aggressive type of brain tumor and there's no cure. Dr. Elmond is confident he can get most of it with surgery, but I'd have to go through chemo and radiation. Most patients with this type of tumor only live twelve to eighteen months even after surgery, and only five percent live longer than five years. Surgery, chemo, radiation…they only buy me time. And there can be complications with the surgery. Things can change for the worse, even if I…"

"What are you saying, Barrett?" she asked, her voice sounding very far away.

"You know exactly what I'm saying."

"You don't want—you're not going to have the surgery, are you?"

"I haven't decided."

"Bullshit," she spat. "You *always* know. You know without ever asking anyone's opinion, because you keep your own counsel. Would you have even told me if I hadn't seen your missed calls?"

"No," I said immediately. "I wouldn't have shared this with you."

"But you shared it with Sasha."

"He was there when I had a seizure," I pointed out. "I didn't have a choice."

"Have you told Flynn?"

"I was about to. And then the bomb."

"You need to tell him. Now. Call him this minute."

I raised my brows. "Why? So he has something else to worry about? Worry that his wife is dying or nearly dead already?"

"Fucking hell, Barrett," she snapped. "I knew it. I knew you weren't going to have the surgery."

"Why would I?" I asked.

"Why *wouldn't* you. You could be the one that defies the odds!"

"Perhaps. But I'm not really a best-case scenario type of person."

"You've been shot, drugged, kidnapped, and fallen from the second story of a house. They didn't know if you were going to be paralyzed, but guess what? You weren't. You're Barrett fucking Campbell. You defy *all* the odds."

"I haven't told you everything," I said.

"Good God, there's more?"

"If I have the surgery, I might no longer be myself."

"What does that even mean?"

"The tumor is in the part of my brain that controls my personality. So, let's say I survive the surgery and I defy the odds and I live. What if I'm not *me* when I wake up? What will that do to Flynn? To my children? That's as good as dying in surgery, Ash."

"So that's it?" she demanded. "You're giving up?"

"No, I'm not giving up. I'm choosing to live the last months of my life the way *I* want to live them." Despite what she thought, I hadn't truly decided what I'd wanted to do until Ash forced me to talk about my predicament.

I heard a child's pattering footsteps and before I knew it, Iain ran into the kitchen and threw his arms around my legs.

"What is it, love?" I asked him, my arms stealing across his back to offer comfort.

"Bad dream," he muttered.

I managed to loosen his hold on me so I could bend down and hug him tight.

How many more nights would I get to comfort him?

The thought weighed heavily on my heart.

"What was your dream about?" I asked.

He pressed his face into the crook of my neck and shuddered. "You were gone. And I couldn't find you."

"Is he asleep?" Ash asked.

I nodded and collapsed onto the couch in the den.

"What took you so long? It's been an hour."

"I checked in on the others." I'd stared at each of them, memorizing their faces, their breathing patterns, storing up memories and hoping they would give me strength through the coming weeks and months.

Ash looked thoughtful as she pondered my words. "You're not tired?"

"No. The migraine fucked my sleep up."

She rose from her seat and went to pour me a glass of scotch and brought it to me. "It's medicinal."

I took it and then drank a long swallow, feeling the burn and peat in the back of my throat.

"You have to have the surgery, Barrett," Ash said after she sat down. "I've been thinking about it the entire time you were upstairs. And you just can't give up."

"I'm not giving up."

She looked into the flames of the gas fireplace. "You're the glue. You're the one who holds all of this together. Without you…"

"Without me, *what*?" I demanded. "You'll all just fall apart? Don't put that shit on me, Ash. Say what you really mean."

"Fine." Ash looked at me. "*I* won't survive this. If you have the surgery and something goes wrong and you die, then okay. At least I'll know that the woman I've admired my entire adult life was worth the admiration. But if you choose to die, without even trying to save yourself, then you're not the woman I know."

"Fuck you," I said without heat. "Fuck you to hell, Ash. You have no idea what this feels like. Watching your life flash before your eyes. Knowing no matter what you do, there's a bomb in your head that could explode at any moment. Raping your memories, stealing your time." I clenched the crystal glass in my hand, knowing I didn't have enough strength to smash it.

Her eyes welled with tears and her lips trembled. "I'm afraid my marriage is falling apart and I'm afraid you won't be here to help me pick up the pieces."

My anger melted away like snow in sunlight.

"I'm a selfish shit," she blubbered. "I know that. But, oh God, the thought of not being able to confide in you is more than I can handle."

Despite the finality of my situation, I laughed until I cried. And then Ash and I were holding each other as tears streamed down our faces.

Only when my phone rang, did we finally pull apart

and get ourselves together. I took several deep breaths and then answered Flynn's call.

"Hey, love," I greeted, feeling the emotion sweep up my throat, threatening to choke me.

"Did I wake you, hen?" His voice was raspy, and I knew he'd barely slept.

"No. I've been up," I hedged. "Iain had a nightmare, but he's back to sleep now."

"I've got more bad news." He sighed. "The Manhattan and Boston ports were set on fire."

"Both?"

"Aye."

"Sasha's holdings," I stated.

"Aye."

"Fuck."

"Aye," he agreed, tone bleak. "He left already for the States."

"I should call Quinn," I said. "And check in."

"You should. Ramsey's awake."

"He is?" I let out a breath of relief. "Thank God. What the hell happened?"

"Stabbed by a woman. No idea if she's related to all of this or if she was acting of her own accord. Knowing Ramsey, it could easily be a scorned woman."

"Who do you think is behind this?" I asked. My mind searched for a connection, but I wasn't sure there was one.

"I don't know. I really don't."

What did burning ports, a hotel bombing, and Ramsey's stabbing have all in common? Was there even a commonality?

"What are you thinking?" Flynn asked. "You've always been good at putting the puzzle pieces together."

"I've got nothing at the moment. I'm just glad we're all safe if not a little worse for wear."

"And healthy," Flynn stated.

"Healthy…right."

Ash grasped my hand, and I clenched it but didn't look at her. I couldn't.

"How are you holding up?"

"As good as can be expected," I said. "With you in London, it feels... I don't know. I hate that we're all spread across the world right now."

He didn't reply.

"Flynn?"

"I've got to go," he said abruptly.

He hung up before I had a chance to say goodbye. I set my phone down on the table and looked at Ash. "That was weird."

"Weird how?" she asked. Her cheeks were still stained with tears, but her eyes were clear.

"Weird like I don't know." I frowned. "Did you hear any of that? About Sasha?"

"About the ports? Yeah. What the fuck, Barrett?"

I shook my head. "I don't know, but I'm calling Quinn."

"Good. Invite her and Helena to come over. We should all be together."

"Yes," I agreed. "We should."

I met her eyes.

How much longer did we all have together?

Chapter 39

SASHA

FUCK.

I was back in New York, dogged by memories of mistakes I'd made. This concrete jungle chewed up lesser men and spit them out like tobacco from a ball player's mouth.

I felt both alive and dead here.

"The Slovakians are pissed," Dimitri said into the phone.

"I'm sure they are," I replied as I descended the staircase of the jet.

"What should I tell them?" Dimitri demanded.

"Tell them nothing."

"I can't tell them *nothing*. I have to give them something. We don't want to lose their business. If they take their business elsewhere—"

"Are the fires under control?" I interrupted.

"*Da.* Armen checked in. He's paid off the port police and they're giving us some breathing room. There will be an investigation, but it won't turn anything up, no matter what." He paused. "Are you sure you want to come down here?"

"Why? Because I almost died in a fire?" I said in a droll tone. I'd never tell my first in command that I still had nightmares about that fateful night. Showing weakness was never an option. "What about you, Dimitri? You were in a hit and run and yet you still get into cars. You even drag race, *da*?"

He sighed. "All right, Sasha. I get your point."

I wasn't even off the tarmac yet and I felt the frenetic energy of New York pulsing in my veins. It was palpable and I sensed it like a forceful entity. I'd grown accustomed to the serenity of Martha's Vineyard and the few weeks I'd gotten to spend in Scotland had relaxed me even further.

The city lights glowed against the dark sky, and I was momentarily entranced as I walked toward the car. I'd been awake for hours and I was ready to sleep, but there was still more to be done.

My driver opened the town car door for me, and I slid inside the sleek comfort of the sedan. He closed the door and then climbed into the driver's seat up front.

"I'll be there soon," I said and hung up.

It only took about thirty minutes to get to the ports due to the late hour I had arrived, and traffic was minimal. When I got out of the car, tar and oil scented the air. Hazy smoke filled the sky.

I wasn't prepared for the sight that greeted me. Four of my cargo ships were decimated.

It was one thing to know you'd been hit. It was another to realize you were bleeding out from a metaphorical bullet wound.

This was equivalent to a bullet wound to the chest.

Dimitri and a few other rough men were on the pier

having a smoke, talking in low tones in Russian. Dimitri saw me and came to me immediately.

"How many ships did we lose in Boston?" I asked.

"Seven."

I exhaled. "I need to find a fight."

Dimitri cracked his knuckles. "Let's do it."

We went searching for trouble. It wasn't hard to find. By the time the sun was streaking up over the city, Dimitri and I were sitting on the edge of the pier, sharing a bottle of vodka. My knuckles were bloody and raw, and I had the beginning of a black eye.

"Do you feel better?" Dimitri asked.

He passed me the bottle of vodka and I took a swig. The liquor stung my split lip.

"No," I admitted.

Aggressive, jet lagged, a little bit drunk, and angry as fuck.

The fighting had tempered my rage, but it in no way got rid of it completely.

"Fuck, Dimitri." I looked at my second in command. "We've been working for years. It's not just the ships, it's the lost cargo, our contracts, our reputation. We've got to keep our ears to the ground to see who pops up to take advantage of the fact that we're down and out. That'll tell us a lot about who might have done this."

I passed the vodka back to him.

"I'm sorry, brother," Dimitri said.

"Why? This isn't your fault." I looked at him when he didn't reply. "What do you know that you're not telling me?"

He didn't bother denying it. "Something happened a few months ago. At the time, I dismissed it. It's lingered in the back of my mind. There's been a surge of French speakers at the ports."

"Here? Boston?" I asked.

"Both, but especially here." He paused and took a swig of vodka. "Our guys are saying they've come across a new drug on the market. It's synthetic, cheaper than coke or meth, and more addictive."

"Fentanyl?" I asked.

"No. Something different. It's called *Felicité*. Have you heard of the Bouchard family? Alan Bouchard?"

"No. Is he Parisian?"

"French Canadian," he clarified. "One of the richest men in Canada, actually. Involved in politics. And in pharmaceuticals."

"Ah," I said in understanding. "Do you think he's funding the manufacturing?"

"Not sure yet. I have to do some more digging. I got one of my guys in Boston with his ear to the ground."

"One of your guys? Russian?"

"*Da.*"

"Add an Irishman you trust. That'll go a long way for morale."

"Will do."

I frowned, turning something over in my mind. "Have we traced *Felicité* back to the source?"

"We're trying to find a dealer to even question. So far, it's like they've all scattered like roaches when the lights are turned on."

My phone vibrated in my pocket.

"*Myshka*," I said in way of greeting.

"Did I wake you?"

"No. I haven't gone to bed." I glanced at Dimitri, handed him the bottle of vodka, and then got up. My muscles groaned in protest.

"How bad is it?" she asked.

"Bad."

"Will we recover?"

"In time."

She sighed. "Casualties?"

"A couple of guys were injured, but no deaths."

"Good. That's good. How'd you take the news?"

"What do you mean?" I hedged.

"I mean, did you look for an underground illegal fighting arena, or did you just walk the streets?"

"Streets."

"Sasha," she said with a sigh.

"I'm fine, Quinn. I was with Dimitri. He had my back."

"When I see you next, will you be sporting a black eye?"

"And a split lip. And my ribs will be sore. You'll have to fuck me gently."

She let out a chuckle. "I shouldn't reward bad behavior."

"Wish you were here." I pitched my voice lower. "I always want a hard fuck after a hard fight."

"Might I introduce you to your left hand?" she suggested.

"Keep your phone on you," I commanded. "Once I'm supine I'll be calling you back."

"Is it wrong that I love how you come to me all angry and full of adrenaline after you fight? It's like you're a primeval beast."

"You're not helping me battle my lust, Quinn."

She snorted. "Good."

"Are you staying alone in that big castle we just bought?"

"Yeah. It's lonely without you here."

"There is a solution."

"Get a dog while you're gone?"

"Go to Barrett's."

She fell silent.

"What, Quinn? What is it?"

"She's hiding something, and I don't like it."

"So, go over there and confront her."

"I can do that?" she asked in surprise.

"Of course, you can do that."

"Doesn't that go against your whole, *trust her to tell you when she's ready,* thing?"

"Confront her, Quinn. Have it out with her if that's what you need."

"You really mean that?"

"I do," I said. "I can't tell you what's going on with her, but I can tell you that she needs you."

"She's going to think you sent me."

"So what if she does?" I demanded. "Do you love her? Like family?"

"Of course I do."

"If Shannon were acting this way, what would you do?" I inquired.

"I'd march into her house and tell her to stop being a prat and tell me what's going on." She paused. "Ah. Okay."

"Exorcise the truth from her, Quinn. We'll all be better off. Now if you'll excuse me, I've got a bottle of vodka to finish."

"Say hello to Dimitri for me," she said.

"Will do."

I hung up and went back to Dimitri's side, but I didn't sit down next to him, for fear I wouldn't be able to get back up again.

"I'm ready for the Russian baths," Dimitri said. "And a woman."

I tightened my left hand into a fist and sighed. "I'm in

agreement about the Russian baths, but I'll have to pass on a woman."

Chapter 40
QUINN

I STOOD at the threshold of Ash's home, feeling only marginally guilty that I was showing up unannounced. I'd driven to Barrett's house first, with Helena in tow, but the security agent at the gate informed me she wasn't home.

Ergo, I deduced that she was with Ash.

It should've been my first thought. Those two leaned heavily on one another when things were tough, and right now, things were tough.

Part of me had wished that Ash and Barrett had reached out to me so we could all be together during this insane time.

The fact that they hadn't... I tried not to let it hurt my feelings. I tried not to think anything of it, but old narratives ran deep. Barrett and I were close. But she and Ash were closer. Had she confided in Ash what was wrong?

I knocked on the door and gathered Helena closer, hoping to shield her from the slanting sheets of rain.

A moment later, the door opened. Barrett stood in the doorway, her eyes widening.

She frowned for a second and then said, "Quinn. What are you doing here?"

"Nice to see you too," I said sarcastically. "Do you mind letting us in? We're getting soaked out here."

Barrett stepped back, but it was clear she was reluctant to do so. "You're just like your fiancé," she muttered. "He shows up out of the blue, too. You could've called."

"*You* could've called," I said. "But you didn't. I was in the house all alone, sitting in a room with mustard yellow decor and tartan wallpaper with no one to talk to."

"Sorry about that." Her face was wreathed with guilt. "I was—I got distracted. Have you talked to Sasha?"

"Yes. What do you mean you were distracted?"

"I got a migraine. I was down for the count. How's Sasha?"

"He hasn't called you?"

She shook her head.

"That's surprising. I thought he would have," I murmured.

"He doesn't always call me," she said with an eyeroll.

"Yes, he does."

"Is that why you came here?" Barrett asked. "To accuse me of something?"

"Are you looking for a fight?"

"Are *you*?" she asked, raising her brows.

With a sigh, I held Helena out to Barrett. "Will you hold her while I disrobe? I don't want to track mud all over Ash's front hallway."

"No," Barrett said softly. "I can't…"

"Why not?"

"Because I…" She sighed. "Christ. I don't even know how to…"

"You're being squirrely," I remarked as I set Helena down on the foyer rug. It only took a few moments for her to toddle in the direction of the kitchen on her squishy little legs.

Ash was coming down the hallway when she saw Helena and scooped her up. "Think you lost something," Ash said as she came forward, bouncing Helena against her hip.

"Sorry to stop by unannounced," I said.

"No worries. We were just about to go for a swim in the pool. You're welcome to join us."

"Thanks for the invite," I said. "Maybe after I talk to Barrett."

Barrett and Ash exchanged a look. They were best friends who'd known each other for years. They could communicate without words, too.

It was a different sort of intimacy than one shared with a man. No less powerful, but different. It was inherently unique and uncommon to find. Soul sisters were hard to come by. But when you found one who understood you, took care of your heart, and let you vent your anger and anguish, and would cry with you, it was the equivalent of finding gold.

"Talk first, but when you're done," Ash said, "I have a spare suit for you. Did you bring a suitcase?"

"What?" I asked in distraction.

"A suitcase. I assumed you came here to corner Barrett. That means a lot of wine, and that means you shouldn't drive home."

"Going in for the kill right away, aren't you, Ash?" I asked with a smile.

"Things are going to hell in a handbasket," she said resolutely. "Why mince words?"

"Ash," Barrett muttered.

"So, did you pack a suitcase or not?" Ash inquired.

"Yeah, I packed a suitcase," I admitted.

"Use the study," Ash suggested. "I'll have Cranson get your suitcase. Quinn, do you want me to keep Helena for a while? We have more than enough nannies to corral the children."

"That would be great. She's going to need a snack in a bit," I said, handing off the diaper bag to Ash who still had Helena to her hip. "I owe you one."

"I owe you like fifteen," Barrett said to Ash.

"Hey, it takes a village to raise a clan, doesn't it?" Ash said with a trifling smile.

"It does," Barrett said quietly.

Something somber moved through the air, something that had nothing to do with our men or the fires they were putting out.

A gaggle of children ran out of the kitchen.

"Hi, Quinn!" Hawk yelled with a wave as he headed for the stairs. "Bye, Quinn!"

"Quinn!" Iain screeched, but then he too, was gone.

Noah, who was far shyer than the others smiled at me, but then bashfully hid his chin in his shoulder as he trailed after his brothers.

The nannies followed at a slower pace, carrying the younger children in their arms. Carys walked on her own. She was at the age where she was asserting her boundaries.

"You good?" Ash asked Barrett, her tone pitched low.

Barrett nodded.

Ash reached out and squeezed Barrett's arm.

"What the hell is going on?" I demanded. "You guys are acting like someone's dying."

Barrett froze and then she let out a raspy chuckle. "Someone *is* dying, Quinn."

"Who?"

Barrett looked me in the eyes and said calmly, "Me."

"What?" I whispered.

"Not here," Ash commanded. "Little ears. Study. Now."

Barrett took my hand, clasping it in hers and pulled me in the direction of the study. She closed the door once we were inside and flipped on the light. Old dark wood walls greeted me, along with oil paintings of landscapes and a portrait of Malcolm Buchanan.

I'd never met the man, but looking at his painting, it was clear to see his lineage stamped upon his two sons. He was gone, but through them he lived on.

I turned away from the portrait and glanced at Barrett as she stood by the window, staring out at the rain.

"What the hell do you mean you're dying? You can't be dying," I protested.

"I can't?" she asked softly.

The great Barrett Campbell, the woman I'd always viewed as larger than life, seemed to shrink and shrivel before my very eyes. Once, she'd taken up space, her breath and voice filling every crevice in every room she occupied, as though each one was custom designed for her presence alone. She was a force. The human equivalent of dynamite. She lived life like it was all supposed to be one giant *boom*.

But now she looked like a shell of her former self, and I couldn't exactly pinpoint why. There was something about her mannerism, her retreating against my line of questioning that just wasn't *her*.

My mind refused to believe her words, but my body knew. I felt the truth of her statement in my gut, and it felt like I'd swallowed gravel.

"I've been diagnosed with a glioblastoma—an aggressive brain tumor," she said.

I paused a moment, but she offered nothing more.

EMMA SLATE

"Brain tumors don't have to be fatal, do they? I mean, surgery? Can't you have surgery?"

"I can. But even if I have the surgery, I'm probably only going to get twelve to eighteen months. Only twenty-five percent of glioblastoma patients live past the year mark, and only five percent of patients live past the five-year mark. Glioblastomas aren't curable, either. Surgery, chemo, radiation tempers them."

She gave me the prognosis without any inflection or emotion.

"Jesus, I sound like a medical journal," she muttered.

"How long have you known about this?" I demanded.

"I just found out about it a few days ago."

"Ash knows."

She nodded.

"Sasha," I said slowly. "He knows. *Of course*, he does. Was he the first to know?"

"Yes."

"How was he the first to know? Why was he the first to know?"

"He was the one who was with me when I had my first seizure," she said plainly. "He was the one who took me to the hospital so I could get an MRI."

"Barrett," I whispered.

"Don't be mad at Sasha," she begged. "I asked him to keep my confidence. Even from Flynn…"

My eyes widened in shock. "Flynn doesn't know?"

"I went to London to tell him but then—"

"The bomb."

"Yes."

"So, he doesn't know?"

"Not yet."

"God, Barrett—"

262

"No guilt. I don't need your guilt. I'll tell Flynn, but it's not the right time."

"Like hell it's not. The right time is *now*. When do you go in for surgery?"

She blinked once, twice, three times, and remained silent.

"You're not having surgery," I concluded.

"I don't think so."

"Are you serious?"

"Yeah, I'm serious. I've already explained this to Ash," she muttered.

"Well explain it to me, because I don't get it."

"Let's say I have the surgery. Let's say they don't completely fuck it all up and I survive with my personality intact—oh, did I forget to mention that the tumor is growing in the part of my brain that makes me, *me*? And that surgery might affect who I am?"

"You didn't mention that, no," I said glumly.

"Right. So, let's say I survive intact, and I'm still me. It's not just surgery. It's chemo and radiation or drug therapies if that doesn't work. It's watching my children grow while I'm stuck in bed fighting for my life, barely able to do anything. And at the end of it, instead of spending my last remaining months loving my children and husband, I die anyway. What's the point, Quinn?"

"Point? What's the point? The point is to fight to live. Fight to survive."

"None of you understand."

"So, make us. Make *me* understand."

"I'm going to die, Quinn. I just want to live the rest of my life—however long that is—on my terms. I don't want my children to see me with tubes coming out of me, stuck in bed for months on end. I don't want them to see me sick and thin because I can't keep solid food down. I want them to remember me this way, the way I am now. I want Flynn to remember me this way, too."

"Is this for you, or for them?" I asked.

Her gaze narrowed and I knew I'd struck a nerve.

"Fine, it's for me," she snapped. "For fuck's sake, don't I deserve the quality of life *I* want? It's *my* fucking life!"

"Of course you do," I said, instantly backing down. "Quality over quantity. I get it. But what if you could have both? What if you defy the odds?"

"What if I don't?"

"If this were Flynn—if he was the one right now in this situation, what would you want for him? Furthermore, how would you feel if he told a bunch of people about his tumor before telling you?"

"I'd be livid," she said immediately. "Without question. But I had plans to tell him—"

"Plans go awry all the time. You know this. Especially in our world."

She turned to look out the window again. "I would respect his decision. A man in his position… He can't ever be seen as weak. Better to die a king than survive as a beaten dog."

"Barrett—"

"Enough, Quinn," she commanded, her tone unyielding. "Enough. I've made my decision. Please respect it."

I was silent for a long moment, trying to come to grips with the fact that one day all too soon, Barrett wouldn't be here anymore. The tumor growing in her brain would leach everything she was. It would take her body, but first it would take her mind.

We'd be left with nothing but a memory of who she was, even before she was truly gone.

Chapter 41

FLYNN

GIANNA FRISCO LOOMED over me as I leaned back against the plush sofa of the penthouse suite.

"You have to talk to the press," she said. "You've been out of the public eye for years, but you've just been firmly thrust back into the limelight because of what happened at The Rex."

I looked at Gianna. She was a no-nonsense woman with the relentless energy of a Pitbull. She was a New York City native, born and raised in Manhattan. A rare breed. Native Manhattanites had an indomitable will. An inner knowing that they belonged with the best. She'd graduated Magna Cum Laude from Columbia, and before I'd hired her to run PR for The Rex, she'd worked for a multi-billion-dollar tech company.

"Flynn," she snapped. "Are you listening to me?"

"I'm really trying not to," I stated.

She sighed like a mother who was at a loss on how to deal with a recalcitrant child, and it made me think of my own.

I grinned.

"Flynn! For the love of God, pay attention!"

"What am I supposed to say to the press, Gianna?" I demanded.

"The point of PR is not honesty. Never honesty. It's about getting ahead of a story before it spirals out of control. You should've called me immediately after it happened."

I glared at her, but she was used to dealing with people in power positions, so she ignored me and went on.

"Not addressing the press is no longer an option. It's time to calm things down. We're going to play on the emotional aspect of what could've happened but didn't because of your top-notch security team. That takes the pressure off you, and makes you appear compassionate and in control. It also means you're cooperating with the authorities."

"You have it all figured out," I mused.

Her brown eyes twinkled with sharp acumen. "You and Barrett have disappeared from the public eye. I get it. You're happily married, you're raising a young family, and you live in the Highlands. It's a fairytale existence, but the public needs to see you as a loving married couple, a phil-anthropic, loving married couple. You need to do some interviews together. After we handle this mess, of course."

I closed my eyes. "You're not saying what I think you're saying…"

"Yes, I am. You know me well enough by now to predict what I'm about to say."

"You want me to drag my wife all around the world and have us pose as a couple in front of cameras, smiling, sipping champagne and donating money to causes we don't believe in just so people will forget that there was a bomb at my hotel?"

"You can either complain about it, or you can just

know that I'm correct. And don't think anyone will ever forget about the bomb. They just won't know the true details behind it. This is what you hired me to do, remember? I clean up messes, and whether you like it or not, you have a big fucking mess on your hands. Now, the only way to clean something of this magnitude up is for you to do your thing with the authorities, and then for me to shove you in front of the public eye in a way that allows us to control the narrative. It's all about the narrative."

I had brought her into the SINS fold because she'd needed to understand the true complexities of my life and how I ran my empire. She hadn't balked when I told her the truth.

I'd upped her signing bonus.

"How long do you expect this PR jaunt to last? Give me a timeframe."

"Couple of months."

"Months," I muttered. "Christ, woman, we have four children."

"So, bring them along. That'll be even better. We'll show you as a loving, committed family man."

"I *am* a loving, committed family man," I groused.

"You're also a criminal," she pointed out.

"Barrett and I care about causes. You know we do. We just can't make them public."

She ignored me and continued to speak, "And I know you're really gonna hate this idea, but I know someone at *Home and Country Magazine* I'd like to introduce you to. If we can get them into your home to do a spread, it would go a long way toward humanizing the whole family."

Barrett was going to hate this, but she would go through with it if it meant saving The Rex and our reputation. Because above all else, we had to protect the SINS.

I scratched my chin. "All right. Set up the press conference for tomorrow morning—late morning. Invite *The Times*, *The Tribune*. Invite them all. I don't care."

"I'll take care of it," she said, straightening her black blazer and then grabbing her black leather briefcase off the coffee table. "I'll be back later with a prepared statement. We'll need to go over it until it's ingrained in your head."

"Fine."

She headed for the elevator. "Oh, and Flynn?"

"Hmm?"

"Shave before tomorrow's press conference. You look like hell."

"You're lucky you're damn good at your job."

Her heels clacked across the wooden floor and then she entered the private elevator. "Seriously, Flynn. I've got this. Trust me."

The doors closed with a soft chime, and I was alone.

I rubbed my forehead, feeling lightheaded. I'd barely eaten anything and had a cocktail on a nearly empty stomach.

I picked up the phone and dialed Barrett.

"Hello, you."

I heard the noise of laughter and splashing water in the background.

"Where are you?" I asked.

"Ash's indoor pool. It's been raining here all day and the boys were in desperate need of burning off energy. They've been taking turns doing cannon balls off the diving board."

I could hear the amusement in her tone. I missed her. Missed them all.

"How are you?" she asked. "I can feel your tension through the phone."

"I spoke with Gianna."

"Ah, *Le Pitbull*."

I laughed and it felt good. "I'm talking to the press tomorrow. Gianna has this covered."

"What can you possibly say that won't make them ask questions?"

"They'll ask questions no matter what," I said. "To divert them, Gianna suggested that you and I focus on a positive PR campaign to revitalize my image, The Rex's image, and to portray us a loving family while the authorities get to the bottom of who was behind this."

"We *are* a loving family," she pointed out. "We just happen to be criminals."

"I said the exact same thing."

She'd pitched her voice low so there was clearly no danger of the boys overhearing. At some point, they'd learn the truth, but not for many years. No use opening that can of worms before any of us were ready.

"I told her you were going to hate the idea," I said.

"Blamed it on me, did you? You hate the idea too."

"Of course I do. We're exceedingly private for a reason."

She paused for a moment and then she said, "I think it's a good idea."

I sighed. "I can't find any fault with it, either."

"Did she have any specifics about what she wanted from us?"

I was surprised by Barrett's willingness, but I wasn't going to dig deeper about it. "A few, but she did suggest inviting *Home and Country Magazine* to our house so they could do a spread on the family. You know, billion-dollar hotel empire owner, his sexy loving wife, his doting children. That sort of thing."

"You forgot one smelly sheep." The sound of her

laughter was exuberant. "So, when is this press conference being held?"

"Late tomorrow morning."

"Be careful, Flynn. They're vultures, and this is a juicy story. Word of advice, find a female reporter and turn on the Campbell charm. She won't be able to resist it and it will give the rest of them pause before grilling you."

"Thanks for the pointer, hen."

"When you're done with the press, does that mean you'll be able to come home?"

"Aye. I'll be home tomorrow evening. Come hell or high water, I've spent enough time away from you and the bairns."

"We miss you."

"How are the boys? How's Piper?"

"Everyone's fine, we're fine. Don't worry about us."

"You sure you miss me? You don't sound like you do," I teased.

"Tomorrow night, I'll lay my naked body on top of yours and show you how much I missed you."

"I'll hold you to that," I said, my voice husky.

She fell silent for a long moment.

"Hen?"

"When you get home, there's something I need to—crap, Hawk! Stop trying to drown your brother. Flynn? I've got to go. Call me tomorrow and tell me how the press conference went."

She hung up on me. I lowered my phone and stared at it, frowning. Why did it feel like every time I was on the phone with her, she was close to telling me something, but always got interrupted or sidetracked?

When I got home, I was going to sit down with my wife and get to the bottom of whatever was bothering her.

Chapter 42

BARRETT

"OUT OF THE POOL," I yelled at Hawk. "Now!"

"Mam," he whined.

"I told you not to beat up on your brothers. And if you can't play nice, then you don't get to play at all."

Sulking, Hawk dog-paddled toward the stairs. Iain stuck his tongue out at his brother, but the moment he saw me watching, he retracted it.

"Barrett the bad ass," Ash said from the shallow end. Carys was in a flotation device, splashing the water with her fists, her giggles echoing off the high ceiling.

Quinn had been asleep on a lounge in the corner but came awake with a start and she looked around in a moment of panic. When she realized nothing was truly amiss, she settled back down.

My nerves and patience were frayed. I wanted to go home. I wanted to take the boys and Piper and wait for Flynn. I knew the moment he walked through the door, I'd spill everything. There would be no finesse, no easing him into the truth. But maybe that was how it was supposed to be.

I was sitting on information that would change the course of his life forever. It was why I hadn't balked at the idea of PR for The Rex. Even though my time was limited, I wanted to pretend like it wasn't. So, I would jet set with my husband and children, I'd give the interviews, I'd smile for the cameras and journalists, and only behind closed doors would I continue to deteriorate.

Hawk ascended the stairs and dripped water where he stood. He shook his head, reminding me of a dog after a bath, spraying water droplets everywhere.

I grabbed a towel on the edge of the chaise and went to him. Unfortunately, I didn't see the puddle in my path. My foot slid through it, and I immediately lost my balance. I twisted my knee on the way down which threw off my center of gravity even more.

"Barrett!" Ash cried.

"Mam!" came Hawk's worried voice.

"I'm okay," I said, gritting my teeth against the pain.

"Everyone out of the pool," Ash commanded.

"Careful," I called out as I heard manic splashing from the pool.

I felt steady and confident hands grasp my arms, helping me sit up. It was Quinn, and she was crouched down next to me.

"I'm fine," I assured her.

My children stood with their towels around their wet bodies, peering at me with wide, scared eyes. Parents weren't supposed to fall. To fail. To get hurt. We were supposed to be infallible.

I forced a smile. "I just had a little accident." I opened my arms to them and before I knew it, I was enveloped by thin, little boy arms. Noah snuggled up against me, reminding me of what he'd been like as an infant.

I had memories of them, but I wouldn't have any new

ones. They would be frozen at this age until I died, and my memories, thoughts and wishes crumbled like dust.

Just like my body.

I couldn't stop the flow of tears that escaped without my permission.

"Why are you crying?" Iain asked, pulling back to look at me.

"Am I crying?" I hastily wiped my cheeks.

Noah nodded.

"I'm hurt," I said. It was technically the truth.

"Where?" Hawk asked. "Can I kiss it and make it better?"

I smiled and nodded. "Here." I pointed to my knee

Hawk leaned over and gently kissed the tender spot.

"Anywhere else?" Noah asked.

I touched my right knee.

"You already said that hurt," Hawk reminded me.

"It hurts a lot," I said, my smile wobbling. "It needs a lot of kisses from you to make it better."

Ash made a choked sound, but she trapped it in her throat. Her own emotions were clearly demanding to be let out, but because she was an adult, a mother, like me, we put our feelings aside, or mashed them down to put on a brave face.

She turned away and focused on getting Carys out of her floatie and then stripped her out of her bathing suit before wrapping her in a towel.

I glanced at Quinn, who'd backed up enough to give my boys room to crowd me. She looked somber. Everything she wanted to say reflected in her eyes.

I shook my head ever so slightly and then turned my attention back to my boys.

"How do you guys feel about going home?" I asked them.

"Aye," Hawk said, sounding just like his father. "I miss home."

"Me too," Iain said.

"Are you sure that's a good idea?" Quinn voiced, her tone full of concern.

"It's a great idea," I assured her with a smile. "I've got the nannies to help me with everything I need."

I raised my eyebrows at her, as if daring her to continue.

She clamped her mouth shut. Reluctantly, Ash nodded, but then she shot Quinn a look. Quinn shrugged, as if silently saying *Barrett's going to do what Barrett's going to do.*

I didn't have control over a lot of things. The tumor rooted in my brain would kill me; it would wring every drop of my life from me. But I had control over how I chose to spend the last few months I had on this earth. And that included sleeping in my own bed when I wanted to, making love to my husband every chance I got, and getting my affairs in order.

I struggled to stand, but then Iain and Noah clasped my free hands with theirs, steadying me. I looked at my children, my beautiful boys who were made in Flynn's image.

"Let's go home."

"I don't like this," Ash said, hugging me to her.

"I know." I pulled back. "But I can't have you watching me every moment like you expect me to…detonate."

She winced. "You make it sound like you're a ticking time bomb. And haven't we had enough of bombs?"

I sighed and then turned to Quinn. "Are you going to give me shit about going home?"

Quinn shook her head. "I know there's no point in trying to talk you out of something once you've made up your mind."

"Are you angry with me?"

"Yes."

I nodded. "I can live with that."

The nannies had packed up the boys and Piper into the massive Suburban. Angus was waiting to chauffeur us home.

I fiddled with the collar of my coat and stared out the window of the den. The rain had abated, but everything looked gray. The sky. The brick walkway leading out front. Life.

"Are you going to stay here?" I asked Quinn.

"Yes." Quinn cleared her throat. "Neither of us feel like being alone right now."

I needed to be alone. Desperately.

I gave Quinn a side hug because Helena was on her hip, and then I cradled the crown of Helena's head. I brushed my lips across her forehead and closed my eyes.

I wondered if Quinn and Sasha would have more children.

"I love you," Ash said, jarring me out of my wayward thoughts. "You know that, right?"

"Of course, I know that," I said.

"I…" She sighed. "I don't know what to say."

"Right now, all you have to do is say goodbye and let me walk out the door. There will be plenty of time later to talk."

"What if you don't come back?" Ash asked quietly. "What if this is the last time we see you? What if something unexpected happens?"

"If that's what happens, then tell Flynn I love him."

"Barrett," Ash whispered, her voice strained.

"I can't, Ash. I can't be strong for you right now. As much as I want to. I have to be strong for myself."

My gaze darted from her to Quinn.

For all intents and purposes, they were my sisters. God-willing, they would be there to see my children grow long after I was gone. They would be there to help Flynn figure out how to live a life without me.

"I'm getting maudlin," I commented. "I need to get the hell out of here before I start weeping."

"Weeping doesn't sound like such a bad idea," Quinn said.

"If I start crying, I don't know if I'll stop," I admitted.

Ash took my hand and gave it a squeeze.

There wasn't anything more to say, so I opened the front door and left.

I climbed into the Suburban and was getting situated when Hawk asked, "When's Da coming home?"

"Tomorrow," I said.

"Good. I miss him," Hawk said, taking a finger and trailing it down the glass window.

"He misses you," I assured him with a smile.

"What's for dinner tonight?" Iain asked.

"Spaghetti and meatballs," I said.

"And garlic bread?" Noah prodded. "Please?"

I grinned. "And garlic bread. Maybe a salad."

"Vegetables, gross," Hawk muttered.

"Do you want to be tall like your Da?" I asked him.

"Aye."

"Then you'll eat a salad."

Flynn was still larger than life to the boys. To them, their father was a superhero, a legend. They looked up to him, wanted to be him.

It tugged on my heartstrings because one day, they'd see Flynn not just as their father, but as a man. A man who made mistakes. A man who took risks. A man who made choices that shaped their world.

God, I need a drink.

Angus pulled into the multi car garage and then parked next to the Shelby Cobra. Flynn and I had plans to the take the red speedster with a white racing stripe for a drive up the Scottish coastline, but we hadn't gotten around to it yet.

Soon.

"Do you want me to get Piper?" Julie asked.

I nodded. "Yes, thank you." I waited for Angus to get out and then I turned to Julie and said, "After the children are in bed tonight, I need to speak to the three of you."

"Are we in trouble?" Bella asked.

I smiled and shook my head. "Not at all."

Chapter 43
BARRETT

"I know you told us not to do the dishes," Suze said. "But you really don't want spaghetti sauce to sit."

Bella wiped her hands on a dishrag and then folded it into a neat square before setting it on the counter. "It went quickly with the three of us."

"Thanks," I said, my appreciation genuine.

Dinner had been boisterous, and I'd almost forgotten, for just a couple of moments, that I was dying.

But now the children were in bed, tucked in for the night and I couldn't use them as a form of distraction. The rain had picked up again and the wind howled like a morose woman that had lost her true love.

"Let's go to the den," I said.

The three young women followed me, and when we got to the den, I signaled for them to go in first. I closed the sliding doors behind me so in the off chance one of the boys ventured downstairs, they wouldn't be able to over-hear what we were discussing.

I went to the liquor cart. "What would you three like to drink?"

Julie cleared her throat. "We don't drink when we work, per your rule."

"This is an extenuating circumstance," I said. "So, what will you have to drink?"

"Glass of red for me," Bella ventured to say.

"Yeah, I'll have the same," Suze stated.

"Might as well make it three," Julie added.

"Have a seat," I said.

The three of them perched on the couch like three little swallows sharing a branch. They were clearly uncomfortable. Whether it was because I'd offered them a drink or I intimidated them, I didn't know.

I deftly opened a bottle of red. I gave them their glasses and then poured myself a scotch. I sat on the couch directly opposite them, grasping the crystal like a lifeline.

"What I'm about to tell you requires your utmost discretion," I began.

"We've already signed NDAs," Bella said. "When you hired us…"

I nodded. "I know. This isn't like that…this is different." I took a deep breath and plowed forward. "A few days ago, I was diagnosed with an aggressive brain tumor. I've had a seizure already and I've been advised by my physician that it's not safe for me to care for my children the way I used to any longer."

Their stunned faces peered back at me. Julie was the first to gain her composure. "That's why you've been having me carry and feed Piper. You haven't held her…"

I nodded.

"Does Mr. Campbell know?" Bella asked.

"Not yet. When he gets home tomorrow, I'll tell him. The reason I'm sharing this with you now is because I need your help."

"We'll help," Suze exclaimed. "Anything you need. For as long as you need it."

"I need the three of you here. Full time. I need you to move into the main house. You'll be compensated accordingly." The young women were fresh out of college, had no long-term boyfriends, and shared the carriage house behind the manor.

"You already are more than generous," Bella said. "I'm not even concerned about that."

I smiled. "Word of advice? When someone offers to pay you for your time, don't balk. Accept it."

Bella's cheeks flamed with heat and then she nodded.

"There are guest rooms on the third floor," I said. "You're welcome to any of them."

Julie looked at Bella and Suze. "You guys go pack first. I'll stay here and then we can swap out."

I reached into my pocket and grabbed the keys to my Mercedes. I tossed them to Suze. "Take my car. Don't involve Angus. You're the only members of the staff that know now, and this has to stay between us until I tell my family."

"Don't worry, Angus is probably asleep in front of the telly," Suze commented with a wry smile.

I took a risk, telling the three young nannies the truth about my situation, but I was backed into a corner. I needed their help and tomorrow, Flynn would know the truth.

"Thank you for sharing this with us, Mrs. Campbell," Julie said softly.

"I'll have a lot to go over with you over the next few days. At some point, I will be hiring private nurses, but that won't stop you from seeing me at my worst. This is going to get ugly. There's a good chance you're going to see me foaming at the mouth at some point in the near future. You might as well call me Barrett."

Julie opened her mouth like she wanted to say something, but at the last second, took a big swallow of wine instead.

"You can ask, you know," I said. "You don't have to bite your tongue. That's why we're here."

"It's none of my business. I work for you. I'll call you Barrett because you've asked, but you're entitled to privacy. I know how much you and Mr. Campbell value that."

"Thanks, Julie," I said quietly. I rose from my spot on the couch. "Do you mind keeping an ear out for Piper? I have some things I'd like to…"

"I don't mind at all."

I exited the den, still carrying my glass. Instinctively, I looked to the stairs, wondering about my children, wondering how they were going to survive losing a parent at their young age.

Would I fade from their memories with the passage of time?

Would Flynn put picture frames of me holding each of them next to their bedsides so they could stare at me before they went to sleep? Or would that be too much for them to bear?

I took a sip of scotch and trekked down the hallway to Flynn's study. I loved the room, with its expansive ornate desk, leather bound books, and the scent of peat lingering in the air. I turned on the light. A warm glow dribbled the furniture in masculine ambiance.

One of his favorite sweaters hung on the back of his desk chair. I set my glass of scotch on the desktop and then reached for the garment. It was worn and faded gray, an odd garment for a billionaire, but something he cherished and refused to get rid of. I brought it to my nose and inhaled. His cologne lingered in the wool, and I closed my eyes, silently asking his forgiveness.

Forgiveness for keeping my condition from him for as long as I had. Forgiveness for not including him in my choice of whether or not to have surgery. Forgiveness for leaving him before we were old and gnarled.

"You're wasting time," Igor said, startling me from my thoughts. He leaned against the edge of Flynn's desk.

"I'm wasting nothing." I took off my own sweater so I could pull on Flynn's. It wasn't the same as having his arms around me, but it made me feel better.

And yet, for the first time in my life, even if Flynn were here to embrace me and whisper words of comfort, I realized they would just be empty—lies that everything was going to be okay.

"Your death will change them," Igor said.

I bowed my head, not wanting to meet Igor's eyes.

"Ash is hanging on by a thread. Her marriage is on the brink of collapse."

"That's not my fault."

"No. Not technically. But she's constantly comparing her relationship to yours and Flynn's. She finds hers... lacking."

"Again, that isn't my fault."

"She knows she could get through anything as long as she has you by her side."

"Spare me the guilt trip." I picked up my glass of scotch and took a hefty swallow, wanting to drown out the truth in Igor's words, but knowing I couldn't.

"Quinn doesn't know what she wants. She says she does, but she's never decided who she wants to be. You were supposed to help her become a queen."

"Stop it," I begged. "Just stop it. Don't burden me with this. Don't put all of this on my shoulders."

I walked to the fireplace mantle and ran my fingers across the marble. Igor's accusations were manifestations of my own. They were poisonous darts puncturing my heart.

"And Sasha," he went on. "He held you in his arms while you had a seizure. He forced you to go to the doctor. Now you're going to force him to watch you wither away and die. You're the potential and hope he has never lost. If you die, you will change him forever, too."

Tears gathered in my eyes and emotion clogged my throat.

"And your children… They're going to grow up without a mother. Your daughter will never know you. She'll grow up in a house of grief and anger, because you dying will knock the entire family off course. Flynn will crumble. He'll become a bitter man. You're the only thing keeping him from becoming completely ruthless. If you die, he'll lose his humanity."

"Shut the fuck up!" I yelled, unable to endure anymore. I threw my glass of scotch at the fireplace. Crystal shattered and brown liquor splattered across the stone floor.

My breathing was harsh in my own ears, and I gripped the mantle as tears trailed down my cheeks. I prayed my children were still asleep. I prayed the nannies hadn't heard my meltdown.

I prayed I wasn't really dying.

But I knew my prayers would go unanswered.

Flynn kept an antique liquor cart fully stocked. I went to it and made myself another drink.

Igor looked solemn and resolute, dressed in a black suit like he was about to attend a funeral.

I began to recognize his ghost as a symbol of the sickness spreading inside me and determined then and there that I would think of him only as the Angel of Death from that moment on.

I set my new glass of scotch on Flynn's desk and then took a seat in his chair.

"Go," I told Igor. "Please."

After a long quiet moment, Igor said, "I'll go. For now."

I waited until I was sure he was gone before opening the desk drawer and pulling out a sheet of heavy cream-colored paper and Flynn's favorite Montblanc pen.

And then I began to write.

Chapter 44
FLYNN

I sat on the balcony of the penthouse suite and stared out into the cold, rainy night.

English rain was different than Scottish rain.

It was subtle, but there was a difference in the air. A tension in the wind.

My phone rested on the glass table next to me and vibrated when it lit up. I'd been fielding calls for the past few days, and I was sick to death of looking at my cell phone. What I wouldn't give to pitch it over the balcony railing and watch it fall to the street below and have a cabbie run over it.

But I was Flynn Campbell, and I couldn't disappear. As much as I wanted to.

I picked up my cell and saw Barrett's name.

"Hen," I greeted. "It's late."

"Da."

I sat up straight. "Hawk?"

He sniffed, like he'd been crying.

"Hawk, what's wrong? Are you hurt?"

"No," came his muffled reply.

My pulse pounded in my ears. "Why do you have your mother's phone?"

"Da, you have to come home," he pleaded, sounding far younger than he normally did. Hawk was all swagger and bravado, but something had him spooked.

"I'll be home tomorrow," I promised.

"No, Da. You have to come home now. It's Mam."

"What's wrong with your mother?" I asked, attempting to keep my anxiety tamped down.

He started to cry.

"Hawk," I commanded. "Tell me what's going on. Right now." When he didn't reply, I snapped, "Is she sick? Does she have a fever? Is she throwing up? Like when you had the flu?"

"No." His voice sounded very far away. "I heard Bella and Suze talking…they said—they said—"

He began to hiccough.

I took a deep breath and forced patience I didn't feel. A knot of nerves had lodged in my stomach. It had been there for days. I thought it had to do with The Rex. Now I was sure it had nothing to do with my hotel.

"Hawk?" I softened my tone. "What did you hear Bella and Suze say?"

He didn't reply for a very long moment. The tension swelled on the other end of the line.

"They said Mam is dying."

Blood roared through my veins. "What do you mean she's dying?"

"Bella said Mam has a tumor in her brain. What's a tumor, Da?"

What the fuck?

"Where are you, Hawk?" I asked.

"On the porch, snuggled under a blanket with Betty."

"Good. Listen, I'll explain what a tumor is later, aye?

But I need you to do something for me. I need you to be strong. I'm leaving London right now. All right? I'll see you in a few hours."

"I love you, Da."

"I love you, too, lad." I hung up with him and pressed the cell phone to my forehead.

Could I really take the word of my seven-year-old son who didn't know what the hell a tumor was?

I lowered my phone and stared at it for a moment. I knew who I could call to confirm what Hawk had told me.

I unlocked my phone and scrolled through my contacts list. My thumb hovered over his name for a moment and then I pressed it.

He answered on the second ring. "Flynn."

"What's wrong with my wife, Sasha?"

He paused as if carefully weighing his words, and then he sighed. "Christ."

"Tell me," I demanded. "Tell me what's wrong with her, like you should've done in the first place, so I didn't have to hear it from my oldest son who overheard the nannies talking about it."

"Fuck. Hawk knows?"

"Damn right he knows," I seethed. "What the hell do you know that I don't?"

"She had a seizure," he said quietly. "A few days ago. I was there when it happened. That's the only reason I know anything. I took her to the hospital."

When he fell silent, I snapped, "Finish it!"

"She came to London to tell you, but then the bomb… She has a brain tumor. It's aggressive. She's refusing treatment, Flynn."

My hand clenched around my cell phone. I felt the metal bend and had to force myself not to throw it just to watch it shatter.

Bile churned in my belly, but I mashed it down before it shot up my throat.

A hazy red veil descended over my eyes.

Without a word, I disconnected.

In less than twelve hours, I would be standing in front of journalists and the press to make a statement that was supposed to cover my arse. It would save the face of my hotel empire. We were supposed to rehabilitate our public image. For years, I'd chosen the SINS over everything and everyone.

But all I could think about now was my wife.

Nothing else mattered.

Like hell she's refusing treatment.

That was not a decision she could make in a vacuum. Not when it came to our life and our children.

I dialed my pilot. He picked up and I said, "I want to leave immediately."

"We can't," Charles responded. "All air traffic is currently grounded due to weather conditions. A storm is blowing through."

"Fuck, fuck, *fuck*."

"Just wait it out, Flynn," he said. "By the time you're finished making your statement, I'm sure the weather will be—"

"I have to get home," I interrupted. "It's an emergency."

"My hands are tied. They won't clear us to fly."

"I have to get home, Charles. It's non-negotiable. I'm going to drive. I can be home in about ten hours."

"Are you sure that's a good idea?" he queried.

"What was that?" I asked, my voice deadly calm.

"Nothing. Never mind."

"That's what I thought." I hung up on him.

Angus was at home with Barrett and the bairns and I

hadn't left The Rex in days. I'd had no use for a driver, and I didn't need one now.

I could drive myself, and I preferred it. I didn't want to talk to another human being. I wanted to be alone to think and figure out how I was going to walk into my house and not lose my shite about my wife keeping this from me.

Why had she kept this from me?

She should've told me the moment she realized something was going on.

I got up and went inside. I'd stopped drinking hours ago in preparation of facing the paparazzi. The last thing I'd wanted to do was look hungover with red rimmed eyes, like I had steadily been drinking for days...which I had been.

Ramsey had been stabbed.

Sasha's holdings at the port had been set on fire.

The Rex was in the middle of a PR nightmare.

Barrett had a brain tumor.

I grabbed my cell phone and made sure I had my wallet in my pocket. Everything else I left. I'd planned for the uncontrollable moments; at every one of my hotels there was an identical silver Aston Martin waiting for me in a permanent VIP spot, fueled and ready to go, maintained by the valet managers. I was a billionaire, and a billionaire always had an escape plan.

An hour later, I was on the outskirts of London. Only then did I call Gianna. It was nearly midnight, but it was her job to take my calls at any time of day.

"Gianna, I'm headed home. There's something I have to take care of."

"What? What the fuck are you—no, no you have to be at the press conference you can't—"

"Family emergency," I said. "And that's all I'm saying about it right now and that's final."

She sighed. "This better be good. I'm going to need something to work with. They're going to be furious."

"Fuck them. This isn't a fucking game, it's my family. I'll be in touch."

I hung up on her. She didn't even attempt to call me back.

My thoughts drifted to my eldest son. Was Hawk asleep? Did he return Barrett's phone? Was he clutching it to his chest, waiting for me to call? Did I want to call and risk waking him up? Or was it better to let it be and just show up? I wanted to comfort him, but I wasn't even sure I could do that over the phone.

My cell rang, jarring me out of my thoughts and I recognized the private, secure line from my office.

"Hello."

"You're awake," Barrett said in surprise.

"I am," I said. "I'm always awake, it seems. Why are you calling me from the study?"

"I can't find my cell phone."

"Hawk has it. He called me not too long ago. Is there something you want to tell me?"

Her breath hitched. "Tell you? Tell you what?"

"I don't know. Maybe you could tell me why I found out about your fucking brain tumor from our seven-year-old."

"How did he—I didn't tell him!"

"The nannies were talking and he overheard. I called Sasha and he confirmed it. Why the hell didn't you tell me?"

A horn beeped from the car behind me, but I wasn't going to go faster. The rain was steadily sprinkling, and the conditions were getting worse. No doubt it would turn torrential soon.

"Was that a car horn?" she asked.

"Aye. I'm on my way home."

"Home? But the press conference—"

"Gianna's handling it."

"Why are you driving home?" she asked. Her voice sounded far away and small.

"Shite weather for flying. Couldn't get clearance to take off."

"Oh."

"I'm hanging up now because I have to concentrate on driving. But when I get home, you're going to tell me everything. Do you understand?"

"Yes," she croaked. "I'll tell you everything."

"Like you should've done the moment you knew."

She was silent for a moment and then she said, "I love you, Flynn. Drive safe."

Chapter 45

BARRETT

I SET the heavy vintage phone in its cradle, my heart galloping in my chest.

Flynn knew.

Flynn knew and I hadn't been the one to tell him.

All I did was hurt him. I tried to shield him, I tried to protect him, and in doing so, I wounded him more.

The drive would take hours—hours of him stewing, getting angrier and angrier.

He was livid, and when he arrived, we were going to have it out. A verbal brawl.

I'd take it. Whatever he threw at me, I'd take it, beg him to forgive me for keeping it from him for so long. And then hope he understood my decision.

I thought about calling Sasha, but I didn't have the reserves. He'd been put in an untenable position and out of loyalty to me, he'd kept my confidence. Only when Flynn had come to him did he finally speak the truth.

I didn't blame Sasha. Not at all.

I'd been holed up in Flynn's study for hours writing letters by hand. Even though my fingers were cramping, I refused to stop until I finished the last letter. My note to Flynn was the longest.

I finally ventured out and went to check on the children, peeking in on them, just to take a moment to watch them sleep. I started with Piper. I ran a hand across her back and gently touched the smooth skin of her cheek.

Iain slept with his mouth hanging open, one arm flung over his head, a leg resting on top of the covers. Noah was the opposite. He was tucked in, almost swaddled.

Hawk wasn't in his bed, but I didn't panic. I checked my bedroom, but he wasn't sleeping in the center of the king-sized bed. I thought about where he would be and then I smiled, having an inkling. I traipsed down to the enclosed porch and found him curled up with Betty, a thick wool blanket tossed over them. Hawk clutched my missing phone to his chest.

I gently took the cell from him and contemplated waking Hawk so I could put him to bed but decided not to disturb him. Carrying him was out of the question. I could have a seizure and drop him.

The rain rapped a gentle rhythm on the roof.

"Mam?" Hawk whispered.

I stilled and then crouched down next to him. "Did I wake you?"

"No." His eyes opened, and even though the enclosed porch was bathed in darkness, the terrace torches gave me enough light to see his face. "Do I have to go back to my bed?"

I smiled and ran a hand across his head. "No, my love. You don't. You can sleep here."

"Will you stay with me?" He sounded afraid.

"Did you have a nightmare?"

Hawk nodded.

"We have to move Betty," I said.

He spoke to the sheep in Gaelic, and she quickly got down from the lounge. Hawk wiggled over to make room for me and then I slid beneath the blanket. He instantly rolled into my side, and I cuddled him against me. I called for Betty, and she jumped back up, but settled at our feet like she was a family dog.

"Am I squishing you?" I asked him.

"No."

Soon, his breathing was deep, and I thought for sure he was asleep, but then he asked, "Mam, are you dying?"

The terror in his voice rammed apart my soul. How was I supposed to have this conversation with my son? How was I going to make him understand? How was I going to explain to him the complexities of the universe that even I didn't comprehend?

And then I realized what I had to do.

"Sit up," I said softly.

When he was facing me, I took a deep shuddering breath. "I know you heard Bella and Suze talking, didn't you?"

He nodded.

"I'm sick. Very sick."

His eyes widened in his face. "Is it the tumor? Is that what's making you sick?"

I could murder the nannies for making me have this talk with my son before I was ready to.

"Yes. There's a tumor growing in here." I pointed to my cranium.

"What is a tumor? I asked Da and he didn't tell me."

This was part of my penance. I'd kept the truth from my husband and now I was going to have to tell my seven-year-old son alone.

"Mam?" Hawk prodded, reminding me that he was waiting for an answer that was far too complex for his age.

"A tumor is like a bump. You know when you hit your knee, or your elbow and it gets red and swollen? Well, that's what I have inside my head."

He frowned. "How did it get there?"

"It started off very small, and it was nothing. But then it got bigger and kept growing."

Hawk nodded slowly. "How do you get it out of your head?"

"I can't get it out of my head. It will stay there."

I was walking a very thin line as a parent. There was being truthful with Hawk, and then there was outright scaring him.

He flung himself into my arms and started to cry, big, soul-wracking sobs that shook his young body.

"I don't want you to die," he whispered.

I brushed a kiss across the top of his head. "I know, love. I know."

"Will you go to Heaven?"

I was pretty sure I'd be going to Hell for all the things I had done, but I would not use my child as my confessor. It might've been a good idea to speak to Father Brooks.

"What do you think?" I asked instead.

He nodded. "Aye, you'll go to Heaven. Will I go there, too?"

"Some day. But not for a long, long time."

"How do you know?"

"Because I do," I lied.

I knew nothing, and perhaps making a promise I had no control over wasn't the smartest move, but he needed comfort more than anything.

"Let's lay back down and listen to the rain," I suggested. "Your dad is on his way home."

"I know, he told me. I miss him."

"Me too."

He tucked himself into my side, his warm little body a solid comfort even though he was crying himself to sleep. I remained awake long after he'd gone quiet, dreading the reckoning that was coming.

Knowing I was going to face Flynn.

I fell asleep to the sounds of Scottish rain drumming on the roof, my eldest child cradled in my arms.

My phone beeped, jarring me awake. I was careful not to jostle Hawk as I searched for my cell which was nestled between us.

It beeped again and again. Frowning, I peered at the alert on the screen.

"Oh, shit," I murmured.

Chapter 46
FLYNN

THE RAIN TURNED TO SNOW. I should've listened to Charles. I should've stayed in London, went ahead with the press conference, and gave the storm time to blow out.

But I just couldn't. Not after finding out about Barrett's brain tumor.

Now, it was the wee hours of the morning, my visibility was fucked, and I was driving along a treacherous road that was known for having some of the worst accidents in the UK.

I slowed my speed as I approached the bridge.

The windshield wiper blades were swishing back and forth to keep the glass clear, but the snow was thick and heavy.

Weak beams of light appeared in my rearview mirror, and they were rapidly approaching. I laid on the horn to alert the other driver, but their speed didn't change.

"Shite," I muttered. I pressed on the brakes to light up the car and alert the driver behind me, but due to the slick bridge, my wheels spun, and I lost traction.

I blasted the horn again, but it was futile.

An old farm truck careened into the back of my car and we slid in tandem to the bridge railing. But the truck was too heavy to stop, and with the slick, icy road and no traction, the truck propelled both vehicles through the guard rail over the bridge.

As the impact occurred, my airbags detonated and dazed me for a split second. I braced for impact as the Aston Martin fell into the river.

As the car plummeted into the water below, my head hit the airbag a second time, and my seatbelt slammed into my chest, pinning me to my seat. My teeth rattled and my vision was spotty. A waterlogged tree limb had impaled the windshield in the center of the car and cold water gushed inside.

I reached for my seat belt, but my right arm felt like it had been pumped full of concrete and refused to move. The dashboard didn't give off enough light to allow me to see to get my bearings. The water was freezing. My lungs burned as they struggled to draw air.

My vision wobbled in and out as water continued to fill the car.

I unlatched my seatbelt with my left hand and then reached for the door handle, but I didn't have the power to wrench the door open against the force of the water.

I'd been on death's door before.

But this? This was different. This was like watching my life end in slow motion. Powerless to stop it.

I thought about my wife.

"I understand, Barrett," I said. "I understand, why you didn't tell me. God, forgive me."

River water swirled up to my chest.

I could no longer fight.

My eyes closed, and everything went dark.

Chapter 47

BARRETT

"HAWK, WAKE UP," I commanded, shaking my son awake while I dialed the head of security.

"Wha—"

"You need to go upstairs and put on your clothes. Warm clothes," I added. "Do you understand?"

He nodded.

"Good, then wake your brothers and tell them to do the same. Find the flashlights in your bedside drawers. Hurry."

He scrambled off the lounge and ran to the door. It opened with force, hitting the door stop as he ran out of the room. Betty jumped down and ran after him. I was too distracted to command her not to.

"Barrett," Tony said as soon as he answered my call. "I have no idea what the fuck is going on with the system. The monitor shut off and then flashed back on, and I just thought it was because of the storm. We've got those backup generators so the system can't go down for very long and I wasn't worried at first. But my guys patrolling the grounds aren't answering their radio checks anymore."

"This is a security breach," I said.

"Aye," Tony agreed, his tone bleak. "Someone has gotten through our—"

Static filtered through the phone.

"Tony?"

The line beeped and then went silent. I looked at my screen. My phone had dropped the call.

"Fuck," I said, scrambling up from the couch and running into the house.

The moment I had seen the alert on my phone that several of the security cameras had gone down at the same time, I knew it was more than just something electrical. I felt it on a gut level.

There were too many events that had occurred in the last several days to be coincidence, and I didn't believe that our state-of-the-art security system would accidentally fail now.

I didn't know my enemy. I didn't know who was at my gate. But I did know I had to get my children to safety.

I rushed up the stairs and hit the light switch on the wall when I got to the second floor, but I didn't stop. I ran to the third floor.

"Julie! Bella! Suze," I called, and then I pushed open a bedroom door.

"What's wrong?" Julie asked, her voice tinged with sleep.

I turned on the light. Her hair was askew, and her cheek was creased from the pillow.

"There's been a security breach," I said. "You need to get the kids out of here. *Now*." She jumped from the bed just as Bella and Suze filled the doorway. I looked at them. "Did you hear that?"

"Yeah," Bella croaked. "I heard it."

"Get dressed," I commanded. "And then meet me on the second floor."

They attempted to move out of my way, but in doing so, collided with each other, looking like lost little lemmings.

"Whatever you do, stay calm," I said. "We don't want to panic the children."

"I'll get Piper," Julie said.

I nodded.

The lights flickered and then went out, pitching us all into darkness.

"Shit," Suze muttered.

"Double shit," Bella added. "I can't see in front of my face."

"Mam!" Hawk yelled. "The lights went out!"

"Do you have your flashlights?" I hollered back.

I had my phone in hand and I turned on the flashlight feature which allowed Julie enough light to find her phone and do the same. She illuminated the hallway for Bella and Suze.

I took the stairs carefully, not wanting to trip on my own two feet. When I made it to the second floor, I called out for the boys. Their doors were open, and Noah and Iain popped their heads out. Noah held a flashlight in one hand, and it blazed brightly. Thank goodness for little boys who liked tents and nature, who always had flashlights nearby. Thank goodness their father was Flynn Campbell and he had taught them to be prepared.

They were dressed in jeans and thick wool sweaters. Their hats and coats were by the front door.

"Where's Hawk?" I asked them.

"He went to Piper's room," Iain said. "He didn't want her to be scared."

Iain's voice trembled, letting me know he was terrified.

301

"I need you to be brave for me," I said. "Can you do that?"

He nodded.

"Good," I murmured. "Now, I want you both to go to my bedroom and sit on the bed and wait for me. Okay?"

Noah grasped his twin's hand and hauled him toward the master bedroom. I went to Piper's nursery and found Hawk with his own flashlight, standing at Piper's crib, singing her a lullaby.

He stopped when he realized I was in the room.

"That was sweet of you to come to Piper so she wouldn't be afraid." I placed my hand on his shoulder. "I've asked so much of you, Hawk. But I need you to do something else for me. I need you to be strong for your brothers and sister. I don't want you to tell them what we talked about earlier, okay?"

"Okay, Mam." He wrapped his arms around my waist and hugged me tight. Betty had made herself comfortable in the rocking chair.

"I'm here," Julie said in the doorway, a sense of urgency in her tone.

"Iain and Noah are in my bedroom. Will you go to them?" I asked, looking down at Hawk. "We'll bring Piper in a moment."

Nodding, Hawk released me and then headed for the door. Betty jumped down from the rocking chair and trotted after him. Julie ran her hand across his head before he disappeared into the hallway.

"Piper's going to be hungry, but we don't have a lot of time." I gently stuck a pacifier into her mouth, praying it would soothe her for the time being.

"How are we supposed to get the children to safety?" Julie asked.

"There's a secret tunnel," I explained as I rushed from the nursery toward my bedroom.

"A secret tunnel?" Julie repeated as she followed me.

"It'll take us underground beneath the castle."

"I didn't know you had a secret tunnel."

"That's why it's called a secret." I entered the room and looked around. The boys were huddled together, looking terrified and gruesome in the illumination of their flashlights.

"Open the chest at the foot of the bed. You'll have to use the wool blankets to keep you warm."

While Bella and Suze went to the chest, I trekked into the walk-in closet and rushed to the back wall where there was a heavy wooden armoire. I opened the doors and pushed aside the gowns I'd once worn to galas and charity events. I reached my hand up to the interior shelf, searching for the hidden button. When I found it, I pushed it, and the back door of the armoire slid open to reveal a staircase built into the wall.

"Cool!" Iain called out. "It's like the wardrobe leading into Narnia!"

"Hush," Bella said, wrapping Iain in a Campbell tartan blanket. "We have to be quiet. Like we're playing a game. Can you do that?"

He nodded, his young face eager. He thought this was an adventure. He had no idea of the danger. Good.

I shoved my feet into a pair of boots and grabbed one of Flynn's coats that hung in the closet.

"Can we take Betty?" Hawk asked, his finger sifting through her wool.

"I'm sorry, love, but we can't. She might make a noise," I said to him.

"Piper cries," Hawk pointed out. "She's loud. So why can't we take Betty?"

I shooed the boys toward the open doorway that led into the tunnel. "Betty can come as long as you promise to keep her quiet. Okay? Let's move."

Bella went in first, followed by Hawk and Betty who stayed by his side. Julie went next. The twins held hands and descended. Thankfully, there was enough light from the flashlights to brighten the way.

An explosion boomed in the distance.

"Hurry," I urged. Suze jumped forward and I trailed behind her.

I closed the armoire's hidden door and listened for a moment, but I couldn't hear anything. Piper began to cry, and Julie tried to shush her. It only seemed to inflame Piper more.

The automatic lights didn't switch on, but Hawk illuminated the way with his flashlight.

We arrived at the end of the tunnel and there was a wrought iron handle sticking out of the rock. Suze paused but a moment, and then grasped it.

If it weren't for the handle, the door would've been undiscoverable. It had been painted to look like the stone walls of the tunnel.

The exit was shielded by boulders and rocks, so anyone walking along the beach would only see a craggy outcrop. We stepped out of the tunnel onto the sandy beach of the firth. I closed the door and it blended into the wall, completely hidden.

Another loud explosion echoed through the night and a moment later, the sky lit up with flames.

"Barrett," Julie gasped. "The house——"

"It doesn't matter," I said, forcing away crushing sadness as I watched the roof of the house catch fire.

A smidgeon of pain flashed through my skull. "You guys need to go. Now. Get the kids to safety."

"Where do we go?" Julie asked as she bounced Piper, still trying to quiet her down.

"Doesn't matter. Just get them safe." I rubbed my forehead.

I felt it. Another seizure was coming.

I crouched down and opened my arms. My children rushed to me, and I embraced them quickly, my tears falling on their hair.

"I love you," I said.

"Mam." Hawk's eyes were wide.

"Go," I urged. "Go now."

Betty tried to nudge in for affection and I gave her an absent pat before pushing her away. A wave of dizziness washed over me.

Suze grasped Hawk's hand and Bella took the twins'.

"I'll see you all soon," I lied.

Julie met my gaze, and her eyes said it all.

I quickly brushed a kiss to my daughter's cheek and then they took off, running across the beach. With fire in the sky behind me illuminating my family, I watched them grow smaller and smaller in the distance.

My world was burning.

I fell face first into the damp sand as the seizure gripped my body.

A veil of darkness slid over my eyes.

I breathed in the scent of the sea, the charred smell of ash on the wind. I heard the waves crash against stone.

And then I heard nothing.

Nothing at all.

Chapter 48
BARRETT

HE WAS SINGING to me in Gaelic, a lullaby he used to sing to our children in the middle of the night when they had trouble sleeping.

My eyes slowly opened.

The singing stopped.

"Barrett?"

I heard the chair scrape across the floor as he stood up and suddenly, he was in my line of sight. His face was covered in stubble and his blue eyes were blood shot.

"You're here," I whispered.

"Of course I'm here."

I blinked, but my lids were sluggish.

"Where are the kids?" I asked, panic crawling up my throat.

"Easy. They're at Ash and Duncan's. Everyone is fine."

Relief swam through me. "Where am I?"

He paused for a moment and then he explained, "You're at the hospital. You've been in and out of it for a few hours. I'm glad you're finally awake."

"The hospital?" I repeated. I remembered the night of

the fire and fleeing the house. The memory of collapsing into the sand rushed back to me.

"How did I get here?"

Flynn's blue eyes were steady as they stared at me. "Jules called the fire department and told them you were on the beach near the house. They found you and brought you to the hospital."

"Oh." My brow wrinkled as I tried to make sense of time and space. "We fought. That night."

"Aye."

"Hawk told you…about my brain tumor," I recalled.

He took my hand and waited. "He did."

"You were on your way home, weren't you?"

"I was, aye."

I exhaled. "I was going to tell you the night I came to The Rex, but the bomb…"

"Easy, hen. Don't work yourself up."

"I don't want to have the surgery. The tumor is in the part of my brain that could affect my personality, and even if it's successful, I have a slim chance of living past the year mark."

Flynn peered at me and remained silent.

"Say something," I demanded. "Please say something. Even if you yell at me. I should have told you first. I shouldn't have waited. I—"

"Hen," he said slowly. "You've already had the surgery."

His words took a moment to puncture the thick fog of emotion that had washed over me. "Love, you've been in the hospital for two weeks. They removed your breathing tube a few days ago and they've been weaning you off the sedatives to try and wake you up."

"Weeks?" I whispered. "I've been here for weeks, and I've already had brain surgery?"

"Aye."

"But—but I don't understand! How? Didn't Ash tell you I didn't want the surgery? Didn't she make it clear that I—"

"I didn't make the decision about your surgery," he said. "Sasha did."

"Sasha? He's not my medical directive. You are."

"You made Sasha your medical directive in case I was unavailable. Remember?"

I blinked lethargically. "Now I remember. You were unavailable? Why?"

"I was in a car accident on my way home."

"Flynn!" I cried.

"Easy. You have to stay calm."

"Stay calm! You were in an accident! I've had brain surgery. I—"

"Hey." His tone was commanding and forceful. "I need you to take a breath. Good. Another one."

When I had myself under control, I asked, "Please tell me what happened. I can take it."

"I was driving over an icy bridge, and a truck smashed into me, sending both our vehicles over the railing and into the river. A good Samaritan driving behind us stopped and rescued me. If it hadn't been for him, I would've died. Aside from a concussion and mild hypothermia, I'm actually fine. No worse for wear."

"It's a miracle," I murmured.

His parents had died in a car accident when he was a teenager, leaving him an orphan. Malcolm Buchanan had taken him in and raised him alongside his own sons.

How ironic that Flynn had almost died the same tragic way.

"Flynn." I tugged on his hand, urging him closer to me.

He stood and then leaned down to brush his lips across my forehead. "Needless to say, I was unable to make any decisions for you. Ash called Jack for the medical directives."

"Sasha went against my wishes," I said. "He knew I didn't want to have the surgery."

"If it makes you feel any better, I would've made the same decision for you," he announced.

"Despite that not being what I wanted?" I asked. "I resent him."

"Resent all you want," Flynn said tightly. "You're alive. And you're still you. My surviving a car accident isn't the only miracle, Barrett."

I closed my eyes. I was in information overload, and I could hardly process any of it.

Brain surgery.

Flynn in a car accident.

Two weeks of my life gone without me even knowing.

Decisions taken away from me. Decisions made for me, about my health, about my wants.

"I don't want you to worry about anything, Barrett," Flynn said quietly. "I want you to focus on healing. Everything else can wait."

"What about the house?" I asked suddenly.

"It's being handled."

"And The Rex?"

"Also being handled."

"What about—"

"Hen, I'm begging you. Rest, aye? That's all you have to do. Rest, get well, and everything else will be taken care of."

My lip wobbled. "What about the stuff between us?"

"Stuff?"

"You were the last to know about my tumor. And I wasn't the one to tell you."

He sighed. "Aye."

"Do you forgive me?"

He paused for so long I was afraid he wouldn't answer. I was drifting off to sleep when he said quietly, "I don't know, Barrett. I really don't know."

Chapter 49
FLYNN

I DIDN'T MOVE from her side until I was sure she was asleep. I let go of her hand and stretched my arms over my head. My muscles groaned and my bones creaked.

I felt fucking old.

Despite the car accident, I had no broken bones or significant injuries.

People talk of seeing a white light.

All I'd seen was darkness.

A nothingness, devoid of anything at all.

And then suddenly I'd been awake, as if nothing had happened, as if no time had passed.

I'd lost my phone and wallet in the river, but they'd identified me by my fingerprints. I'd called Barrett's cell as soon as I could, but Ash had answered it. She'd told me that Barrett had just had the surgery and had been wheeled into recovery.

My wife had had brain surgery and I hadn't been the one sitting by her bedside.

It had been Sasha.

He'd flown back from the States after making the call

for her to have the surgery, and he'd been the one sitting by her bedside when I walked into her room.

Without a word, he got up and left.

It had been two weeks and I hadn't spoken to him about it. Two weeks of waiting to see if my wife would pull through. Two weeks of not caring that the house had been set on fire or that Gianna had taken the podium at The Rex press conference and fielded questions from the press.

It had taken everything I had inside me to even call my children.

What the fuck was I supposed to tell them?

Your mother might die?

Your mother might live?

The fact that Barrett had survived the surgery didn't surprise me. The fact that Barrett still seemed like *Barrett* didn't surprise me, either.

I wasn't sure what the future held for us and that was terrifying.

Dr. Elmond had removed most of the tumor but had warned me that she would still need radiation and chemo- therapy. He'd sat me down and explained her diagnosis, prognosis, and what to expect in the coming months. Glioblastomas weren't curable and we'd need to be vigilant for any signs and symptoms that the tumor was growing again.

He'd expounded the probability of her living past the five-year mark.

Quinn, Sasha, Ash, and Duncan had been keeping vigil in the waiting room for two weeks, rotating in and out one or two at a time. Since they began attempting to wake Barrett up, everyone was there constantly. I blinked tired eyes when I saw Duncan rise from his chair as I walked into the waiting room.

"She's awake. Well, she was. She fell back asleep, but

she was lucid. She remembers everything, and as far as I can tell, she's still Barrett."

There was a collective sigh of relief.

"Brother," Duncan said, coming toward me and grasping me in a strong bear hug. "You look like hell."

"He smells like hell," Ash said with a watery smile. Her statement didn't stop her from embracing me.

"I need to tell the nurse to page Dr. Elmond and let him know that she's awake," I said.

"I'll take care of it," Quinn said. As she walked past me, she took my hand and gave it a hearty squeeze. I squeezed it back.

"I don't want to leave her," I said. "But we have business to discuss."

"Quinn and I will stay, "Ash volunteered. "You guys talk and sort out our future."

Chapter 50
BARRETT

THE DOOR to my hospital room opened and Ash strode in a few feet and then stopped. "You're awake," she said.

"Dr. Elmond was just here," I said.

"Oh." She paused, like she wasn't sure what to say.

"Where's Flynn?"

"He needed to discuss some things with Duncan and Sasha. He'll be back."

I wasn't sure I was ready for Flynn to return any time soon. The confrontation between us had been tempered and it felt like a reprieve.

"Okay." I peered at her. "You're not asking about what Dr. Elmond said."

"I figured if you wanted to tell me, you'd tell me."

"Convenient," I muttered.

"What?"

"I said that was convenient," I snapped, finally finding some fire.

"Why are you pissed at me?" she demanded.

"Because you knew."

"I knew what?"

"You knew I didn't want the surgery and you let Sasha approve it anyway." I sighed. "Do you remember how hard it was on me when I was bedridden the last time?"

"I remember."

"That's going to be me again. Only worse. Because now I'll be puking up my guts while toxins run rampant through my veins to kill what's left of this thing inside me that wants to kill me. I didn't want this, Ash. I didn't want sickness and vomit, and that *smell*. God, that smell of disease. It's horrible."

I closed my eyes for a moment before opening them. "It's all too much I can barely stand it. Flynn told me he'd have made the same decision as Sasha, if he'd been able."

"We were all in a panic when we couldn't get a hold of him. None of us knew what to do. After you wound up in the hospital, and we knew what the medical directives specified, a decision had to be made immediately. Sasha gave the go ahead for your surgery. You have to understand we didn't even know where Flynn was until after you were in surgery."

"Do you agree? With Sasha's decision?"

"Yes."

"Why?"

"Because the Barrett of old would've fought like hell. Which leads me to believe that you not wanting to fight was just another symptom of your tumor."

"What?"

"You said brain tumors can affect personality. I've never known you to back down from a fight, and when it came to your own health, your own survival, you just *accepted* it. You accepted your death like it was a foregone conclusion."

I fell silent as I pondered her words. Was it true? Did I not want to fight because the tumor itself had changed me so drastically? Or had I really made my peace with living out the last few months of my life on my terms?

"I guess we'll never know," I said quietly.

"I guess not. I'm glad, though. That you're here. That you're still you." She gave me a watery smile.

I couldn't help but smile back, tears gathering in my eyes.

"Is there not just a tiny part of you that's relieved?" Ash asked.

"Relieved? About what?"

"Relieved that the decision was taken off your hands? Relieved that the surgery has already happened?"

"I don't know. Maybe. Yes? I guess?" I blew out a breath of air. "Will you give me a mirror? I want to see the…damage."

"You sure?"

"Yeah."

With a sigh, she riffled through her shoulder bag and pulled out a compact. She flipped it open and held it out to me so I could see my reflection. My entire head was shaved and on the left side of my skull was a thick C-shaped incision that had been stitched closed. The only color on my pale face were my red eyebrows.

"Oh God," I whispered and hastily closed my eyes. "You could've warned me."

"I asked if you were sure if you wanted a mirror," she said. "And besides, you don't look that bad."

"I don't look *that bad*? What are you talking about? My fucking head is shaved."

"We've had two weeks to get used to it," she said.

Her comment was casual, and yet it reminded me that they'd all had time to adjust to a new reality already and I hadn't.

But I was alive. And that was everything.

Chapter 51
FLYNN

WE'D RENTED rooms at an Inverness bed and breakfast ten minutes from the hospital. As much as I wanted to see my children, they were safe in Dornoch, an hour away. I spoke with them on the phone every night while trying to field questions that I didn't have the answers to.

"I need a shower and shave," I said to Duncan and Sasha. "And then we'll have a meeting."

Sasha and Duncan nodded.

Thirty minutes later, the three of us were in the sitting room. The French doors were closed to give us privacy, a roaring fire chasing away the chill in the air, with tea and sandwiches on the coffee table.

"You look better," Duncan commented.

Sasha snorted. "Like hell he does."

"I think it'll take a few months before I don't look like shite," I muttered. I'd stared at my reflection after shaving off the beard, wondering when I'd lose the haunted look in my eyes.

I'd been on death's doorstep many times before, but I'd never actually died. I hadn't yet processed my accident. I'd shoved it aside and focused on Barrett. For now, she was the front and center of my life, and everything else would have to wait.

"Let's get to the business so I can head back to the hospital," I remarked. "I don't want to leave her for long."

Duncan nodded. "The Prince of Monaco is behind the attack on The Rex, as well as the attack on your home. Hadrian's source confirmed that the prince wasn't happy that we were opening a hotel in Monte Carlo and refusing to give him a cut of the casino. So he set up bad press for The Rex, knowing the Monaco council would back him up when he suggested not letting you do business in their country."

Duncan took a sip of his coffee before continuing, "Hadrian approached the council and explained the situation. Needless to say, the council was not happy. They were looking forward to a Rex Hotel in Monaco and all the kickbacks it would bring them. Bluntly put, they do not stand with the prince on this matter. In fact, it was made clear that they would be happy to do business with us, if only the prince would stop trying to get in the way…"

I reached for a tea sandwich. "Assassination?"

"Aye," Duncan said.

I nodded. "Quietly, and without fuss. I don't need a big revenge plot to prove a point. I want this finished."

"Thought you might." Duncan said as he scratched his raspy jaw. "I already gave Hadrian the go ahead. He did, after all, marry into a certain family that is known for their discretion in these types of matters."

"Good," I said.

"What are you going to do about your house?" Sasha asked.

"I've hired a contractor to see to the repairs while Barrett is healing. I want them done as soon as possible so when Barrett is released, she can recover in her own bed." I looked at Sasha. "I never did thank you for what you did for her. For making the call for her to have the surgery."

"It's the least I could do. I'm sorry I knew about the tumor before you," Sasha said.

"No more apologies," I said. "And for the record, I would've made the same call."

"Glad to hear it," he said. "How pissed is she about the situation?"

"Too soon to tell," I replied. "When the sedatives wear off and her head clears, I imagine an emotional explosion the likes of which we've never seen."

"What about you?" Duncan asked. "How pissed are you?"

"Livid. But you can't yell at your wife who's had brain surgery." I clenched my jaw. "How are things at the ports?"

"Dimitri found the fucker that orchestrated the attack, but he's just the middleman. We're really after Alan Bouchard. We're putting a plan into place to take control of Bouchard's routes. We'll wipe them out and once again be the main player on the Eastern seaboard."

I nodded.

"I've talked to Ramsey," Duncan said. "His stabbing was in no way related to the SINS. It was personal. He's found out where the woman—Lex—lives and has eyes tracking her, so there's no way for her to run. When he's healed, he'll take care of her."

"Why did she stab him?" I asked.

"That's still unclear."

"Where is he recovering?" I took a bite of the sandwich.

"An undisclosed location. He's safe," Duncan replied.

I nodded and swallowed. "If that's everything, then I need to get back to the hospital."

Chapter 52

SASHA

SHE WAS STARING INTO SPACE, and I wasn't sure she'd even heard me come into her room. I sat in the chair by her bedside and waited.

Waited for her to rain hell down on me for making the call that saved her life.

"God damn you to hell," she whispered.

"*Da.*" I sighed. "I thought that would be your reaction."

"Thank you."

I frowned. "I don't understand."

Barrett's head turned and her eyes met mine. "You gave me another chance at life."

I rubbed the back of my neck. "I don't understand. I thought for sure you'd be pissed as fuck at me."

"I am pissed as fuck. This was not the outcome I expected. But I don't think I'm allowed to be angry at you. We've been in this situation before. Only, you were the one lying in the bed and you were begging me for something."

"You were strong enough to deliver it."

"Are you saying you weren't strong enough to let me die?" she asked pointedly.

"You had a chance at life. I wasn't going to be the one to end it. Besides, you made me your medical advocate in case Flynn was unavailable. Thanks for telling me, by the way."

She sighed.

"Dr. Elmond told me the probabilities and the risks. I made a decision. I went with my gut. Pure gut instinct. I *knew* you'd live Barrett. I knew you'd still be *you*."

"You're kidding me." She raised her eyebrows. It looked comical considering she had no real hair line anymore since they'd shaved her head. "You based my entire future off of *gut instinct*?"

"I stand by my decision."

She paused for a moment and then nodded slowly. "You told Flynn."

"No. I confirmed what Hawk had told him. It should've been you."

"I know."

"You're not mad at me for that."

"Was that a question or a statement?"

"Statement. We have history."

"Yes."

"You've seen me at my most vulnerable."

"I have," she agreed.

"I sat by your bedside until Flynn came. I never left."

Barrett reached her hand out to me. "We're family, Sasha. Always. Nothing will ever change that."

I took her hand. It was warm, reminding me that she was alive.

"How are you feeling?" I asked.

"Like I just had brain surgery."

"Barrett," I warned.

"Confused. Tired. Angry. Hopeful. Resentful. Grateful. Wishing I was out of this bed. Knowing I'll be stuck here a while longer yet. Missing my children. Missing my husband."

"What are you talking about? Flynn is here."

"I don't mean *here* at the hospital." She paused. "I mean he's holding back."

"About what?"

"He's acting like he's not even mad that I kept this from him, and I know that isn't the truth."

"I think he's just too busy being relieved that you're out of surgery for him to be angry."

"Hmm. Maybe."

"Have you tried talking to him?"

"I hadn't thought of that, no," she said with an eye roll. It made me smile.

"So…we're good?" she asked.

"You tell me."

"We're good."

"I'm glad you're still with us, Barrett."

"That makes two of us, Sasha."

Chapter 53
BARRETT

FLYNN HANDED me a green cap made of Merino wool. I slid it over my bandaged head and looked at him.

"Well?" I asked.

"Beautiful."

"Yeah, right," I muttered.

"How's your energy today?"

"Okay."

He sat on the edge of the bed and took my hands in his. "I want to say something."

I mentally braced myself. "All right."

Flynn's gaze was steady when he peered at me. "I got you pregnant on purpose. After Dolinsky... I knew your birth control lapsed. I took advantage of it."

"Oh."

"I didn't think you'd stay if it was just for me." I was silent long enough that he finally demanded, "Say something."

"Is this why?"

He looked at me quizzically.

I bathed my dry lips with my tongue. "Is this why you haven't rained down hell on me even though I lied to you about the tumor?"

He clenched his jaw, and I knew I was correct.

"No more free passes," I said quietly. "For either of us."

"It's that simple, is it?"

"Were you hoping I'd get mad at you for your admission and then you'd have the excuse to get mad at me back? Finally blow up at me for all the wrongs I've done?"

"I don't know what I was hoping for," he said, voice low.

"Are you sorry that you got me pregnant on purpose?"

"No," he said immediately. "I don't regret it. What about you?"

"Do I regret you getting me pregnant? No, not even a little bit."

"Good, but that's not what I was referring to."

"Oh, you want to know if I have remorse over not telling you about the tumor." I swallowed. "Yes. Yes, I regret my actions. But apologizing…it feels like going to confession. Like, you can do all these wrongs, but the moment you say *I'm sorry*, everything is suddenly forgiven. But the damage has been done."

He squeezed my fingers. "It was your brain they cut into."

"So, you're giving me a bit of grace?"

"I don't know, Barrett." He let go of my hand and then got up and started pacing across the floor. "I just—fuck! I feel sick inside. Why didn't you tell me you were having hallucinations?"

"Did Sasha tell you about those?"

He nodded.

"Did he tell you the details of my hallucinations?"

"No."

"They were about him."

"Him? You mean Sasha?"

"No. About Dolinsky."

His eyes blazed. "Dolinsky."

"Yes," I croaked.

"Why, Barrett? Why didn't you tell me?"

"Because everything between us always comes back to him...and inevitably Sasha. I couldn't burden you with that. Not after all this time."

Flynn's brow furrowed. "Why him?"

"Hmm?"

"Why do you think your hallucinations were of Dolinsky?"

"Because I associate him with death."

Flynn took a moment to digest my words and then he said, "You were scared. To have the surgery."

"Yes. I didn't like my odds of survival with the surgery. The recovery process is going to be a nightmare. Chemo, radiation, tubes and wires sticking out of me. I didn't want the boys to see that. I didn't want you to see that."

"Because you thought you wouldn't be the outlier and live past the year mark."

"Yeah. I wanted to choose. How I was going to die. At home, with my family, with all my hair." I flashed him a sad smile. "Versus a skinny living corpse."

He flinched.

"Well, what's done is done, and I'll see it through now." I stared at him. "I can't have this between us. Please, Flynn. Tell me I haven't lost you."

He rushed to my side and gently cradled my cheeks in his hands. "You could never lose me. Ever."

"Then kiss me, Flynn. And remind me that we're both

alive. Remind me that there isn't anything we can't over-come together."

His eyes darkened. "Woman, you are my everything. And I'll spend the rest of my life proving it to you."

Epilogue #1
ASH

A few days later

I SAT IN THE STUDY, a drink in my hands, waiting for my husband to say something. It had been days since we'd had any time alone together, and to be honest, I was afraid for what was to come.

He looked tired.

He looked worn.

He looked...*older*.

"Before you say anything," I blurted out, disturbing the silence, "I want to say that I love you. I don't care about anything else. I don't want to lose you or our family and the life we've built together."

Duncan took a sip of his drink, his gray eyes glittering in the firelight. "I don't deserve you."

"What? That's not what I—"

"Woman, let me speak," he said, his voice low and rumbly. It made my stomach cartwheel with excitement every time he took that tone because it meant...well, it usually meant a round of rough intimacy that cemented us back together.

"I've been a stupid git. I thought I wanted... I don't know, something else. A different life. A different purpose. Hell, a purpose I recognized." He frowned. "But all this shite with Barrett, I realize how lucky I am to have you. I wouldn't trade what you and I have for anything else. I swear, Ash."

He set his drink down on the coffee table between us and then he stood up and came to me. He gently took my glass from my hands and set it down next to his. And then he was hauling me up into his arms.

This was the man that I knew. The take charge, commanding, confident man I'd married.

He dragged me in front of the fireplace and then his lips claimed mine. I was delirious with want. I wondered if there was ever a time I wouldn't want this man.

We pulled apart so we could remove our clothes. We stared at one another and then Duncan's hands cupped my breasts, his thumbs teasing my nipples. He leaned forward and kissed the hollow of my throat.

My knees weakened and I collapsed onto the rug in front of the fireplace.

Duncan followed me down, covering my body with his.

I stared into his eyes as I traced the lines of his jaw, his forehead, his hair line. I studied him like I was memorizing him because if life had taught me anything, it was that you didn't know when or if these moments came ever again.

I brought his mouth to mine and kissed him with all the longing and love I had in me. For the years of our marriage, for the children we were raising, for the milestones and the heartaches we'd lived through.

And when he slid into me, achingly slow, I closed my eyes and savored the feeling of us being one. My skin flushed from the heat of the fire, our bodies writhing in tandem as we brought each other to the peak of pleasure.

Duncan crumpled on top of me, his breathing harsh and labored in my ear. Finally, he rolled off and settled next to me.

I curled into his embrace and placed my cheek on his chest.

"That didn't solve our problems," Duncan said. "Despite how good it was."

"Why not?" I asked, lifting myself up and staring into his eyes. "Why can't that have solved all of our problems? I'm sick of talking, Duncan. That's all any of us do. Why can't we just start fresh, wipe the slate clean, and move forward?"

He grasped my chin with his thumb and forefinger and brought me to his lips for a kiss. "I'd like nothing more, lass."

"Then let it be," I said. "From this moment on, the past doesn't exist. When we fight in the future, neither one of us will bring up old resentments."

"I have no resentments."

I paused for a moment and then smiled. "Neither do I."

"Swear it."

"I swear it."

He grinned. "Kiss me again, woman. And let me show you how much I adore you."

Epilogue #2
QUINN

I FINGERED the gold wedding band as I sat by the bay window in the master bedroom of the home Sasha and I had bought in Scotland.

It was dreary and cold, and I nuzzled deeper into the blue silk robe.

The door to the bedroom opened and Sasha came in. He was dressed in a pair of black trousers and a burgundy sweater.

I smiled up at him. "Good morning, husband of leisure."

"Good morning, wife of leisure," he quipped, leaning down and kissing my forehead. "You're still in your robe. Everything all right?"

I nodded. "Just sitting here. Thinking."

"About?"

"When are we telling people?"

"Telling people," he repeated.

"That we got married in the hospital chapel a week ago?" I asked.

He gently nudged me away from the wall, but only so

he could take a seat behind me and then wrap me in his arms. His hands settled on my belly.

"We should probably tell them before you start showing, *da*?"

"*Da*." I smiled up at him. "Are we allowed to be this happy?"

"Allowed?" he snorted. "Don't you think we've sacrificed enough to get here? To this moment?"

"Yes, sacrifice." I shook my head. "You want a boy."

"A girl would be fine, too. Just as long as you both are healthy, I don't care."

"Liar."

"I'm not lying," he insisted. "I do want a boy, but it's not indicative of my happiness."

I sighed, leaning my head against his chest. We were silent for a while as we watched the rain fall, fat drops hitting the glass window.

"I don't want to hold my breath," I said finally. "I'm not sure I trust the good fortune currently smiling down on us."

"Dimitri is handling everything on the coast. I'm here with you and Helena. Our family is safe. Barrett is healing quickly. Why am I—the Russian—trying to placate your worries? Shouldn't it be the other way around?"

"Probably," I agreed.

I traced the wedding ring on his hand, loving the symbol of our bond against his skin.

"How does it feel to have a new last name?" he asked.

"I was yours long before our last names ever became the same," I reminded him.

His hand slipped into my robe and cupped my breast. "I want to take my wife to bed," he whispered, his voice raspy with want.

I undid the sash of my robe and let it fall open. "This bay window bench is as good as any bed."

"Who says marriage takes all the fun out of a relationship?" Sasha asked.

I lifted myself up and turned to face him. My hands went to his fly, and I slowly unclasped the button. "Marriage to me is a lot of fun."

I lowered the zipper of his pants and then reached into his boxers to extract him. "Should I prove it to you?"

Epilogue #3

RAMSEY

I SWIRLED the glass of whiskey and then brought it to my nose. I inhaled deeply, held it in my lungs for a moment, and then released my breath.

The gas fireplace in the living room of the Idaho mountain lodge cast a bright, welcoming warmth. The high ceilings made me feel free, and one entire wall was made almost entirely of glass, showing off the Rocky Mountains and the snow-dusted pine trees.

I took another sip of whiskey and began to scroll through the documents on my tablet that Genevieve had sent me on Ainsley Rivers.

My phone rested on the couch next to me and began to ring. I picked it up immediately.

"Burn my house down yet?" Elijah Padgett asked, his Irish accent thick and garbled.

"It's still standing," I commented. "How is it you have a place like this that you never use?"

"I use it," he protested. "Just not often."

"Well, thanks for offering it up as a safe house."

"Seems the least I could do if I want to get in bed with your family."

"We can do business together, but stay in your own fucking bed," I quipped.

"You still need your hot little nurse to help you piss?"

"Fuck off. I'm sitting on your fifteen-thousand-dollar couch, drinking your five-hundred-dollar bottle of Irish whiskey, and enjoying the fruits of *your* labor."

"It's a twenty-thousand-dollar couch," Padgett snapped. "Try not to bleed all over it."

He hung up on me.

I grinned and tossed my phone aside.

And then I got back to reading.

Ainsley Rivers had worked on The Fifteenth Floor of The Dallas Rex for just over a year before abruptly quitting. I didn't remember hiring her, so Genevieve must've been the one to take care of it. I read through all the documents, including Ainsley's obituary.

There was no mention of a woman named Lex.

Anger boiled to the surface of my skin. The woman had played me. She'd taken me for a ride and then stabbed me, leaving me bleeding out to die.

When I faced her again, there would be hell to pay.

Epilogue #4
BARRETT

FLYNN SHUT the door to the house. I leaned against him, feeling tired and weak.

"You can't even tell there was a fire in here," I commented.

"The damage wasn't as extensive as I originally thought. Installing the sprinkler system to automatically turn on in case of smoke detection saved a lot. The Persian rug had to be replaced. And I spent a small fortune to have everything repainted. I wanted the house finished so that…"

"So that I could recover in peace," I finished for him. I pressed my head to his shoulder. "Thank you."

"Let's get you upstairs."

"It's so quiet," I said as I allowed Flynn to bear the brunt of my weight as he helped me walk.

"I'm not sure how to tell you this, but I sent our children off to be with Moira and James."

"You *what*?" I demanded.

"You can yell at me after I get you upstairs to bed."

We took the stairs slowly and by the time I got to the top of the landing, I was winded.

Flynn opened the bedroom door and a chorus of *surprise!* rang out. Our boys bounded off the bed and came to me.

I shot Flynn a look which only made him smile. Jules approached us with Piper in her arms. God, I missed her. Missed all of them.

"Okay," Bella announced. "Let's all head downstairs and give your mom time to settle in."

There were presents on the bedside table. Some were beautifully wrapped, no doubt the work of the nannies. The other gifts, gifts I knew were from the boys, were a mess. Scotch tape, blue ribbons, and far too much wrapping paper. Those would be the gifts I opened first.

Flynn helped me into bed and then settled down next to me.

"Tell me it's all going to be okay," I whispered. "Tell me we're strong enough to get through this. Tell me I can survive the treatments that are coming."

"You can survive them. You *have* to survive them. Because I don't have a life without you, Barrett."

I looked him in the eyes.

This man was my world, my everything.

"Thank you," I whispered.

"For what?"

"For walking through hell with me."

"Woman," he began. "I'd burn it all to the ground to save you. That's how much you mean to me."

"Well," I lifted my hand and touched his cheek. "If anyone knows how to rise from the ashes, it's us."

"Phoenixes, aye?"

"Aye," I agreed. "We're not done yet, Flynn."

"We've only just begun." His lips quirked into a smile.

"Are you tired? Do you want me to leave so you can go to sleep?"

"In a bit. But for now, I want the boys, and Piper, in here. I don't want—I can't have my entire life change. I have to be present. They have to know I'm not going anywhere."

He gently kissed my lips and then gingerly climbed off the edge of the bed. He went to the door and slipped out into the hallway.

Flynn wasn't gone long, and he returned with Piper in his arms, and the boys trailing behind him.

"Gentle," he said to them.

"Get up here, ruffians," I said with a smile. "I need kisses from my favorite men."

The boys climbed up onto the bed, being as mindful of my condition as they could be at their age.

"Are you dying?" Hawk asked.

"Not today, love," I said.

He took my hand and brought it to his lips. "We'll take good care of you, Mam."

"I know you will." I smiled.

Noah snuggled down next to me, his head on my pillow. "Is this okay?" he whispered.

"Better than okay," I whispered back.

Iain curled up on my other side. "Can I see your scar? I want to kiss it and make it better."

I reached up to remove the wool cap on my head. Iain brushed his lips against my bandaged incision.

"Thank you. It feels so much better," I said. "But I'm going to need kisses every day, okay?"

"Okay," Iain said, settling back down.

I looked at Flynn. His smile was tender as he gently patted Piper's back. "You want to hold your daughter?"

Tears prickled my eyes. I never thought I'd be able to

hold her again. I opened my arms and Flynn placed Piper on my chest.

I breathed her in.

I couldn't control the future. I couldn't live for it either. I had to live in the present. Because at the moment, I had everything I needed.

Life had brought me strife and fear. It had also brought me love and a family.

"What are you thinking about, hen?" Flynn asked, taking a seat at the edge of the bed. He searched for my ankle over the cover.

I sighed. "How lucky I am to be alive."

He squeezed my ankle and let it go. "You're the heart of this family, Barrett. We're nothing without you."

"We need you," Hawk said. "So you have to get better."

"I'll get better," I promised, feeling emotion thicken my throat. "I've got too much to live for."

Additional Works

The Tarnished Angels Motorcycle Club Series:

Wreck & Ruin (Book 1)
Crash & Carnage (Book 2)
Madness & Mayhem (Book 3)
Thrust & Throttle (Book 4)
Venom & Vengeance (Book 5)
Fire & Frenzy (Book 6)
Leather & Lies (Book 7)
Heartbeats & Highways (Book 8 - preorder)

SINS Series:

Sins of a King (Book 1)
Birth of a Queen (Book 2)
Rise of a Dynasty (Book 3)
Dawn of an Empire (Book 4)
Ember (Book 5)
Burn (Book 6)

Additional Works

Ashes (Book 7)
Fall of a Kingdom (Book 8)

Others:

Peasants and Kings

About the Author

Wall Street Journal & USA Today bestselling author Emma Slate writes romance with heart and heat.

Called "the dialogue queen" by her college playwriting professor, Emma writes love stories that range from romance-for-your-pants to action-flicks-for-chicks.

When she isn't writing, she's usually curled up under a heating blanket with a steamy romance novel and her two beagles—unless her outdoorsy husband can convince her to go on a hike.

www.ingramcontent.com/pod-product-compliance
Lightning Source LLC
Chambersburg PA
CBHW021245190726
48289CB00005B/1503